CW00498921

HUNTER

THE ROYAL PACK TRILOGY: BOOK 2

ANNE K. WHELAN

LIZ CAIN

CLAN WHELAN
PUBLISHING

Cover design by MiblArt

Who wants to fit in? Normal is overrated anyway.
Liz Cain

Do not overthink, just do it.
Anne K. Whelan

ABOUT THE AUTHORS

Anne and Liz are the co-founders of Clan Whelan Publishing (CWP). They believe in the power of stories and know firsthand the challenges that self-published authors face when trying to get their work out into the world. Anne teamed up with her friend Liz to create CWP in order to make a positive impact in the lives of authors and readers alike. Liz has always been an avid reader and jumped at the opportunity to help more stories be published.

Together, Anne and Liz make it easier for readers to discover new fantasy romance and paranormal romance, including paranormal women's fiction, stories in one place. They have always aspired to help people in any way they can. By joining forces, Anne and Liz are able to do just that. Their mission is to help their authors navigate the indie publishing world and continue to bring their stories to life, with or without CWP.

If you are interested in being the first to know about our upcoming new releases, sign up to CWP newsletter.

PROLOGUE

Twenty-one years earlier

Solus sat in his kitchen and stared out the window while Aine was out with the warriors; she had achieved First Warrior, and he should be proud. At sixteen, she was the youngest to achieve such an honor. But here he was without a wife and stuck with the unforgettable image of his newborn son, lifeless in his arms.

Arwen had insisted she could survive the birth; she was strong enough. But, she was so stubborn and the price had been her life. She transferred her powers to him as they had prepared for as she died, but all he could feel was her loss. The power was only meant for those born of the royal bloodline and not to be passed to another. The process of transferring the power outside of the bloodline corrupted it, and he would have to fight that corruption while he held it.

Solus sighed deeply and let it out through his nose, then jerked as a knock at the door broke his reverie. He blew out a breath and growled; he could feel the darkness swell within him.

"Solus, it's time to get out and take up your duties!" Arwen's father, Conrad, shouted through the closed door.

Solus marched to the door and threw it open, snarling, "I will come out in my own damn time!"

Conrad stood before him. After Arwen had died and Solus had hidden away to grieve, Conrad resumed the role of Pack Leader. This was his position before he stepped back to allow Solus and Arwen to lead the pack when she was still alive.

"Wallowing will not bring them back. We need to hunt, but there are hunters in the area. We can't stay too close to home, and you're our best tracker. I need you...the pack needs you." Conrad reached out to put a hand on his shoulder, "I grieve for her, too," but Solus slapped it away, and Arwen's father slumped.

"I need time to grieve. Your needs are not important to me." Solus almost turned away, but a growl in Conrad's throat brought his attention back to his leader.

"You will obey me. I know you and Arwen shared Pack Leader duties with me, but with her gone, I am still in charge." Power radiated through the entrance to their small house. "The pack comes first, and we need to hunt. You WILL join us."

Solus fought the effect's influence but wasn't strong enough; only Arwen had had the power to stand up to her father. His knees shook before one gave, then he knelt before his leader.

He gritted his teeth and spat the words, "Yes, sir." Conrad nodded and left.

Solus ground his teeth and wrenched himself off the floor with the dark power his mate had given him swirling around him. What she had done when she gave him the power was against their laws, and Solus knew he would bear the consequences alone. A tinge of madness rose to the surface, and the thoughts he'd been having made more sense. It would take time for him to build up the power, time he didn't have.

He watched the old wolf leave. Conrad's ideas were outdated, and the pack was deteriorating under his rule. To have to hunt miles away from their home was becoming difficult. They should take what they needed from the humans that didn't know they existed.

Conrad didn't want Aine trained in her powers claiming she would be too dangerous. Arwen had said that Solus would need to protect Aine from Conrad as they grew. She would need her powers to protect the pack when she became Pack Leader.

Why should Conrad make the decisions? Aine needed training, and the humans needed to be put in their place. *They have everything, and we're left with scraps.* He'd had the argument with Conrad many times. Maybe it was time he did more about it, especially to protect Aine.

Solus looked down at his hands and saw the black smoke curl around his fingers. Arwen had taught him some of what it meant to have her power, but he'd only really understood once he used it himself. Aine was next in line to rule when Conrad passed, but maybe he should take over leadership before Conrad destroyed them all.

He watched the smoke, mesmerized as it encircled his palm. It seemed to speak to him, to tell him his decision was right. He could feel it. He prepared to leave and meet Conrad with Rolan and two other warriors. Solus eyed Rolan and gave him a barely perceptible nod, which Rolan returned.

It took them half the day to travel to one of their hunting grounds, but Solus appreciated the distance from the pack.

Conrad gave the order to start the hunt, and Rolan joined Solus. The two warriors loyal to Conrad left, and Conrad went in the opposite direction; the Pack Leader always hunted alone, and Solus usually took Rolan.

"Rolan, my boy," Solus said. "It's time."

Rolan gulped and nodded. "You'll take the leadership?"

"Yes. This pack is ripe for the taking, and my daughter is too young to lead. Conrad made a mistake taking it from me after Arwen's death. Even if Aine takes the title, I'll be able to guide her to make the right decisions." Solus looked at Rolan. "You can help me with that. I see how she looks at you."

Rolan grinned when Solus walked over to a rock, pulling out a long bag and removing a rifle from within. He had taught the boy to shoot for this one task and placed rifles at each of their hunting grounds, just in case.

"I'll make you proud." Rolan looked up into his master's eyes.

"No one left alive; the pack must think it was humans." Solus watched Rolan swallow before he nodded, then took out his own rifle before leaving to follow Conrad's two warriors. He had his own part to play.

Solus tracked Conrad to a cave. It smelled of old bear, but the trail was cold. Moss covered the rocks on the entrance, and the ground was made up of hard-packed dirt.

Conrad, in his light grey wolf form, sniffed the entrance and snorted. Solus took up his position above the cave entrance and aimed. As his finger tensed to squeeze the trigger, his foot shifted, and the loose soil above the cave gave under his weight. His finger slipped, and the crack of the rifle startled Conrad. Solus slipped down the side of the cave entrance, his bullet flying wide. He shifted quickly to face Conrad in his onyx black wolf form.

Solus huffed and shook himself. Conrad's wolf form was tense, growling before him.

Traitor, why would you betray us? It is not my fault Arwen died.

I am doing this for Aine.

The two shots did not come as a shock to him, but Conrad whipped round to face the direction the two warriors had taken. Solus was positioned perfectly, and he lunged for the pack leader's throat, jaws wide, biting down hard. Blood flooded his mouth, but a slight twist from Conrad stopped him from being killed outright.

Conrad howled as his power poured from him. Solus was thrown back hard from the explosion of dark magic. It blew them apart and, a sickening crack sounded from his rear flank, followed by sharp pain. Numbness spread through Solus's limbs as he hit the cave entrance. He looked up to see Conrad weaving towards him, blood gushing from his neck until he collapsed a few feet from Solus.

What have you done? Conrad's mental voice was weak. Solus watched the flow of life drain from his eyes.

By the time Rolan found him, their leader's eyes stared blankly to the sky. Solus had tried to move, but his hind legs would not obey.

"Master, you're hurt!" Rolan ran towards him in human form, the rifle slung over his shoulder.

"My back..." Solus coughed. "I think it's broken."

Rolan ran forward to help him up, but Solus couldn't move.

"You'll need to get Vernon," Solus said weakly. "He's not far from here. Then you'll need to skin Conrad's body and burn it to hide the evidence of the bite. Are the other two dead?"

"Yes, I skinned them already." Rolan swallowed hard as he tried to contain a heave, his hand on his stomach.

"Then go. Don't just stare at me, you'll have to tell the village I died. I'm too wounded to make it back," Solus growled. "It'll take everything Vernon has to heal this, and the pack will question his methods. Better that I rule from the shadows than as a cripple."

Rolan nodded before he left to fetch Vernon. Solus pulled his power around his body and let it hypnotize him to dull the pain.

He would hold his powers. Even if it killed him to try.

1

Eloi crouched and faced the tall shifter before her; she could clearly see the aggressive intent in his eyes as he circled to her left. Careful to keep her movements subtle, Eloi shifted and prepared to block. When the well-trained warrior launched towards her, she pivoted to align herself behind him. As he struck where she had stood, Eloi clipped the back of his knee. The warrior face-planted in front of her, and Eloi moved to subdue him. The warrior grunted as she put him in a lock, preventing any retaliation.

"Nicely done, Eloi!" Lachlan praised from the edge of the arena.

Eloi focused and tried not to be distracted, but the warrior took advantage and flipped her off him. They circled each other once more. Nyko and Eloi had trained together since she began her combat training. At seventeen, she was older than her mother had been when Aine was promoted to First Warrior. Lachlan held that position now as her mate, but he delegated to Eloi regularly.

Eloi watched Nyko for his tell, a slight twitch in the

direction he would launch himself. She could have easily felt his intentions with her mind, but Lachlan said that was cheating, so instead, she waited for Nyko to make his move. He feinted left, which Eloi anticipated; she beautifully executed another headlock she had worked on. Eloi felt her mother enter the clearing and relaxed her hold when Nyko tapped out.

"Take a break—good work, Eloi. Nyko, we can talk about what you think went wrong after you've run laps." Lachlan dismissed them and, with a sickening love-struck smile on his face, approached Aine. Nyko made vomiting noises in Eloi's ear, and she slapped his hand away.

"Why do they still have to be so mushy?" Eloi got frustrated at how Aine and Lachlan could be. It was good to see her mom happy, but did she have to be so obvious in public all the time? It was disgusting. As Pack Leader, Aine should be less emotional around the pack, but she and Lachlan were always all over each other. *Gross.*

"Do they ever come up for air?" Nyko flicked her ear.

Since the day the hunters invaded, and Rolan died, Aine and Lachlan took Nyko under their wing. They felt he needed a more traditional upbringing to ensure he wasn't taken advantage of, especially after what had happened with Rolan.

Nyko's parents had died when he was younger, and he'd always been the village orphan. He was like a brother to Eloi. An annoying, pain in the ass, always around and taking her things kind of brother. She tried to look annoyed, but Nyko had a way about him. She couldn't stay mad at him for long.

Eloi watched Aine and Lachlan. Despite the years that had passed since they had mated, they could barely keep their hands off each other. The girl sighed and turned to get a drink. She looked around Sumter—it was so different from the day Rolan's supporters attacked. With her water, she walked through the village, away from Nyko and her parents. The pit that had held Lachlan prisoner was gone, the meeting area was now used for fight training, and a building had been erected.

Lachlan's family of hunters ended up settling in Burntwood Falls after the attack, and the townsfolk hadn't been too happy to discover there was a settlement of shifters nearby. So, Liam, head of the Hunters and Lachlan's father, educated them on the secret settlements all across the country. As a result, they eventually conceded to let the hunters stay as a deterrent. But, of course, it also helped that they took up Lachlan's role of keeping the wild animals at bay.

Liam still hoped that Lachlan would leave the shifters and join them. Relationships were strained, but with the help of Phil, Lachlan's best friend and owner of the diner on the edge of the town, some of the folks in Burntwood Falls came around. They helped to modernize the houses in the village, and Aine became more relaxed about sending wolves out into the world. The humans from town even visited on occasion, usually just the younger people from Burntwood Falls and those who had known Aine.

Eventually, a tenuous relationship had formed between the Hunters, the town, and the shifters in Sumter. Lachlan worked hard as a liaison between them all, and he even thought Liam would eventually come around to working with the shifters. Eloi laughed. That man was as hardheaded as Lachlan. She continued to walk towards the edge of Sumter, to her favorite spot, where she always practiced.

There was a small pond to the north, with a waterfall tumbling in from a high rock. The sound of the water soothed Eloi; she sat, closing her eyes, and listened. She had been practicing reaching out with her sense as her mother did. Although she didn't have Aine's reach, she could feel some of the pack on the edges of the village as they worked. She especially liked to watch the younglings. They had childish freedom and joy that was a pleasure to experience.

Eloi stretched her reach out into the forest, examining the surrounding area for any disturbances. The Faction, a rebellion shifter group led by Rolan before his death, had been raiding the settlement over the previous three years; they even kidnapped some villagers each time. They had not been seen since, even when Aine or Eloi tried to reach them, they were lost to the pack connection. Eloi had watched her mother's heart break each time it happened. Lachlan begged Aine to bring in some of the hunters to find them, but she refused, still not trusting them.

A disturbance on the edge of her reach caught Eloi's attention. She pushed out with her power, as her mother had taught her, and managed to stretch a little further. Four shifters approached from north of Sumter; Burntwood Falls lay to the east, so it wouldn't be anyone from the town.

Eloi quickly stood and tilted her head in the direction of the newcomers as they entered her range. They didn't seem to be malicious—more tired from a long journey. They didn't feel like the shifters that normally attacked. Eloi connected to her mother to show her what she saw.

I'll send warriors out to meet them, Eloi. Don't head in that direction. Come back to the village.

Eloi sniffed. *I'm not a child, I'll meet up with the warriors.*

Eloi, I'm not telling you again. Head back to the village.

Eloi groaned loudly and turned back towards Sumter. As she slowly walked, she kept track of the newcomers. There was one female and three males, all shifters from what she could tell. She concentrated so hard that she didn't notice a tree before her until a sharp pain hit her in the face.

"Ow, stupid tree!" Eloi rubbed her nose and took a deep breath. She didn't know how her mother managed to connect to so many and still carry on with other tasks. She shook her head and sniffed hard to clear her nose, then felt again for the small group, reaching for the warriors coming to meet them.

Alarm shot through Eloi as she realized they were no longer alone. A group of seven shifters moved quickly towards them, and she could feel their malicious intent from here.

THE FACTION!

Eloi screamed through her mental connection with her mother and managed to include some of the pack close to her. Aine's shock bled down the bond they had, and the Pack Leader sprang into action. Eloi felt the warriors on the way to meet the group shift and race to defend them. She changed direction; the thinning trees became thick again as she shifted and sprinted towards the point where the groups would all converge. Leaping over a fallen trunk, the Eloi felt the power of her limbs propel her forward. Light brightened the area ahead as she approached the road.

She burst through the trees, blinking to adjust to the light. Scanning the area the newcomers were being attacked, Eloi saw two of the five warriors take down one of the Faction. Black blood oozed onto the road as the wolf fell dead before them. A dark grey wolf, almost as large as the warriors, grabbed one of the three males from the group of five. His face contorted when teeth pierced his leg; half-shifted, his scream came out as a howl as his head hit the ground with a sickening crack. A second wolf from the Faction grabbed his other leg, and his companions were helpless as they fought their own opponents. His body then disappeared into the darkness of the trees, away from the village.

Eloi took in the scene, mouth open. The Faction wolves' coloring seemed dull; black veins spiderwebbed from their eyes and across their bodies, most apparent in the light gray wolf closest to her. The attention of three of the Faction was on the warriors and the small group they defended. The female shifted into a red and black wolf, as had her companion with similar colorings alongside her. They fought with the warriors against the enemy. The last in the group, a dark brown wolf, had been separated and fought two of the Faction wolves. He howled when one clamped on his leg in an attempt to drag him into the woods like they had his companion.

This group was the closest to Eloi, and she launched herself towards the light grey wolf which gripped the brown wolf's leg. She felt dark magic leak from his mind, his saliva dripping like black tar from his jaw, all the wolves attacking as though rabid. Eloi went straight for the throat of the wolf and tore. A copper tang infected with a rancid taste burst in her mouth. As she felt his life slip away, she spat the foul liquid and shook her head. The wolf fell still, and another five warriors joined them from the village.

The fight was brutal but ended quickly as the other warriors joined, causing the attackers to outnumber skilled warriors. Eloi surveyed the area. There were no casualties from the warriors, but one of the male newcomers had a nasty bite, and one was missing.

"Eric!" the female wolf half-growled as she shifted back. She screamed the name again into the woods and took a step towards the trees where their companion had been dragged off.

"He's gone, Ciara." A lean, muscular man in his twenties, blond hair cut close to his scalp, hugged her close; she sobbed and turned into him, her body shaking. He closed his eyes and grimaced as she yelled the name again. Eloi examined the area, still in wolf form.

Mom is gonna kill me for not going back to the village. She couldn't help but feel smug about her kill, though. Then, she felt Aine and Lachlan approach the group and slunk back to the edge of the woods, hoping they wouldn't notice her.

"Report," Aine commanded. A rough bearded, sandy-haired warrior stepped forward.

"Five of the Faction are dead; two took off with one of the strangers. One of the strangers was nearly taken, but we killed the two who had him. He could do with medical attention. These two seem okay." He gestured towards the sobbing woman, then Eloi. "Eloi took out one while we took out the other four."

Aine's eyes snapped to her daughter, her mouth set in a thin line, and Eloi tried to hold her head high when she saw the anger flash in her mother's eyes.

I told you to come back to the village.

Eloi remained silent; anything she said would make it worse, and better not to argue in front of the warriors. Even if they couldn't hear the mental exchange, it would be obvious from their body language.

"Thanks, Jason." Aine turned back to the warrior. "Let's get these three back to the village before there's another attack."

The female looked up from the man she sobbed against towards Aine and Lachlan. Lachlan stepped up beside Aine to assess the scene. His eyes swept over the dead wolves then landed on the female. He gasped.

"Ciara! And Conor! What are you doing here?" He strode forward to embrace the two shifters and looked them both over for injuries. The male let out an uneasy laugh before he spoke, his accent similar to Lachlan's.

"Actually, we were looking for you." Conor cleared his throat. "We heard your family had come after you, and with the way things were..." His voice trailed off. Ciara lifted her head and stared at Lachlan.

"Hello, Kind Warrior," she said. "Not how I expected to be meeting you again." She sniffed and wiped her eyes, attempting a weak smile. "But it's good to see you, all the same."

"The girl you rescued when you left your family?" Aine stepped towards the newcomers.

"Yes, Ciara and her brother, Conor." Lachlan clasped the other male by the shoulder. "And this is Gary. I lived with them for a while after I left my father."

Aine's gaze swept over the group, and she smiled. "Let's get back," she said. "Seems like they have a story to tell."

Conor led his sister following the warriors, his friend Gary limping after them. The road had been built to bring in supplies from Burntwood Falls more efficiently, and the smooth surface would make the journey back to the village easier for the injured man. Lachlan took Aine's hand, and Eloi noticed his small squeeze; her mother's face softened, and she smiled up at him. Eloi used the distraction to slink past them and join the warriors ahead. She didn't shift, thinking that if she stayed in wolf form, it would delay her mother's unavoidable lecture.

The trees lining the road on either side thinned as the village approached. The small group had nearly made it to safety before they had been attacked. A large fence was erected as a defense against the Faction attacks; Eloi resented the enclosure. It felt more like a prison than a safety measure. However, once inside the perimeter, she felt the group relax, and other shifters came forward to help the siblings and Gary towards the medical center.

Aine followed the group inside the building, and Eloi followed curiously. She had heard some of the stories from Lachlan about his family and was curious to meet the girl he had rescued. She would be in her early thirties now but was only a teenager when she was taken and tortured by Finn, Lachlan's older brother.

Eloi stared at Ciara's blonde hair and blue eyes. Her arms were muscular, and her body toned. She looked strong and powerful despite the redness in her eyes. Eloi admired her strength. She had just lost a friend, and here she was before the Pack Leaders looking confident. Conor stood at his sister's side, a grin on his face as he looked at Lachlan.

"I won't be so easy to tackle to the ground now." Conor gave Lachlan a cheeky wink as he spoke.

"Not that gangly teenager anymore, are you, boy?" Lachlan stepped forward to shake Conor's hand and pull him in for a hug. Eloi shifted into human form and approached the group, wary of keeping Lachlan between her and her mother. Aine's eyes narrowed when she saw Eloi come forward, then she turned her head to the three newcomers.

"Welcome, all of you. It's rare for us to have visitors to the pack," Aine said with a smile.

"I'm Ciara, and this is Conor, as you know." Ciara paused and gestured towards their third member. "This is Gary." Gary waved weakly, a thin sheen of sweat shining on his brow, and he sighed as he sat down in a chair next to one of the beds in the room.

"Eric was taken, he..." Ciara swallowed hard and closed

her eyes a moment before she continued. “He’s my mate, and we have a son who stayed with my parents. He will be heartbroken. We have to get Eric back.” The woman tried to stifle a small sob.

“We’ve heard rumors of your pack out here, living amongst humans, and that Lachlan’s family had settled nearby.” Conor continued for his sister. “The Faction has been bringing followers over from Europe. We heard their leader, Rolan, was calling all wolves to fight for their freedom.”

“Rolan?” Aine’s hand flew to her mouth as she gasped. Lachlan tensed and recoiled as if struck.

“He’s alive?” Lachlan put his arm around Aine. “His body was taken, but we assumed his supporters wanted to bury him in their own way...” then almost inaudibly, “I killed him... we buried him. How is this possible?”

“Maybe it’s a different Rolan?” Ciara shrugged.

“It feels right. When his grave was found dug up and the body missing, it didn’t sit well with me, but it would make sense for them to try and bring him back.” Aine folded her arms over her chest and leaned into Lachlan. They both looked up as Eyolf entered the medical center.

“I heard we’ve had another attack.” Eyolf looked over at the group. “And some visitors, it seems.” The older wolf looked over the siblings before his gaze fell on Gary.

“I think this young man needs some medical attention.” He walked over to Gary and put a hand to his forehead. “He has a fever.”

Tania, a petite girl with long, brown hair, one of the trainees Caroline had taken under her wing, came over to assess her patient. Ciara and Conor watched in concern until Eyolf walked towards them.

“Eyolf, this is Ciara and Conor. Lachlan spent some

time with their pack after he left his family." Aine frowned. "They've just told us that Rolan still leads the Faction."

"I always knew that boy was playing with dark magic. But resurrection...there's always a cost." Eyolf closed his eyes and shook his head, his lips curled in disgust. "He must be working with someone extremely powerful for them to bring him back."

"So, it's possible?" Lachlan took a step, unconsciously moving towards Aine.

"Yes, but as I said, it's very dark magic, and there's always a cost. Usually, the life of another in exchange for the one being brought back."

"The rumors are they are amassing an army to enslave the humans. I'm not going to lie; it *is* tempting." Ciara shrugged when her brother gave her a sharp look. "Well, after the way we've been treated. It would be great to live in freedom."

"It wouldn't be freedom." Aine's voice was harsh. "It would be another form of enslavement. Rolan was controlling his supporters through his magic. They become his puppets, slaves."

"I noticed the ones that attacked us today had black saliva and veins all over." Eloi gestured in the air with her hands, clearing her throat when her mother looked over. She gave an awkward wave to the siblings. "Hi, I'm Eloi. Aine is my mom."

Ciara grinned and looked between them. "You can tell."

"The wolves today had darkness in them?" Aine walked around Lachlan to face Eloi. The girl braced herself for a lecture and flinched slightly.

"Yeah, I could feel the darkness coming off them. It was almost like their minds weren't their own. Their blood tasted funny too like it was diseased." She straightened her back and waited for her mother to speak.

There was a loud crash from across the room. Eloi looked up to see instruments and equipment slide across the floor as Tania struggled with a flailing Gary.

"What the—?" Lachlan surged forward to help Tania hold Gary down. The newcomer lunged for Lachlan, his teeth clicking as his jaw snapped at Lachlan's arms, where he held him down. Saliva dripped from his face, the same black as their attackers.

"Gary?" Conor's voice shook as he called his friend's name.

"Here, help hold him!" Lachlan shouted. Tania stepped back, allowing Conor to take her position. Then, she rushed over to a cabinet to prepare a sedative.

"Gary, calm down!" Conor begged.

Gary's arms lashed out, and Conor struggled to hold him. He jerked to the side, nearly crashing into Tania as she returned with a syringe in her hand. Quickly she plunged the needle into Gary's neck, and the effect was immediate. His eyes rolled into the back of his head, and his entire body went rigid, then relaxed on the bed. The group held their breath as they waited for him to move.

"What the hell?" Eloi's voice rang out in the quiet room.

2

The smell of damp and moss tickled Rolan's nose. Seated on the makeshift throne in the center of the largest cavern, he stared out at the shifters working around the area, refugees that had escaped various settlements after being attacked by "hunters." Mostly bare rock surrounded them. Oil lanterns created an eerie atmosphere, providing light for those in attendance. He hated being down in these caves.

Many tunnels led to smaller areas, webbing out into smaller caverns used for living quarters. Rolan missed the air and openness of living in the country. The lack of sunlight and dreary interior were starting to get to him. He was the face of the revolution, the Faction. Solus was not ready to make himself public and continued to use Rolan as his puppet.

"Maybe you shouldn't sit there, sir." Taylor, one of the guards, approached him. "You've tried to take his seat a few times now, and you always end up being punished severely."

Rolan winced as he thought about the last time. "True."

He sighed and rested his head on his fist, leaning on the arm of the stone throne. "The refugees, have they been settled?"

"Yes, sir." Taylor paused. "I know our numbers took a huge hit after the attack on Sumter three years ago, but do we need to attack these villages to create the refugees? It doesn't seem right."

"Sacrifices must be made for the greater good." Rolan gestured around the cave and watched the groups as they worked. Taylor was right. Their numbers had fallen drastically three years ago when they attacked Sumter. The O'Reilly hunters were an unexpected barrier, for which the Faction had not accounted when they planned the attack of the Aiobhan pack. Rolan ground his teeth. Most of that day was blank. He had woken a few days later, but the sickening crack as Lachlan killed him still gave him nightmares.

"Don't get too comfortable," a deep voice spoke quietly from behind the throne. Rolan turned to watch Solus approach. "You are not ready."

Short, black hair streaked with silver glowed in the soft lantern lights. Emerald eyes, identical to his ex-mate's, burned into Rolan. He could feel the pulse of power, a call for submission. Rolan gritted his teeth as he fought the urge to surrender. Failing, his body moved of its own accord, stepping down from the stone chair and bowing his head to the older wolf.

A smile played on Solus's face. He had broad shoulders and a large build compared to Rolan's lean muscle. Rolan would not beat him in a direct attack; he would have to be more cunning to defeat him. That is if he could overcome the call from the dark power within his master.

"More followers will arrive today. The stronger half will join our trainers. The weaker will be...taken to my chambers; I have another use for them," Solus's voice was stern.

He looked past Rolan to the workers in the area as he took his place on the stone throne.

"Yes, sir." Rolan could not help but obey. "We have a new addition—he is loyal to a pack in Europe and refuses to join."

"You know what to do, Rolan. Why do you hesitate?" Solus gestured toward him.

"He is strong; it would be a waste to—" Rolan cringed at Solus's expression.

"You believe you can change his loyalty?" His leader raised an eyebrow.

Rolan kept his head down and held his breath. "Give me a little time."

"Very well." Solus looked back at Taylor, who kept a blank face.

"He was taken from a group on their way to Sumter," Rolan continued. "If we have his loyalty, we may be able to infiltrate the pack again." He dared to look up at Solus, whose brow furrowed before he spoke.

"Still want to destroy them, Rolan? You need to learn to let go. There will come a time when we can take over Sumter, but we need more power. Rumors are that my daughter's power has grown tenfold since you left." Solus's eyes met Rolan's. "I have use for her, do you understand?"

Rolan flinched as the last word vibrated through him. "Yes, master," he balked.

"Good, now bring the selected to me." Solus quickly stood and headed toward his rooms.

Rolan slowly backed away, his gaze glued to the ground as he left the cavern. The nearest tunnel on his right would lead him to the group of new wolves that had joined them. His laugh was bitter as he thought about how Solus scouted packs in the area. If he found them a promising group, or if they had a resource he needed, then "hunters" would attack. Refugees would then be "rescued" by the Faction and taken in.

"The desperate are susceptible, Rolan," he said in mimicry. "I can use their pain and loss to encourage them to join the Faction."

Solus wasn't wrong; the Faction has grown and now spread throughout North America, waiting... always waiting. Rolan had no idea what their leader had planned—it's taken decades to reach this point. The old wolf had patience, that was certain.

The tunnel Rolan followed narrowed briefly, then opened into a smaller cavern with a large hole in the ceiling. Dust spiraled in the sunlight that trailed down from the opening, and Rolan's eyes closed briefly; he sighed, soaking in the warmth. Murmuring around him brought his attention to the forlorn group of mostly teenage boys. One woman in her late twenties sat in the corner, her knees drawn up to her chest. Her vacant stare was fixed on the patches of sunlight in the corner of the room, and she didn't seem to notice Rolan's approach.

"Name," he demanded. She flinched at his harsh word and curled deeper into herself with a whimper.

"I won't ask again." Rolan put as much authority into his voice as he could. He was about to step forward when she spoke.

"Olivia." Her voice was quiet and small. Dirty and greasy brown hair hung in bedraggled clumps, partially covering her face. Rolan crinkled his nose as he watched her shrink into the wall, and an idea struck him.

"Come with me." He attempted a kind voice, but it came out strained. The girl paused before standing and following, eyes downcast. Rolan moved quickly from the cavern.

Several minutes passed as he led the girl deeper into the caves, glancing back often to make sure she still followed.

Taylor diligently watched the entrance to a small crevice, one of many in a row toward a dead end. Rusted iron bars latticed each opening—Solus's dungeon within the caves. The crevices were small, with barely enough room for one wolf. Finally, Rolan stopped, and with a look, the guard retreated towards the dungeon entrance.

"See this prisoner?" Rolan spoke quietly and gestured towards the end crevice. At this distance, the wolf wouldn't hear him. He turned towards the girl to see her nod. "Your task is to look after him, make him feel at home. Understand?"

Without a word, the girl nodded again. Rolan grinned; she was as a female should be. Docile and willing to serve.

"Tell him about your experience with humans, bring him to our side, and you will be rewarded." Rolan raised a hand to stroke the girl's cheek, and she cringed at the touch. He sniffed and scowled. "You'll need a wash first. Taylor, take care of that!" he shouted after the guard.

"You begged to be let in, Olivia. We promised you safety. Perform this task, and you will be safe here." Rolan walked past the girl. "Taylor, the guard up there, will set you up with the other girls; they will show you the ropes. I think you'll fit in very well."

Rolan briefly explained the girl's presence to Taylor, who responded with a quick nod.

"You think it'll work?" the guard asked flatly.

Rolan frowned. "It might. Solus is determined to turn them all, but we need some with strength to lead our warriors. Feed the girl rumors of the packs in the area and the atrocities they commit. If she believes them, then he will believe her."

"It's diabolical, sir. Now I know why Solus brought you back." Taylor's blank face did not change as he turned to retrieve the girl. Olivia hadn't moved as they spoke in hushed tones, and Rolan hoped she wasn't too meek to pull off this task.

~

ERIC LISTENED when a whispered conversation took place near the entrance to the dungeon. He couldn't make out the words and growled in frustration, rising from the rough stone floor. His gaze swept over the small crevice and iron bars that cut him off from freedom. He was brought to the caves earlier that day, dragged away from his companions on their way to Sumter.

Ciara wanted to find the hunter who rescued her years ago; she had information she wanted to pass on to him. Eric vaguely remembered the man—sad and quiet, he stayed with their pack for a short time after the rescue, leaving with the assurance that he was always welcome. Eric's father died in the attack on the hunters to rescue Ciara, and he knew that Lachlan's mother also died that same day. He avoided the hunter as they both grieved, too angry to form a connection.

The rock closed in around Eric in his cell; the feeling of being underground made it hard for him to breathe. The wolf that grabbed him hadn't broken the skin when he was taken, but his leg hurt from being dragged. Eric twisted and felt a dull pain at the back of his skull; he reached up and probed through his shaggy hair at the small lump with his fingers. At some point, his head must have hit a rock, or he had been knocked out.

As he assessed the rest of his body for injuries, he listened for anyone coming down the cave tunnel to his cell. Then, the sound of shuffling feet caught his attention, and he turned to face his cell door. A slight girl with damp hair that could have once been blonde cowered at the entrance to his cell. She quickly placed a tray of food on the floor and slid it under the door. The smell of beef and mashed potato made Eric's stomach grumble in protest and his mouth water.

The girl stepped back and rubbed her arms. She looked freshly cleaned in a simple, obviously second-hand, white top and jeans. Her blue eyes observed Eric as he slowly approached the tray and sniffed.

"It's not poisoned," the girl whispered. "I made it myself."

"Might just check that for myself." Eric inhaled deeply and couldn't detect anything foreign in the food.

"It needs salt." The girl gave him a shy smile and leaned against the wall opposite his cell.

"You going to watch me eat?" Eric pulled the tray forward. Looking at the girl, he realized she was barely skin and bones herself. With a sigh, he pushed the tray back under the cell door. "I think you could use this more than me."

She hesitated a moment before she grabbed the tray and started shoveling the food into her mouth. Eric looked on, astonished, as the girl devoured the meal while kneeling before his cell door. He lowered himself to sit cross-legged before her.

"Hungry, huh? They don't feed you much here, then?" He waited patiently for her to finish and answer. The girl looked up apologetically.

"I only just got here," she spoke softly. "I've not had

much chance to eat yet. They wanted me to make sure you were okay first."

He frowned. "I'm Eric. What's your name?"

"Olivia," she said quietly.

"When were you taken, Olivia?" Eric kept his voice gentle.

She frowned at him. "I wasn't taken. I had to beg them to bring me in. I..." She took a deep breath. "I couldn't take hiding from the humans anymore."

"Why would you come here? Aren't there other packs that you could have gone to rather than the Faction?" Eric watched her back up towards the wall opposite his cell and pull her knees to her chest. She rested her chin on them, her eyes glistening with moisture.

"I've been rejected by packs my whole life. They don't want to take in someone who will be a liability. My whole family was killed in an attack by hunters and rabid shifters. At least the Faction has a place for me—they are fighting the packs that treat others with cruelty." Her voice trembled.

"That can't be right; our pack in Ireland never rejected a shifter." Eric moved towards the bars and watched Olivia, but she shrugged and didn't answer.

"I heard the Faction has been taking shifters against their will, I mean..." Eric paused. "Look at me, I didn't want to come here. They took me from my mate. We were on our way to find a friend of ours who settled with a pack around here." He frowned and looked around, "That is, if I'm still in the area I was taken."

"You mean Sumter? I heard they have a corrupt leader who brainwashes her pack and makes them weak." Olivia curled her lip in disgust. "The leader, she even brainwashed a human hunter into helping her, and she's with him. It's disgusting. We shouldn't mix with humans like that. And a hunter? What was she thinking?"

"That doesn't sound right." Eric sighed and leaned towards the wall near the bars. He lifted his hands to rub his face. "My mate is with them; I heard they were good people. Lachlan and Aine are mated; they were meant to be together."

"Everyone around here knows they aren't. The Faction has been defending against them—they attack us and reduce our numbers." She nodded firmly.

Eric shook his head, his stomach churned. "If what you say is true, then my mate is in danger. I need to get to her!" Eric stood frantically and called for the guard, who ignored him.

"Calm down. I'm sure they will help you if you ask." Oliva rose quickly but didn't come within arm's reach.

"Tell them I need to speak to someone. Why are they holding me here? They haven't even told me!" Eric shook the bars on his door, and Olivia backed away from him towards the guard.

"I'll go get someone," Oliva said, unsure. She turned, and Eric watched her figure disappear down the corridor of cells towards the guard.

~

ROLAN WATCHED Solus observing the group as they entered the ritual chamber. A large stone altar was situated in the middle of the circular room and held a copper bowl. Two more caves attached to this chamber, one of which led to Solus's quarters. Rolan had brought five wolves from the newcomers, members of the group who were either too sick, too old, or too weak to waste time training.

"I'm going to offer you an opportunity. This will help you become strong and help my pack." Solus's words caught their attention. Rolan watched the thin streams of dark smoke trail off Solus and towards the group. They looked pathetic and frail in front of the two powerful shifters.

Rolan curled his lip as the group cowered towards the edges of the room. Once the smoke made contact, the group relaxed, and Rolan waited for Solus's persuasion to start. The participants had to perform the ritual willingly.

"I have an honorable task for you." Solus's voice drifted over the group thick with power. Their heads snapped to look at him with rapt attention and adoration. "I need you to join a special section of my warriors. You will be important in the upcoming war."

Rolan snorted. It didn't matter what Solus said; the group was under his power and would do anything for him.

"Will you join me?" Eager heads nodded, and an older man with white hair stepped forward.

"What can I do to help?" His hands twitched in front of him as Solus released his power. The group pressed forth, eager to do their master's bidding.

Solus stepped toward the bowl on the stone altar. He drew out a penknife, and without flinching, he sliced his palm. A viscous fluid, thicker than blood, poured from his wound. Rolan wrinkled his nose as dark power surrounded the fluid. Solus closed his eyes in concentration. Rolan tried to discover how their leader performed this ritual on many occasions, but even being in the room, he was still clueless. The fluid flowed around the bowl, the surface of the liquid writhing, as Solus lifted the vessel into the air.

"Drink," he encouraged the group.

Greedily they approached, fighting for the first sip.

Rolan took the bowl from the last in the group to drink. The drained bowl was returned to the altar.

The man with white hair licked his lips and stared at Solus with wonder. His wide eyes clouded, and his grin never faltered as black veins spread from his mouth over his face, then down his neck. As the darkness devastated the man's body, his expression never changed, nor did his gaze waver. Rolan saw the effects wash over the rest of the group, and Solus stepped forward, hand outstretched. The old man's expression changed to one of rapture when the hand touched his head.

"Five more for my dark army." Solus grinned at Rolan. "We nearly have enough, but we need more if we are to take over all the packs in this area."

Rolan took an involuntary step back at his master's manic expression, but it disappeared when Solus shook his head. Dread left a heavy feeling in his stomach as he led the five dark wolves from the room to a cavern further in, where the other turned shifters lived.

They settled in with the others, sat like statues, staring into space. They would remain like this until commanded; once Solus let them loose, they would become rabid, and only he could control them unless Rolan could figure out a way to circumvent his grip.

3

Aine surveyed the medical room to see that everyone was silent and staring at the unconscious shifter before them. Horror twisted her insides as everyone watched Gary's still form.

"What just happened?" Conor's lean frame cautiously approached his friend. Slowly he placed the back of his hand on Gary's forehead. "He's burning up, even for a shifter."

The silence stretched; each face around the room shared the same blank expression. Aine shifted as each gaze eventually fell on her.

"Let's limit how many people know about this. I don't want to scare the rest of the pack, and Gary needs treatment. Tania, what do you think?"

"If I didn't know any better, I'd say he has rabies. He's acting rabid, and he definitely has a fever." Tania slowly approached Gary, her posture wary. Lachlan walked behind her and started to pick up the objects that had fallen to the floor.

"We need to get his temperature down." Tania turned to Eloi. "Can you get me water and some towels?"

Eloi nodded and turned to quickly leave the room. Aine frowned and looked out the window.

"We need to limit the number of people around him. I'm worried about others getting bitten if this is the result. Tania, you'll have to keep him restrained and sedated for now." Aine held up her hand as Ciara and Conor opened their mouths to object. Neither spoke. She then turned to Lachlan. "Have you heard of anything like this before?"

"No, but then my family wasn't big on keeping shifters alive long after we captured them." Lachlan cleared his throat and shifted uncomfortably. "Most weren't captured, especially if they were rabid. So we always put it down to them going crazy."

Aine shifted her gaze to Eyolf, who had so far avoided making eye contact. He gave a slight nod and tilted his head towards the door, and she looked to see who was left in the room. Ciara and Conor stood together, their faces full of concern as Tania examined the bite on Gary.

"Conor, Ciara." Aine crossed the room to them. "I'm sorry for your friend, but my pack's safety comes first. We will do everything we can for him and make him comfortable. You've had a long journey. Come with me, and I'll get you settled in one of our houses."

"Thank you." Conor put his arm around his sister, who nodded. "Sorry to bring this to your door."

Both siblings were quiet as Aine led them to one of the empty houses. Their village had expanded over the last three years, but shifters were often taken when the Faction made their attacks. They had plenty of accommodation now in Sumter as a result, but Aine's heart ached for those that had been lost. With this new development, she was more determined than ever to end the Faction—which meant working with the hunters.

Aine sighed and looked back towards the medical building where Lachlan and Eloi were helping Tania; Eyolf had wandered in the direction of his house. She would do anything to protect her family and her pack.

"It's not much, but I hope you'll be able to make yourselves comfortable. If you need anything, ask a member of the pack." Conor and Ciara, both looking pale, nodded with tight smiles. Aine left them to settle in and headed towards Eyolf's house. The old man knew something, and she hoped it would help.

WHEN AINE WALKED through Eyolf's door, he was already waiting for her at his kitchen table. They'd had many discussions in this room about their pack's future. Today felt different. A sense of foreboding gripped Aine, and a shiver ran through her. Eyolf's eyes were dark and turbulent, his mouth thin as he swallowed.

"That bad?" Aine looked to her mentor. He shifted in his chair and sighed.

"I hoped I'd never see this." His glance was in the direction of the medical building. Then, brushing hair from his face, "There is a reason that the legends about werewolves all center around bites."

"Really? I always thought that was something the humans made up." Aine leaned forward with her hand on the table.

"It's dangerous to use dark magic unless you're one of the original families. Your line has protections against it.

However, those outside your bloodline can be corrupted by it."

"You mean they go crazy like Rolan was starting to?"

"Pretty much." Eyolf looked tired, and for the first time, he looked his age. He rubbed his face with his hands and exhaled.

"One of the worst shifter wars nearly wiped out all the original families. The Aoibhans barely survived. One shifter discovered a way to infect his followers—he turned them into puppets. They're obedient, stronger, and more lethal than his other wolves. Once infected, they become a shell, mindless without a master, and can be used to overwhelm a pack. Their bites infected his enemies and turned them to his side if they didn't kill them first."

"How do you create them? Is there a cure?" Aine could feel her heart hammering in her chest as she waited for his answer.

"It sounds like Rolan discovered the magic. I'm not sure exactly how they're made, but what I do know is that a shifter would have to somehow use their own blood to infect the host with darkness from their power. It would temporarily weaken the master, but ultimately, the more they create, the more powerful the master would become. Your family could purge the infected wolves from what my records say, but most would die anyway. It became too dangerous to cure them as it appears the process weakened the person trying to heal and killed at least one." Eyolf's eyes met Aine's. "Don't even think about trying it. We can't lose you, Aine. It's too risky."

"I can't sit by and simply do nothing." Aine looked up at Eyolf and quickly stood. "I know you think I can't do it, but I'm so strong now, and I have been practicing and can control my power."

"Aine, please. Let's do more research before you try anything. Don't charge into the unknown without thinking." Eyolf grabbed her hand.

"Well, now, that doesn't sound like me." She smiled at him and squeezed his hand. "Look into it, but don't be too long. With this kind of thing, I believe, the sooner you can treat it, the better. I'll talk to Lachlan about this, but we shouldn't tell the others yet. I don't want to give them false hope if we can't help."

The air outside felt cool on Aine's face as she left. She admired the scene around her, at what they had built over the last three years. Though working with the humans in Burntwood Falls had been a risk, her pack was more comfortable than they'd ever been.

Aine closed her eyes and felt a cool breeze on her skin. She sighed heavily before making her way to see Lachlan; she needed to talk to him about his father.

~

LACHLAN WATCHED Ciara pace the kitchen of the house the siblings were staying in. Her gaze would periodically glance in the direction of the medical building. She had seemed so young when he left Ireland eighteen years ago, but the woman she had grown into was astounding.

It had taken time for her to recover from his brother's torture. Lachlan helped where he could, despite a difficult start with the pack; no one wanted to trust the hunter who stayed with them. Ciara had introduced him as the "Kind Warrior," a fable from the pack's past. A prophecy of a hunter who would mate with a shifter and the conflict between shifters and hunters would finally end. He hadn't believed her when she explained the stories to him, but he was more open to the idea since meeting Aine.

"So, you mated." Ciara's gaze fell on Lachlan as she passed him.

"As did you." Lachlan shifted and turned to stare out the window. An awkward silence fell between them. When Ciara stopped, Lachlan turned to look at her.

"I remember when I hoped that I was the shifter you would mate, that we could bring balance to the world together." Her laugh was light. "I must have seemed like a foolish little girl to you."

Lachlan chuckled. "Not foolish, just young. I was far too old for you… It's been too long; I should have contacted you more. I feel like…." He paused. "I feel like I let life run away with me a bit. I was in a haze, and the years just slipped away." He ran his hands down his face.

"You were like a ghost when you left us, only half there." Ciara's smile was small. "I'm surprised any packs accepted you in Europe."

"So am I. I look back now, and I can't for the life of me figure out why any of them trusted me." Lachlan's gaze pierced Ciara's. "I was a hunter. For all they knew, I could have been a spy. And no letter should have granted me access."

"It's the prophecy, Lachlan. Our packs have been without hope for so long. You saved my life and earned the trust of our pack."

Lachlan scoffed. "Many of them *didn't* trust me or want me there."

"But I knew you could be trusted—even losing your mother was part of the prophecy. I knew when you returned that night that she would be gone." Guilt flashed in Ciara's eyes.

"What?" Tension spread through Lachlan's body. "Why didn't you warn me?"

"It was already too late." Silent tears escaped Ciara's eyes as she watched him. "It had all been written."

Lachlan growled. "I could have saved her." He felt an awareness from Aine; she was heading towards the house. He closed his eyes. "I need to go."

"Lachlan, I..."

"No, Ciara, I can't right now." Lachlan strode towards the door, his chest heaving. "I'll talk to you later."

Aine came into view, a frown on her face as she caught sight of him. Lachlan kept his pace slow as he approached her, his fists clenched.

What's wrong? Even after three years, it still made Lachlan jerk when Aine spoke inside his head.

Old wounds. Lachlan opened his arms and sighed when Aine leaned into him with no hesitation. He looked in the direction Aine had come from, and his brows drew together.

What has Eyolf been hiding now?

Same old, same old. Aine shrugged in his arms. *There is a way for me to heal this sickness using my power. He knew more than he told us and knows more still.*

So many secrets. What's his excuse this time? Lachlan's sigh was content as he held Aine, the tension melting from his body.

You know his opinion on too much knowledge. Aine shifted as Lachlan waited for a chuckle which never came. *If I try to heal this sickness, chances are it won't work, and it could kill me in the process.*

Lachlan stiffened. *Then you don't try it, no matter what. You hear me? I can't lose you!*

He tightened his grip on Aine, and she held him just as tight. Through her, Lachlan felt a disturbance amongst the shifters posted near the northern border. First their curiosity, then their horror.

"Aine!" Lachlan exclaimed, but she was already moving. He felt her call to arms roll through Sumter.

The Faction returned, this time with reinforcements.

AINE FELT the vitriol of poisoned minds approaching, more invading from the Faction than had ever been sent before. A desire to do harm and take from her pack overwhelmed her senses and caused nausea to run through her. The alien thoughts invaded her head and called to the now roiling and bucking darkness within her.

She stumbled as she approached the northern border, her warriors already in formation. The edge of the trees before them seemed to darken, wind rustling through the leaves. The need to shift pulsed within her and recoiled from the dark power. Lachlan stood firm beside her, and she drew from his strength.

"You know what to do." Her eyes met each of the lead warriors while Nyko and Eloi fell in behind Lachlan. As her shifters from the border broke the tree line, frantic in their escape, black smoke rose around them. Aine felt the horror of one of her shifters reverberate through her when he fell and was dragged back into the trees. His cry was brief before it cut off.

She swallowed thickly as she watched the shifter disappear, another taken from her pack. Silence fell as the remaining two shifters who watched the north fell in amongst the warriors' ranks. Growls rang out through the trees, and the air vibrated. Aine held her breath as more than fifty wolves slowly stalked out of the trees.

Aine looked out at her warriors, their numbers now in the low thirties since the battle three years ago. Most of them were young and had already experienced too much violence. She strained to gather her power within, ready to defend her family. Tension rolled through her pack as the enemy before them approached.

She moved forward to position herself between the pack and the Faction. While drawing herself up to strike, a howl echoed from the trees as smoke swirled violently around them. It was their signal, and the rabid wolves began their charge.

Darkness struck the wolves before her, and Aine unleashed her power; like a torrent, it swept over them. The beasts slowed, limbs outstretched towards her friends and family. Then, as if moving through molasses, they inched closer. A cry escaped her, and Aine pumped more power into the dark smoke around her enemy. She could hear her warriors breathe around her while they waited for her signal to move in. Sweat stung her eyes.

Aine! Stop! It's not working! Lachlan's call felt muffled and far away. The power shifted, and it felt more like the wolves were pulling it from her. Aine fought to cut off the flow and drag the power back inside. Her limbs shook, and she threw her hands toward the power in desperation. Finally, the world tilted as the last of the dark smoke absorbed back into her, and Lachlan's arms caught her.

"Go!" Lachlan's shout made Aine jerk in his hold.

"I need to help!" Aine struggled from his grasp, legs trembling as she stood.

"You need rest." Lachlan reached for her again, but she had already turned toward the fight.

The warriors fought hard, despite the odds. The wolves attacking from the forest fought with ferocity but were untrained. Aine's heart clenched as she watched Eloi shift and throw herself into the fight, her pale wolf shining brightly. It was almost the same pure white of her own.

"Where are they all coming from?" Aine frowned, eyes scanning the trees.

"I don't know." Lachlan picked up his spear from where he had dropped it. "Let's go—I know you won't sit out. I've got your back."

Aine stopped resisting the urge to shift. Her jaw ached as it lengthened, muscles twisting, bones reshaping, then she gracefully dropped to four feet. Her strength seemed to return as she ran forward, powerful muscles carrying her into the fray. Lachlan was on her heels as they joined the fight.

~

ELOI FELT the snap of bone between her jaws, the wolf before her going down. She quickly discovered that snapping the neck was the only way to slow these demons down. She could feel Nyko on her flank, defending her side. The enemy wolves had the same coloring and veins as those that attacked Ciara and her group on the road.

She watched as Jason led a group of warriors further into the enemy. She stepped forward to follow, but a yelp had her head turning sharply.

Axel, a young warrior who shouldn't have been in the group, fell to her right. Front paws scrambled as he was dragged along the ground toward the trees. Nyko followed Eloi as she changed direction and sprinted after the young wolf. She nearly collided with an adversary when her path was blocked by a huge grey female. Eyes completely black and smoke encircling her body, the grey wolf's saliva dripped black from her jaw.

Eloi recoiled and lunged to the wolf's left, Nyko to the right. By the time the grey female had been taken down, Axel was nowhere in sight.

Did you see where they took him? Nyko's voice was frantic in Eloi's mind.

No. Eloi's reply sounded small, even to herself.

We can't leave him!

There are too many, we must protect the village! Eloi turned back to the fight. Despite the dwindling numbers of the enemy, the pack was still outnumbered.

Eloi felt the pack rise to a challenge from her mother. Aine had shifted and was exerting her influence on the pack. Like a battle cry, the call to defend their family and friends energized the warriors. Nyko looked back once more to the trees where Axel had disappeared before following Eloi back toward the fight.

The warriors formed a barrier between the enemy wolves and Sumter. Nyko and Eloi filled the gaps in the ranks and turned to face the trees once more. Warriors were interspersed within the enemy, overrun, and injured. A whine escaped Eloi, and she turned to Aine.

Mom!

I know, Eloi. My power isn't working. It's like they were feeding on it.

Aine howled, and the warriors moved forward as one, each wolf feeling the intentions and movements of the others.

A shot rang out from the east, followed closely by a volley. Shock reverberated through the pack, but they held their line. Enemy wolves in front of them fell. A piercing howl echoed through the trees, and the rabid wolves turned to flee, some clamping their jaws around injured warriors and dragging them with them.

Lachlan surged forward, he wielded his spear piercing the heart of a wolf that had turned and lunged towards him. Five of the pack were being dragged towards the trees; he felt Eloi reach his side, and together they sprinted toward their fallen comrades. Lachlan pumped his legs harder, but one by one, they disappeared. With his heart hammering in his chest and Eloi panting beside him, they gained on the final warrior being taken.

Jason scrambled desperately, his black fur matted and wet with blood around a large bite in his flank. His eyes met Lachlan's, and the spear hurtled towards one of the wolves dragging the warrior. Eloi leaped at the second wolf and Jason fell still, breathing heavy. When Lachlan approached to help, Jason's growl vibrated the injured shifter's body.

"Still don't like me, huh?" Lachlan ignored him and helped the wolf to his feet, and Eloi leaned against his side, allowing him to limp back toward the pack. Lachlan let out a long breath and turned toward the east. His father and a group of hunters stood along the eastern tree line waiting, rifles at the ready. Running a hand through his hair, he turned to approach the group. His heart was heavy, and a weariness ran through his body as he forced himself to take each step.

"Bit of trouble you're having." Liam's cocky grin spread across his face.

"You were tracking them?" Lachlan looked to the hunters in the group. Most were men he didn't know. Thankfully his brothers weren't among them, though he did miss Cillian.

"From the north, I think they are staying in the cave

systems. Good thing we were here." Liam kept his face blank.

"Coming around to the idea that not all shifters are bad?" Lachlan held his breath as his father grunted, mumbling something under his breath. "Let me see to the pack, then I'll meet you in town."

By the time Lachlan returned to the pack, Jason had shifted into his human form. With his shirt removed, the bite that had been evident when he was being dragged into the forest was stark against his human skin. Aine examined it, her brow creased and face paled.

"We need to get you to the medical building," she said. "This doesn't look good."

It's the same as Gary. Aine's sorrow drifted through her mental link with Lachlan. Her eyes shot to Eloi and towards the rest of the pack.

"Has anyone else been bitten?" she asked, scanning her warriors.

4

Lachlan pulled into the drive of his old house. After he'd permanently moved to Sumter, and his father made it clear he wasn't leaving, Lachlan offered Liam the house. It felt strange knocking on his old front door.

The front of the house looked overrun with plants and foliage, but it felt like it could have been days since he left instead of years. He looked towards Phil's diner, just out of sight, missing the days he would walk over and see his friend. Guilt flooded him as he realized he'd neglected Phil the last year. The big man would occasionally come and visit him in Sumter, but he hadn't been back into town in a while.

The door opened, and Lachlan turned to face Finn. His brother scowled. "What do you want? You're not welcome here."

"I have a meeting with Liam." Lachlan kept his face passive and his hands at his sides. The last time he had seen Finn, he'd gotten sucker-punched. Lachlan defended himself, and eventually, Finn had to concede defeat; there was no love lost between the two.

Finn's lip curled up into a sneer. "He's in town." The door slammed in Lachlan's face.

Lachlan sighed and turned back to his truck. He stopped before he got in and walked past it; the diner wasn't far. He smiled when he pushed the door open and looked around at the booths.

"Lachlan, good to see ya, man!" Phil removed his apron and walked around from the counter. He pulled his friend into a bear hug and clapped him on the back. "It's been too long."

Lachlan couldn't help his grin. "I know; I should have come sooner. How're you doing?"

"Been hanging out with Cillian a lot. He reminds me of you." Phil gestured to a booth, and they took a seat. There were a couple of customers in the diner, but with it being late afternoon, it wasn't busy, and no one paid them much attention.

"Cillian is the most like our ma; I reckon that's why my father keeps him close," Lachlan said fondly.

"How are the girls? You should bring them more often. I miss them, though I guess I could visit more too." Phil winked at him.

"They are well—we are having a few problems, though," Lachlan told Phil about the recent attacks. "I'm going to see Liam, see if he's open to supporting us. I'm hoping that because he will be fighting rabid shifters, he will see my side and agree."

"Hmm, I don't see why not. Cillian said he's really coming around. Eloi helps. He finds her irresistible." Phil laughed. "Last time she was here, she spent the whole time calling him grandpa. He got all grouchy, but I did catch a smile at one point."

"She gets under everyone's skin, hard not to adore her," Lachlan chuckled. "Fancy coming into town with me?"

"Nah, I have to be here today. Got inventory to take care of," he groaned.

They chatted a while longer until a family came in, and Phil got up to help his staff. "Don't be a stranger," he said, clapping Lachlan on the back. "I miss you coming in here."

"I promise I'll be back. Probably later to pick up food on my way home. Eloi won't forgive me otherwise," Lachlan teased.

The drive into Burntwood Falls didn't take long. He spotted a few hunters on the way and wondered at how things had changed in just three years. Once he'd parked outside his store in town, he walked toward the bench that used to be his favorite spot. He wasn't surprised to find his father now sitting there.

Lachlan watched across the street as Maddie and her husband left Maddie's store; he could never remember the man's name. Maddie offered a tentative wave and Lachlan smiled back at her.

Liam raised an eyebrow at the exchange. "Friends of yours?"

"Yeah, I should come back into town more." Lachlan sat next to his father.

"You look tired, son. You're not getting enough rest. Probably could use help with those monsters." Liam cocked his head.

"I've been saying the same thing to you for three years." Lachlan ran his hand through his hair. "They're getting bolder, and this last lot.... More like zombies than shifters."

Liam nodded. "Yes, they seem to be infected with... something. Reminds me of rabies."

"You've seen them, then? Was anyone bitten?" Lachlan gripped the edge of the bench.

"Yeah, we've patrolled the woods and encountered them. Some bites, but they're superficial wounds. We heal faster than most, so it's not been an issue." Liam shrugged.

"Your hunters weren't infected?" Lachlan's brow furrowed.

"Infected how?"

"We've had a couple of shifters infected. It turns them, and they attack their friends, anyone. Aine's spoken to our historian, and this same thing devastated packs in the early shifter wars." Lachlan thumped the side of the bench. "Only Rolan would dare use such a weapon and risk uncontrolled infection."

He paused, swallowed, and looked at his father. "Aine's power could cure them and possibly kill her at the same time. I don't want her to risk it, but you know how stubborn she is."

Liam's eyes darkened. "Now that doesn't sound good. Why are you telling me?"

"Because we need to work together. You keep asking me to come back to you, but it can work both ways. Work with the pack. The time you've been here, they haven't attacked humans; they've defended the area. You have to admit it would be advantageous to have shifters on your side." Lachlan relaxed his features and looked around the town. "This area will need hunters *and* shifters to survive these attacks. We need to pool our resources."

"What would your lady shifter's pack say about that?"

"They're reluctant, but do you blame them?" Lachlan shifted. "Our family has a reputation. There's a shifter visiting from Ireland. You would remember her as the girl Finn tortured, the one I helped to escape that night."

"Finn?" Liam barked. "That son of mine is a bully. I wish I'd seen it before and reined it in. That is my failing. He's getting out of hand."

Lachlan didn't look at his father and remained silent. He looked at the sleepy town and almost envied their lives. Though if they didn't stop the threat from the Faction, this town would no longer enjoy these calm days. He rose.

"I know things are strained between us, but you're still my son. I don't know where I went wrong with you. Or maybe what went right...." Liam scrubbed his hands down his face. "I'm getting old, and I can feel it. You need to be the one to take over. Finn—well, he's Finn. The others don't have the strength to lead. I didn't see it before, but you do."

Lachlan froze. "I don't want to lead the hunters."

"That's what makes you the best choice." Liam watched his son.

"I'll think about it. We are better off working together, and if I did take over leadership, you know I'd work with the shifters. I know it'll be hard to overcome decades of conflict between hunters and shifters, but I've found a history where we worked together for the benefit of both groups." Lachlan chuckled at the stunned look on his father's face. "If I'm to lead the hunters, and I'm not saying I will, you need to start working with us. You know where you can find me. Send some of the younger warriors to test the water."

Lachlan strolled back to his truck, a breeze whispering across his face as he opened the door. When he looked back at Liam, the older man's face was pensive, and Lachlan hoped they could come to an agreement.

Nyko waited in a dark corner for Eloi to come from Eyolf's home; he shrunk back into the shadows and tried to keep his breath shallow. The moon rose above the settlement, a waning crescent barely visible in the sky. Perfect conditions for someone to sneak around and blend in. He watched the small figure stroll down the street between the houses toward their home and grinned as she drew closer to his hiding place.

His muscles coiled as he prepared to spring out at her; with a giant leap, he aimed to tackle her. But, with a quick sidestep and strategically placed hand, Eloi turned the tackle into a throw, and Nyko was on his back. His brow furrowed as he stared up into Eloi's face.

"Damn, I thought I had you that time!" Nyko rubbed the back of his head and groaned. Eloi held her hand out to him and helped him to his feet, then laughed.

"Better luck next time," she smirked at him.

"You're not supposed to sense for me during these exercises. That's not fair," Nyko grumbled.

"I wasn't; you just get overexcited and give yourself away just before you jump out. I hear you move." Eloi winked at him, and he nudged her with his shoulder. She stumbled slightly and pushed him back.

"Hey, you big bully!"

"Better than a spoiled brat," Nyko laughed.

Eloi had once hoped he would see her as more than an annoying little sister. But in moments like these, she cringed when she thought back on her crush.

"What's for dinner?" Eloi strode toward the home they shared with Aine and Lachlan.

"Lachlan went to the town, so probably Phil's burgers." Nyko's stomach growled audibly.

The pair bickered as they approached the house; it was

quiet, with only a tiny glow emitting from a light near the back. He followed Eloi into the entranceway and looked towards the kitchen. He frowned when he saw Aine at the table, head in her hands. Eloi abruptly stopped at his side.

"Mom?" Eloi walked over to her mother's side and crouched next to her.

"I'm okay, just worried about Jason and Gary." Aine paused. "I should help them, but the risk outweighs the chance of saving them."

"Can I help, Mom?" Eloi stroked her mother's arm.

"I don't know...maybe. Your power is almost as strong as mine was at your age," Aine said, rising. "We will have to consult with Eyolf, see what he's discovered from his research on the bites."

"Can I do anything?" Nyko hovered near the door, and Aine smiled at him.

"I don't think so. It's something that has been noted before in our history. But books will only tell you so much without practical experience." The leader looked between the two of them. "Just don't get bitten. I couldn't bear to lose either of you." She pulled them into a hug.

The front door creaked as it opened, and Lachlan walked in, holding takeaway bags from the diner.

"Burgers, anyone?" He walked through to the kitchen and dropped the bags on the table. Then, moving to the counter on the other side, he crouched to reach for plates in the cupboard. "Eloi, grab the cutlery, please."

As they sat down for the meal, Nyko watched each of them. Eloi snuck glances at her mom, and Lachlan watched each of them. Eventually, his gaze caught Nyko's, and he offered a small smile.

"Didn't manage to outwit her, then," Lachlan chuckled. Nyko groaned as the tension broke.

"How could you tell?"

"Because you'd be bragging about it if you'd got her." Lachlan looked across to Eloi. "He got too excited as he was about to jump out at you, didn't he?"

"Yup." Eloi took a bite of her burger and groaned. "This never gets old," she mumbled around her mouthful.

"Eloi, swallow before you speak." Aine smiled at her daughter, her eyes sparkling.

"Uh-huh."

They ate in silence, with an odd moan from Eloi as she ate her second burger. Nyko watched Aine; she twisted her hands in her lap and hadn't eaten much. He'd never seen her this nervous.

"How did it go with your father?" Aine asked Lachlan, her lips thinned and hands stilled.

"He wants me to take the leadership of the hunters. I told him if I did, I would be working with shifters. He's actually considering it."

Aine sighed. "Better than nothing, I guess."

"Give him time; he's come quite a long way in three years. Although, Finn may be a problem." Lachlan shrugged and sighed heavily.

"That doesn't surprise me." Aine took his hand, and they sat in silence. Nyko shifted uncomfortably; Eloi rolled her eyes.

"Mom, we need to talk to Eyolf to see if we can combine our power to help Jason and Gary." Eloi looked between Aine and Lachlan as Lachlan's head whipped up to Aine.

"You said you wouldn't try. It's too dangerous." His voice had a note of desperation.

"We need all the shifters we can get, and Jason is one of our best!" Aine let a breath out through her nose. "I couldn't live with myself if I didn't at least try."

"So now you'll endanger Eloi, too." Aine winced at Lachlan's words.

"I can do it!" Eloi yelled as she stood.

"Sit down, Eloi," Aine spoke firmly.

"No, I'm going back to Eyolf. He must know something!" Eloi pushed her chair hard, and it rocked slightly as she left the room.

Aine pinched her brow. "Let her go. Eyolf will talk to her."

Nyko made himself small as he stood and slinked towards the edge of the room, Aine and Lachlan carrying on in quiet tones. Lachlan reached up to cup Aine's face, and Nyko felt his chest tighten as he left. He wondered if he would find a partnership like theirs one day. And he didn't envy Eloi—she had a lot to live up to with Aine as her mom.

Walking out the front door, he took a gulp of air, then began to wander through the village. This late at night, most of the pack members were in their homes. With so little moon out, the stars twinkled clear and bright. His path led him to the medical building, and he could see lights on as he approached the door. When he pushed it open, Tania looked up from Gary, who slept fitfully.

"How are you holding up in here?" Nyko carefully walked into the room.

"Same as before, really. I've had to sedate Jason. Gary is unchanged." Tania sighed and leaned away from the bed. "I don't really know what else I can do."

"Is there really no hope?"

"I've never seen anything like this before. I've tried to break their fevers, but it's getting worse. I can't let up on the sedatives, or they might bite someone, and then we'll have another case." Her hand reached for her necklace and clutched it to her chest. "It's hopeless."

"Nothing is hopeless. Look what we've been through before. Aine will think of something." Nyko hoped he wasn't lying. "She always does."

Tania turned to him. She started to shake, and Nyko gulped. Awkwardly he lifted his arms and placed them around her, and she leaned against his chest. He patted her back, looking at the two unconscious shifters, their skin pale and clammy, Gary moaning as he slept. Nyko closed his eyes and tried to will them to get better.

"Maybe you should take a break, Tania. I'll stay with them. You've been here all day." Nyko gently pushed her back so he could look at her face. She sniffled and looked up at him with wet eyes.

"Thank you, I…I need some rest." Tania slowly turned and left the building.

Nyko picked up a book from one of the bedside tables and sat in a chair in the corner. He pulled another chair close with his foot and crossed his feet on it. He might as well get comfortable; it was going to be a long night.

EYOLF JUMPED as Eloi entered his house, slamming the door, then chuckled as she stormed over to his kitchen table.

"Trouble, youngling?"

"I'm not a youngling anymore, and I wish everyone would remember that!" Eloi exclaimed. She huffed as she threw herself into a chair, folded her arms on the table, and rested her chin on them.

"Hard to not think of you as a youngling when you throw yourself around like you are." Eyolf chuckled again at Eloi's scowl. "What's bothering you?"

"I want to help Mom cure the bitten shifters." Eloi

paused. "I'm strong. If we combine our power, then we may be able to cure them."

"Hmmm." Eyolf's lip twitched, and he tapped his chin with one finger. "It might work. But the risks, Eloi. There's a reason Aine hasn't tried already, and I don't think we should risk you both in that way."

"We can do it; I know we can." Eloi looked up hopefully.

"I'll do some research. You are both powerful, but I don't understand enough about this malady."

"Thanks, I just want to help. What if more of the pack gets bitten? We need a way to fight this!" Eloi hit the table with her fist. "I hate feeling helpless."

"Does this have anything to do with your father being alive and leading the Faction?" Eyolf sat in front of Eloi and took her hands.

"He's not my father. I just have the misfortune of sharing his blood," Eloi huffed.

"Aren't you worried about seeing him again, especially if he's coming after the pack so aggressively?" Eyolf raised his eyebrow. Eloi rolled her eyes, then shrugged.

"We will deal with him like we did last time. Lachlan went to his father. If the hunters are on our side, we will stand a better chance."

"Hopefully." Eyolf's gaze turned wistful. The silence stretched between them, and Eloi took back her hands. A dull headache had started to throb behind her eyes.

"What if we used the medallion? It would increase my power, and then I could help."

Eyolf's face went pale. "Eloi, you would be unconscious for days, and that's if it even worked and didn't kill you. There is a reason your mother won't let you use the medallion. Trust her."

"But I'm not a baby! So why is she holding me back? At

my age, she was leading our pack!" Eloi ground her teeth, and Eyolf rose from his chair.

"I'll find out what I can. But we need to be careful, Eloi. Forget the medallion. You would need time to learn to control that power. Aine barely could at first, if you remember." Eyolf reached out a hand, and Eloi ignored it.

"I hope there is a solution," she said, crossing her arms over her chest. "Those dark wolves are hard to fight. It's like they have no will of their own, like robots and are being controlled. We need all the help we can get."

"I think that's what they're made for, to be relentless." Eyolf's brow creased, and he stared out of his kitchen window into the darkness.

"I'll leave you to it then." Eloi stormed towards the door and left him to his reverie, kicking his fence as she passed. She knew she shouldn't leave, but she needed to be in her quiet place. Without thought, she wandered toward the edge of the village.

~

Nyko jerked awake when a loud crash echoed through the room. The book he'd been holding fell from his hand. Gary thrashed on his bed, still not conscious, but he had knocked over his IV stand. Nyko sent a pulse of urgency towards Aine, hoping she would pick up the message and was not sleeping already. He ran over to Gary to pick the stand back up; fortunately, it was still connected. All he could do was hold Gary in place and hope someone arrived to help him soon. His ears strained as he heard footsteps outside, and a harried Tania pushed through the door.

"What happened?"

"He started thrashing and knocked his IV over. I'm not

sure I can hold him in place much longer!" Nyko's arms strained against Gary's efforts to throw himself out of bed. The injured man's eyes snapped open, and an inhuman growl escaped his throat.

"Hurry, Tania!" Nyko urged.

Tania glanced up as she grabbed a vial and quickly filled a syringe. She administered the syringe into Gary's IV line with admirable efficiency just as his teeth snapped toward Nyko's forearm. Nyko flinched. Gary's eyes rolled into the back of his head, and Nyko felt him relax under his grip.

"Are you okay?" Tania's eyes shone as she looked at him.

Nyko's eyes flicked towards her, and it was then he noticed she wore a thin tank top and shorts. He coughed as his face flushed with heat, then lifted his arm to scratch the back of his head.

"Yeah..." He coughed again. "I'm fine."

Tania blushed as she noticed his gaze but didn't look away. She brushed her hair out of her face and smiled at him. He realized how close they were and held his breath as silence fell between them. Both jumped apart when the infirmary door crashed open, and Lachlan ran in.

"Everyone okay?" His eyes darted around the room.

"Fine, just Gary decided he was done napping. We... disagreed." Nyko gestured toward the unconscious man. Tania crossed her arms and looked self-consciously at the floor.

"Alright then, you have this under control?" Lachlan raised an eyebrow at Nyko, and the boy felt his face heat again. He looked at his feet.

"Yes, sir." Nyko flicked his hand in an awkward salute. He shook his head and groaned.

"Very well. I'll be getting back to my wife." Lachlan

winked at Nyko, and Tania's blush deepened. Nyko stared at Lachlan's back as he left, then turned back to Tania.

"So..." He let his voice trail off. "What now?"

"Erm, I think that Gary is burning the sedative off too quickly. I don't think we can keep him under longer than maybe another day. We need another solution." Tania sighed. "I'm going to go and get dressed. Will you be alright with them for a few more minutes?"

"Sure. When you get back, I can stay and keep you company."

"You don't have to do that." Tania cocked her head and smiled prettily at him. As she turned to leave, Nyko failed to keep from admiring her backside. He gulped and shook his head at himself.

"Sure, but I want to," he said. "You're in here alone too much." He quickly looked to the corner at his chair and approached it, picking up the book he'd dropped in his sleep. A pang of guilt gnawed at him. At least he'd woken up in time; he would have to be more vigilant if he was going to keep watch here.

5

Aine sat in the kitchen, looking out the window as the sun broke the horizon and warming her hands on her coffee. She hadn't had coffee before she met Lachlan and wasn't sure how she had lived so long without it.

Lachlan had warned Aine of Gary's condition when he got back the night before. She hadn't slept all night as she weighed their options. His medallion, and the power it could offer, weighed heavily on her mind, but Eloi wasn't ready.

"You been up all night?" Lachlan yawned in the doorway, shirtless with pajama bottoms that hung low on his hips. "Eloi didn't come home."

"I know, I had hoped she wasn't stupid enough to leave the borders, but she's in her place. I've been keeping a mental link just in case." Aine's eyes burned when she closed them.

Lachlan put a hand on her shoulder, then looked at her and sighed. "You've decided, then?"

"I have to try. Unfortunately, Gary is out of time. I can feel the parasite, or whatever it is, spreading through him, and he's nearly gone." Aine looked up at him. "How can I ignore that?"

Lachlan stepped back to lean against the wall, his arms crossed over his chest. Aine watched his naked torso muscles flex as he moved and licked her lips. He sensed this, and his mood shifted as his lips curved in a half-grin.

"Like what you see?"

"An empty house and my husband half-naked?" Aine cocked her head and raised an eyebrow. Then, she turned in her chair and parted her legs invitingly. A low growl escaped Lachlan as he prowled towards her, and Aine watched him, thinking, *He'd make a perfect wolf.*

As he caged her in with his arms, hands on the table, she lifted her chin. Their faces were barely an inch apart, and their breath mingled. Lachlan leaned in for a slow kiss, so intense that Aine couldn't stop a moan from escaping. Her skin tingled as he ran one hand up her arm, and her core ached. As she deepened the kiss, Lachlan lifted her from the chair; he laughed when he bumped into the doorframe on his way out of the kitchen.

"You're so beautiful, Aine. Have I told you that today?"

"Nope, you're slacking."

"I'm anything but slacking." Lachlan winked saucily as they entered their bedroom. He laid her down on the ruffled sheets and moved his hands down her body. Aine arched into his touch, nipples hardened and sensitive against the shirt she wore. She gasped, surprised when his fingers found a sensitive spot above her hip. His growing need was evident when he leaned down to kiss her. His hands moved up to run through her hair and frame her face.

"You're mine, Aine. I can't lose you."

"You won't," Aine gasped. Primal need gripped her, and

she throbbed, ready for him. Frantically, she pushed down his pants and ran her hands up his muscular body. Lachlan stepped closer to the bed and lowered himself on top of her, their bodies close.

"You are wearing too many clothes." Lachlan kissed down her jaw.

"What you going to do about it?" Aine giggled.

He gripped her shirt and, in one movement, tore it down the front. Aine gasped at the shock of cold air, quickly replaced by the feel of his skin along hers. She moved her hands over his glorious shoulders and arms. He ground his hips into hers as he kissed her, and she felt him hard against her center. The delicious friction caused pulses of pleasure to surge through her.

"Still too many clothes," Aine panted. Lachlan groaned against her shoulder.

"You're killing me, Aine."

She gently pushed him away and freed herself of her cumbersome clothing. Before she could react, he was on her again, pushing her legs open and leaning over her. As he pushed two fingers into her wetness, she gasped in pleasure, his thumb circling her sensitive apex. Aine gripped his shoulder as an orgasm seized her; it crashed over her in waves, and she moaned.

Lachlan's next kiss was full of need and urgency. He slowly slid into her and filled her up, Aine crying out from the intense feeling. Their bodies entwined; he started to move slowly at first but soon lost control. All Aine could do was hold on and savor the feel of her man inside her. She felt pleasure build further; Lachlan's groan nearly tipped her over again; she was so close. Then, with one final thrust, she succumbed, and he quivered over her before stilling.

Each shock of pleasure caused her to shake, sensitive in all the right places.

Lachlan rolled off her, chest heaving as he pulled her hand to his lips for a kiss. Aine smiled at him and rolled over to put her head on his chest. She breathed a content sigh.

"Ready to face the day?" Lachlan's voice rumbled under her ear.

"No, can today come back tomorrow?"

Lachlan laughed and held her close. Aine scrunched up her eyes and let out a breath while he stroked her arm gently.

They lay there in silence until they heard the front door open. Then, looking at each other, their wide eyes turned in unison to their open bedroom door. Aine laughed as Lachlan leaped up to close it, exhaling when he barred the door.

"I doubt either of them would come in here." Aine rose and let her hips sway a little as she retrieved her clothes from the floor. She crinkled her nose. "Can't wear this again."

She tossed the shirt into a corner and dressed in something more sensible. Lachlan walked up behind her and wrapped his arms around her waist.

"Dressing is hard like this," she squeaked.

"Are you trying for round two?"

"That would be nice, but things to do, people to see." Aine grinned wickedly at him.

"God, I love you, woman." He slapped her backside playfully and turned to dress himself.

Aine stretched her body, which ached in the right places. The worries from earlier threatened to invade her thoughts, but she kept them at bay a little longer. She turned to gaze and admire the handsome Irish man in her bedroom, grinning in his direction. Lachlan's eyes sparkled with intensity.

"Aine? Lachlan?" Nyko's footsteps paused outside their bedroom, and Aine smothered a laugh.

"Coming!" Aine walked towards the door and just caught Lachlan's mumble, for their ears only.

"We both just did."

She couldn't suppress her grin, and Nyko groaned when she opened the door. Her face dropped when she saw the look on his face.

"He's worse, isn't he?" Aine tensed and closed her eyes. "I'll be there in five minutes; let me have one more cup of coffee."

AINE ENDED up taking the coffee with her on the way to the medical building. Eyolf intercepted her on the way.

"I've been reading up and—"

"It doesn't matter, Eyolf; if it doesn't help, then I don't want to know. I've made my decision, and I won't involve Eloi." Aine strode past her mentor and walked with purpose.

"I figured as much," Eyolf huffed. "You read the books I gave you about the procedure?"

"It's similar to how I purged the pack, just...more intense." Aine kept her face blank as she entered the medical building. Ciara and Conor stood to one side with somber faces. She schooled her expression and mentally took a deep breath, then walked over to Tania.

"He's burning off the sedative. I don't know what else to do." Tania's eyes were downcast, and she looked tired.

"You have done an admirable job. We haven't seen this before in our lifetime. No one could have done better." Aine placed a hand on Tania's shoulder and gave it a squeeze. "I'll take it from here. You'll need to be on standby...in case this does not work."

Tania's eyes sprang to Aine's, and the younger woman opened her mouth to protest. But Aine gave a slight shake of her head and turned to face the room. Several members of her pack had gathered to see Jason.

"Clear the room," Aine said quietly to Tania, who was wringing her hands. The woman jumped and sprang into action. In moments there were only the unconscious Jason and Gary, Lachlan, and Eyolf left.

"If this kills me, Eloi will have to lead. This is our way, Lachlan—guide her, but you will have to step down." Aine turned to him. As he stepped back, he opened his mouth to say, *"Please don't,"* but didn't finish, his expression careful.

Aine turned to Eyolf. "Are you ready, old man?" she smirked.

"Are you?" Eyolf looked pale but stood regal.

Aine approached Gary. The shifter was already twitching as if the sedative was wearing off again. She sat on the chair next to the bed and placed her hands on his chest. At the first touch, the power pulled into the unconscious man. Aine closed her eyes and frantically grasped at the power to control the flow.

A map of the man's body appeared in her mind, and she could feel the points where her power drew into him. A black hole near his heart drained his energy and his soul. She avoided that area, concentrating around his center, close to his heart, his essence. It was weak, surrounded by a malevolent dark mass. Aine tried to circle a protective barrier around him, but the strands that held him there were fragile. She reached out for his presence, his mind. A ghost appeared before her, looking starved, eyes hollow and barely visible.

Gary?

Who are you?

I'm Aine. I lead the pack in Sumter. Do you remember coming to us?

The ghost looked around bewildered and started when his gaze fell on her again.

Who are you? His mental voice was faint, and his hands shook.

Do you remember Ciara and Conor? They came with you. And Eric?

Eric was taken. Better to be taken... Gary's voice faded, and his appearance dimmed.

Gary, I need you to hold on!

Gary's pale figure looked around again and didn't seem to see her. A tear escaped Aine's closed eye as she looked to the essence inside him. Weaker now, it was barely present against the dark spiderweb inside him.

Aine grasped the essence of the wolf before her and held on for them both. Her energy drained from her faster as she pushed her power into every inch of him. It fought with the parasite, but she could feel Gary's essence quickly fading.

She screamed in frustration and felt more power push out of her, pain lancing through her body, and in a panic, she tried to stop the flow of power. A familiar dark figure loomed over her, the features obscured by shadow. With the shadow's presence, her power pulled out of her faster. The torrent wouldn't slow; she felt Gary's essence give a final pulse, then disappear. Her own energy bled into the void that was once the man.

In desperation, she reached out to Lachlan, his voice drifting softly into her head.

Don't leave me.

Eloi woke with a start; the presence of someone in the area had her on her feet in a second. She looked around frantically but saw no sign of anyone. She rubbed her eyes and blinked at the sunlight which shone through the trees. She lay on the flat rock next to the pool of water; it had become her place and was where she went to be at peace.

But a presence still loomed. She reached out with her mind but couldn't sense anyone. She shook her head and watched the ripples across the small pond created by the waterfall.

Eloi collected herself and brushed off the moss and dirt on her clothes, turning to scan the area one last time before heading home. She reached out with her mind to gauge her mother's reaction, and to her horror, there was a blankness where her mother's presence should have been. She spread her reach further, but she couldn't feel her mother anywhere on pack land.

With a gasp, Eloi shifted faster than she ever had before and sprinted back toward her home. Lachlan wouldn't be far from her, and his mind was in turmoil. The rhythm of her paws thudding on the ground echoed the urgency in her mind.

As the houses came into view, Eloi felt a gathering around the medical center. Her heart sank as she raced forward. Nyko's tall figure came into view, holding Tania close to him as she sobbed quietly. Eloi shifted and looked at the pack, who surrounded the medical building. She raced to the door and pushed it open; it bounced off the wall and narrowly missed hitting her as she sped into the room. Lachlan sat on the floor with Aine in his arms; he clutched her close to his chest.

"I can't...." His voice broke. "I can't feel her."

Eloi slid into a crouch beside him. Her hands scrambled for her mother's chest, and she pushed energy into her. There was no heartbeat, so Eloi pushed her energy into her mother's center. She searched for any sign. Relief flooded the girl as a heartbeat fluttered beneath her hands.

"She's not breathing, Lachlan. Breathe for her!" She looked up at the broken man, her eyes begging him to help her.

"TANIA!" Her voice echoed around the room. The petite woman crashed through the door, tears streaking her red face.

"Yes?"

"She's still here, do something!" Eloi still poured energy into Aine, weariness sweeping through her. But each beat of her mother's heart spurred her on. Lachlan had laid Aine before him, tilting her head back to breathe into her.

"Not too often, Lachlan—here, let me help. Step back, both of you." Tania moved a defibrillator next to Aine. "Both of you need to give me space; I won't be able to help with you hovering. Nyko, you help me. You two outside."

Lachlan led Eloi out to let Tania work. "What happened?" the girl screamed in his face. He didn't look like he knew where he was. She grabbed his face and made his eyes focus on hers. "What happened, Lachlan?"

"She...she tried to save Gary. I can't feel her, Eloi." Lachlan tried to drop to his knees.

"Do not fall apart! The pack can't see you like this. She's still here. Tania will save her;." Eloi felt him hold his own weight, and he took a deep breath. His face was pale, but he nodded.

"Give me something to do."

"Go and find Ciara—she's your friend, right? I'm guessing Gary didn't make it?" Eloi's voice held all the command she could muster. Lachlan nodded and stumbled away from her.

She had kept her connection with Aine, and despite her fatigue, she still let energy trickle down their bond. Eyolf stood in front of the pack. Giving her a nod, he turned to herd the pack away from the medical building.

Eloi gasped as she felt a pulse of energy return from her mother. She let out a breath and glanced meaningfully toward Eyolf. He closed his eyes and let out a long breath, the tension from his shoulders visibly released. Eloi walked around the corner of the building; no one was in sight. She fell to her knees clutching her hands to her chest, her arms trembling. Her eyes stung as she straightened and turned back toward the building. Chest tight, she took one step at a time and pushed the door open.

Aine was laid on a bed. She looked pale and still, but Tania smiled as Eloi entered.

"She's breathing on her own. I don't know how you did it, Eloi, but you kept her alive. She was gone, and...." Tania sobbed and threw herself at the girl.

Eloi hugged her and let her cry. Nyko came into view behind Tania, his face pinched, and he looked ready to drop. Eloi pushed Tania toward him and moved to sit next to her mother. Aine's hand felt cold in her own.

"Will she wake?" Eloi turned to Tania.

"Yes, she's strong. I felt her energy when she came back, that command she holds...you know?" Tania still clung to Nyko, and Eloi smiled.

"Yes, I know. You might want to tell Lachlan she's okay."

"Of course." Nyko's voice was tight as he led Tania out of the room. "Call me if you need me."

Eloi felt the tension leave her body as they exited; tiredness dragged her down. She lay her head on the bed and still trickled energy into Aine through her hand. Her eyes drifted closed, and her head felt fuzzy. As she snoozed next to her mother, a whisper of a thought caressed her mind.

I love you, Eloi.

LACHLAN SAT with his head in his hands. Aine still slept in the medical building. Whatever she had done, Gary hadn't made it. Ciara and Conor mourned their friend. Tania worried about Jason's rapid deterioration, and tension within the pack was apparent. Lachlan still couldn't connect with his wife and mate; his head ached, and nausea stopped him from eating.

"Lachlan, you need to go and get some rest." Eloi walked into the medical building and came to stand next to him. "You're no good to anyone here. Without Aine, you need to reassure the pack. That's your job."

Lachlan scraped his hands down his face and blinked at the light in the room. Eloi had acted above her years and set a great example of the leader she would be. He rose and shook his head.

"You're right, I just...." He didn't really know what he was going to say. "I can't feel her anymore."

"She's there; just give her time. I wish she'd waited for me to help."

"She wouldn't risk losing both of you and leaving the pack defenseless." Lachlan cringed when he looked at his actions over the last day. He strode with purpose towards their family home to quickly shower and shave.

He would touch base with the warriors and see how their defenses faired. Without Aine to give them warning, their borders were vulnerable.

SOLUS WOKE FROM A DEEP SLEEP. He'd performed too many initiations recently and could feel the toll it took on him. The wolves taken from Aine's pack were now securely under his control; still, he needed more.

With each new initiation, his power grew exponentially, but his body paid the price. He groaned as he rose—his mind had been with a wolf bitten by an initiate. The wolf had fought until he succumbed, and instead of turning, he had died. Solus could have sworn he dreamt of Aine, fighting with the wolf to regain control. He had stood over her and watched her drain herself to save the wolf.

He shook his head and swayed. He would visit the prisoner today. The conversations between the prisoner and a wolf Rolan had assigned to serve him had given them an opportunity.

"Master." Rolan appeared in the corridor next to him. "How do you fare?"

"I'm fine, Rolan." Solus gritted his teeth and waved away the concern. They walked on in silence. As the corridor opened into the main area and he approached his pack members, Solus felt some of his strength returning. When he entered the room, his chest loosened, and his stride became stronger. He could understand why his mate's ancestors had insisted on creating packs. Each member's loyalty contributed strength to their leader, the more loyal the pack, the stronger the pack leader's power and influence became. This appeared to increase with each generation.

The corridor that led to the prisoner was bleak, damp with very little light. The rough rock along the walls glistened as water ran down. Solus looked down on the shifter Rolan called Eric in the corner of the cell. He had one leg stretched out and the other bent with his elbow on his knee. He appeared relaxed, but Solus could sense his turmoil as the older shifter approached.

"Rolan, leave us."

"But—" Rolan retreated with a sharp look from Solus. The leader crouched in front of the bars, his eyes level with the captured shifter.

"Eric, is it? First, I must apologize for your treatment here. We had to be sure you weren't with the pack you were heading for or had been influenced by them." Solus sighed and ran his hand through his hair, then slouched his shoulders, letting some of the weariness show.

"Why?"

"You're from the European packs? Well, over here, the pack you were heading for has been capturing shifters and forcing them to stay in that area. Most of the time against their will," Solus growled. "We have been trying to free as many as we can. Unfortunately, you were the only one we could save this time. Our scouts informed me that the leader of that pack killed one of yours, the older male."

"What?!" The shifter lunged forward to hold the bars. "Tell me you're joking. We were coming to them for help."

"I'm afraid it's true. The siblings are fine, they were friendly with the hunter there, and he's protected them...so far." Solus paused. "I'm sorry to tell you this, but this is my fault. The leader of that pack is my misguided daughter. She started using dark magic when she was a teenager, experimenting. I should have stopped her." He put his head in his hands.

"Dark magic? Is that what was wrong with the wolves that took me? But they were your wolves!"

"Refugees that we've managed to pull out of her pack. They can only live a half-life now."

"This can't be happening" Eric scrunched his eyes together, and his knuckles went white as he gripped the bars. "I need to get Ciara and Conor out of there."

Solus wove a little of his dark influence into the shifter's mind; it was easy in the prisoner's weakened state. But, even if he didn't want to believe Solus, he would now. "I need your help to do this. If we can lure the leader out of the settlement, I can bring her back here. She's my daughter, my responsibility. Once she's away, we can free her prisoners."

The imprisoned wolf looked up. "How can I help?"

6

Aine's eyes fluttered, feeling dry, and her throat was parched. She coughed, and pain lanced through every cell in her body.

"Steady, here." She relaxed at Lachlan's voice and felt cool water at her lips. The small sip soothed her dry throat as she swallowed slowly.

"What—?" Aine coughed again, her body protesting.

"Don't talk. I'll tell you." Lachlan came in to view when Aine turned her head towards him. His eyes were tight, with dark circles smudged underneath. She squeezed her eyes closed, and the soreness behind them lessened.

"You tried to save Gary, and Tania thinks you drained yourself. He..." Lachlan paused. "He didn't make it. And we nearly lost you." His voice caught.

Aine straightened her head again to stare at the ceiling. Even that caused an ache in her chest. Nausea crept up from her queasy stomach. She quickly turned away from Lachlan and vomited on the floor beside the bed. The taste of bile had her retching again. Her husband's hands rubbed her back, lessening her discomfort. Slowly, she rolled back flat on the bed, wincing as her weight shifted.

"Try not to move." Lachlan stroked her hair. "Eloi kept you alive; you'd be so proud of her."

Aine swallowed and tried to reach out to Eloi. It was faint, but she could feel her with Nyko. They were training with the warriors. Lachlan's emotions were muffled, his eyes sad, and his hand shook when it took hers.

"I thought I'd lost you." Lachlan squeezed her hand gently, his fingers trembling.

"Won't get rid of me that easy." Aine tried to smile, but her eyes were heavy. "I'm so exhausted."

"Sleep, my love." Lachlan's voice was quiet.

"You should, too." Aine drifted off to the sound of his soft chuckle.

ELOI KEPT a close watch on her mother. It had been three days, and she still appeared weakened. Physically, she was her old self, but Eloi couldn't feel the same strength in the mental bond they usually had. The connection to Lachlan still hadn't recovered, and Eloi could see his agitation at not being able to share energy or feel his mate.

Lachlan and Aine had discussed what happened with Eyolf, who suggested a pack to the north may have more knowledge of the dark powers Rolan used to control the wolves. The shifters in Tivaci used to regularly mingle with those in Sumter, but as technology developed, they became more isolated.

Eloi, Aine, and Lachlan stood on the edge of Sumter. Some of the shifters gathered behind them as they waited for two hunters to arrive. Lachlan heard from his father, and they had come to an agreement. Some of the younger warriors would come and train under Lachlan.

Aine could feel the unease in the pack. When Lachlan first became pack leader with her, not all the shifters had accepted him. It had taken time to earn their trust, and there were still those who didn't like having a human in the pack.

Lachlan stepped forward as two young men walked cautiously into the village. "Thanks for coming."

Eloi's voice arose in Aine's mind. *Liam must really trust Lachlan to send two warriors here, Mom.*

Or they are spies sent to root out our weaknesses and report back. Aine shifted slightly.

"I know this isn't going to be easy for either side," Lachlan said. "But we need to come to terms with our differences to fight a common enemy. It is time to realize that it isn't a case of them or us." He held out his hand. A young man who couldn't have been more than twenty stepped forward.

"I'm a second cousin of some sort on your mam's side. Owen." He took Lachlan's hand and shook firmly.

Lachlan's face slackened before he smiled again. "You have her eyes."

Owen nodded, his face openly curious. Eloi studied him curiously, then turned her head to the second hunter. His hair was lighter, and he looked older, his demeanor suggesting more caution than Owen's.

"Ian. I'll put it out there now. I'm not sure this is a good idea, but I couldn't let the kid run off without me." Ian tilted his head to Owen. "Gets himself in trouble otherwise."

"My younger brother was like that." Lachlan winked. "I know it won't be easy, but Liam said you were probably the most open-minded in the group. You'll need that. I'm not going to tell you it'll be an easy welcome either."

Ian cocked his head. "Figured as much," he mumbled.

"I've got a house for you on the edge of the settlement. I figured it would give you some space. It's close to us, too. I give you my word that you will have no trouble from the shifters here. And we are grateful for your offer to come and join us."

Eloi noticed Aine was quiet and turned to observe her. Her mother wore a slight frown.

Do you need me to help?

I can't get a read on them. Aine sighed. Eloi winked at her, opened herself up to the feelings around her, and concentrated on the two young hunters. Each was nervous and surveying the area for any place that could hide an adversary. But there was a hope and a curiosity that gave Eloi pause.

They were a good choice by Liam if he wanted to mend bridges. Eloi stepped forward boldly.

"I'm Eloi, and this is my mother, Aine. She and Lachlan are pack leaders." She held out her hand as Lachlan had. Ian hesitated, but Owen stepped forward with a grin.

"Nice to meet you." His grip was firm, and his palm cool in hers. Ian stepped up behind Owen and offered his hand. He grunted as Eloi shook it.

"Shall we?" Lachlan gestured towards the house he had intended for them. "I'll get you settled and update you on today's plans."

The two hunters followed Lachlan; Owen looked back at Eloi before he left, and she smiled. Aine moved up beside her.

"Mom, take me with you," Eloi said. "If you can't use your powers, you're vulnerable."

"Lachlan and I are going with the two hunters, and I'll take two warriors. He thinks it will be a good way to build a better relationship. I need you to stay here, with the way things are...." Aine paused. "I need you to stay here in case anything happens to me. One of us always needs to be here. The pack comes first."

"But—"

"No, Eloi, it's my final decision." Aine crossed her arms, and the girl glared at her.

"Nothing will happen to you if you let me help," Eloi said. "We need to use the medallion so my power matches yours. I need to get out in the world more—I feel like I only know Sumter. How am I supposed to be a good leader when I've been so isolated? You're keeping me a prisoner here!"

Aine scoffed and rolled her eyes. "Now you're just being dramatic. That medallion is dangerous, and I don't keep you here."

"Then why can't I leave?" Eloi gritted her teeth, spitting the words.

"Where do you want to go? Would you like to travel to other packs, is that it?" Aine's voice was calm, but Eloi could detect her frustration. So Eloi just shook her head and didn't respond.

"We are leaving in the next half an hour. We will be back before nightfall, hopefully with a way to help Jason." Aine stepped forward to hug her daughter, but Eloi stepped back out of her mother's reach.

"You never listen," Eloi growled, storming away from Aine; her mother didn't follow. She thought about going to the training area to work out her frustration there, but she needed peace. Eloi sighed. The tension over the last few days had disturbed her sleep, and there was only one place where she could rest.

Half an hour later, she lay on a flat rock near her pond. The bubbling water from the waterfall drifted through the breeze towards her. Her tight muscles and the tension in her upper back slowly relaxed as she counted her breaths. She tried not to think about her mother's words; each time she did, she couldn't help the growl of frustration that bubbled inside her. Sometimes she wanted to scream, shift, and run from Sumter as fast as her four legs would carry her.

~

AINE FELT MUCH STRONGER NOW. Just before they left Sumter, a sensation like a pop happened in her head that seemed to clear the block on her power. As Lachlan's emotions rushed back in, she breathed a sigh of relief. The hunters had been stunned when he picked her up in a hug for no apparent reason, while Nyko and an older warrior, Elijah, stood to one side, blank looks on their faces. Aine felt their apprehension at having the two hunters join them. She felt Eloi's fury when she found out Nyko was going, and she still had to stay behind.

Nyko was curious about the hunters but also wary after Rolan's teachings on their history. She had chosen Elijah for his experience. He was slightly older than her and had trained under her grandfather. His hair was greyer than the pitch black it had once been. She had known him all her life and knew he would trust her. Despite his misgivings, he tried with the young hunters.

They took two SUVs north for nearly a day and then hiked when they got to the edge of the Tivaci territory. Aine sensed the settlement ahead of them; the shifters all gathered in one area, but their emotions were subdued.

"Something isn't right; we will approach slowly." Aine turned to nod at Nyko and Elijah. The two hunters exchanged a nod with Lachlan.

"Stealth from here." Aine marveled at the skill of the hunters as their steps became imperceptible. The group moved silently as they approached the edge of the settlement. She put her hand up quickly.

There's a scout up ahead, but he feels wrong...like one of Rolan's wolves.

Aine crinkled her brow and exchanged a look with Lachlan as they mentally communicated. He then turned to the hunters and used well-practiced signals to relay the exchange. The hunters nodded, though they looked at Aine with silent confusion.

Can we get around the scout to high ground? Lachlan looked at Aine expectantly.

She gestured to follow her to a path up toward the west. As they crept higher to the top of a lookout, Aine was surprised that she could feel no presence.

There's no one on the lookout. Aine's stomach churned as they moved closer.

Lachlan gestured to the hunters and the warriors to stay farther down as he and Aine crept closer to the top. At the summit, the couple looked over the settlement. Aine muffled a gasp.

The houses were like those in Sumter, this settlement about half the size. It looked beautiful, hidden by a circle of trees with a water source at its center. But around the village, the shifters were chained to posts and surrounded by the wolves Rolan had sent to take Sumter's shifters. Aine's eyes stung as she looked at Tivaci's inhabitants and the life they were being forced to live. They looked vacant, staring into nothing, and the chains had the black, oily surface that had been on the cuffs used on her three years ago.

She looked to the cave system hidden near the water

source; her suspicions were confirmed when she saw a group of chained shifters being led into the opening in the ground, each holding a pickaxe.

We need to leave.

We need to bring back reinforcements! We can't leave them like this. Lachlan shifted slightly, and Aine could see his knuckles white where his fists were clenched.

I know, but how can we hold Sumter and rescue Tivaci? I can see what the metal for the cuffs is from here. I thought the secret was forgotten, but did you see that group?

Lachlan paled and looked back to the hunters and warriors they'd left behind. He gestured toward them with his head, and they slid down to meet the group. He quickly signaled to the hunters, who nodded.

Aine's heart felt heavy at the retreat, but they couldn't act now; her thoughts were in turmoil. She let Lachlan lead the group as she thought back to the prisoners they left behind. Nyko touched her arm, a look of concern on his face. She shook her head slightly. The boy's body tensed, and Aine found herself shoved behind him. A quiet growl was the only warning before two wolves leaped at the group from opposite directions.

Nyko and Elijah quickly shifted. Aine whirled to watch Lachlan pivot to avoid the teeth of one of the wolves. The two hunters sprang into action, each flanking Lachlan against the wolf. Aine could finally admit the asset the hunters would be to her shifters.

Nyko and Elijah faced the second beast. Aine shook herself and drew on her power, instantly crying out and clutching her head. She heard Lachlan shout but kept her eyes shut.

When she opened her eyes again, Lachlan was crouched in front of her. His hand cupped her face, and he leaned his forehead against hers. Aine felt him push energy toward her and jerked back.

"You'll need your strength," she whispered. Slowly she stood up and looked around. One wolf had been dispatched by the hunters, and the other by her warriors. She assessed both pairs as they stood vigilant and alert.

"We need to get out of here. Can you keep up?" Her question was directed at Owen and Ian.

"You bet." Owen grinned, his eyes sparkling with the thrill of victory.

Aine nodded and shifted; immediately, she felt the fatigue fade away. She shook out her white fur and stood proud next to her shifters. Owen bowed and gestured toward their vehicles. "After you."

The shifters set off, and the hunters kept a steady pace beside them. They arrived at the vehicles quickly.

"Well, that was something." Ian breathed hard but didn't seem winded.

"I know, right?" Owen smiled at his friend, and Lachlan chuckled as he came to stand next to them.

~

Eloi didn't sleep but let herself slowly relax. She was annoyed at how she lost her temper, acting like the youngling she so despised being referred to as. But she needed her mom to see she was ready to take on more responsibility.

The skin on the back of her neck prickled; had she been in wolf form, then her hackles would have raised. A twig cracked sharply behind her, and in one fluid movement, she was on her feet, crouched and twisted to face the direction of the noise. A hiss sounded through the teeth of a boy in front of her.

At first glance, he looked young, but she guessed his age was closer to twenty when she looked into his eyes. His skin was darker than her pale complexion, and his onyx eyes mesmerized her. Crouched on her level, he tilted his head and gave her a cocky grin, and she tensed at his laughing gaze.

"Well..." He cleared his throat. "This is awkward."

Eloi, still anxious, felt around her; he appeared to be alone. His presence barely registered as she sensed the area. He looked amused, and she scowled.

"Good day for sunbathing...." His voice trailed away as he looked up through the thick branches and back down to the shadows on her flat rock. Her scowl deepened.

"Okaaaay..." He drew the word out and looked around. Eloi assessed his build, his large shoulders, toned arms, and muscular legs. She blushed when she met his eyes; he caught her checking him out.

"Like what you see?" he winked.

"No." Eloi shifted her weight to prevent one leg from going numb.

"Ah, she speaks."

"Have you been here before when I'm here? Your scent is familiar. I didn't detect it before, but now you're here..." Eloi shook her head.

"Maybe." He spoke too quickly, and his face reddened. Eloi waited for him to do something, what though, she wasn't sure. The silence stretched between them, and she frowned. Finally, he stood slowly and held his hand out to her. "I won't hurt you; I've just been curious," he said with a shrug.

"Why?"

"You're intriguing. You always come here when you're frustrated, but by the time you leave, you're...calm."

Eloi narrowed her eyes. "I like it here." She moved to her left, towards Sumter.

"Don't go!" he exclaimed. "What's your name?"

"Why?"

"I told you, I'm curious about you." He smiled at her, and Eloi's insides melted. She shook her head as he sat down and crossed his legs. "Come on. I won't bite...much." He laughed.

Eloi glanced towards home but looked back quickly. He hadn't moved, and his eyes twinkled as she slowly sat down herself. His posture was relaxed, but she kept herself prepared.

"So, what is your name?" He grinned at her again.

Eloi jerked her chin at him. "You first."

"Daniel. Your turn."

"Eloi."

"Eloi." He cocked his head and looked into the distance. "What does it mean?"

"I..." Eloi paused. "I don't know; I should ask my mom."

"That's okay. What's your favorite food, Eloi?"

"Burgers."

He looked surprised, then thoughtful. "I prefer pizza, though my brother always says it's just glorified grilled cheese."

"Pizza?" Eloi frowned.

"I'll bring some next time." He winked at her, and a tight, warm feeling started in her chest. "Do you mind if I come back?"

Eloi looked toward Sumter. "Erm..."

"You can say maybe." His eyes twinkled as he smiled at her.

"Okay."

"Okay, maybe, or okay, I can come back?" He leaned toward her eagerly.

"Figure it out," she giggled and quickly stood. "I need to get back."

"See you soon." Daniel winked, his eyes glowed amber and turned slowly.

Eloi tilted her head and drew her brows together as she watched him retreat into the woods. She listened for a few minutes to his soft tread as he walked away. The rhythm too fast for a human, and she gasped when she realized what he was. She couldn't help the smile on her face as she turned for home.

7

Eloi walked back toward the center of Sumter and spotted Eyolf as he watched her. He looked tense, and she saw him blow out a breath, his shoulders relaxing slightly. Eloi stiffened when he approached and fell into step beside her.

"Out so long this time, youngling? We were starting to get worried." Eyolf smiled.

Eloi sighed. "I'm not a youngling. I am nearly eighteen. Why won't you all start treating me that way?" She scowled at him and immediately regretted her outburst.

Eyolf nodded. "It's hard to remember when you've watched someone grow up. I'm sorry young—Eloi. It's a force of habit. Do you feel better?"

"Yes, I always feel better after a bit of space." She gestured toward her home.

"Things are getting rather intense around here. Your mom is only trying to protect you."

"I know, really I do. I'm just frustrated." She looked at the medical building. "Do you have an update on Jason?"

"He's awake and lucid, but the infection is still spreading." Eyolf grimaced. "Tania is trying her best, but we can't see a way to draw it out."

"That's a good sign, though. Gary never regained consciousness, at least not as himself." Her voice was low, and she glanced around.

"I don't know." Eyolf kept stride with her as they entered the medical building. Tania was lining up various stock in one corner, and Jason sat up in bed, grinning at Eloi as she entered.

"Good to see you awake." Eloi returned the grin.

"It's easier to fight when I'm awake." Jason's jaw was clenched as he spoke, and Eloi frowned.

"What do you need?" She took a step closer, and Eyolf stepped between them. Jason flinched.

"Less company, maybe a more secure area...just in case." Jason's eyes flicked to Tania, and Eloi nodded.

"How about we move you to your home? We can post a warrior outside and secure it. You'll be more comfortable and away from other shifters." Eloi spoke firmly, and Jason nodded.

The girl turned to Tania. "Can you organize that?"

Tania nodded, her eyes and nose red. Eloi turned to Eyolf.

"Ask some warriors to help; they will know best how to secure his home." She watched Eyolf leave and then walked over to Tania. She nodded toward the office at the back, away from Jason.

"Are you okay?" Eloi asked as they entered the other room, studying Tania's face.

"Yeah, just tired. I wish there was more I could do. I feel like Gary didn't last as long because I kept him under, but...." Tania paused and sighed. "Whenever we brought him out, he was rabid and would attack anyone near. It wasn't safe."

"You did your best, and that's all we can ask for." Eloi squeezed her shoulder. "Is there anything I can do to help?"

"No, I should really have been training an apprentice." Tania sat at her desk and shuffled some papers around.

"Would you like me to find someone willing?"

"No, it would be more effort than it's worth right now." Tania shrugged. "I'll figure it out."

"Surely having someone to fetch and carry would be better than nothing?" Eloi looked at the disarray around her. "Or to help with the paperwork here. Do you have notes on everyone?"

Tania laughed, "Yes, I like to be thorough. There's no need; Nyko has been helping me." Her cheeks turned pink.

"I bet he has." Eloi winked at her. "Well, if you're sure."

Tania nodded, and her blush spread.

Eloi left the building to find Eyolf waiting outside for her. "I've informed the warriors; they're checking Jason's house over now."

"Thank you, Eyolf." She eyed him warily. "Can we talk? I need your help."

"Shall we go to my house? I think my kitchen knows all the secrets in Sumter." He chuckled, and Eloi smiled at him, nodding. They walked in silence, and once she was settled into a seat in his kitchen, she heaved a sigh.

"My mother refuses to see or treat me as an adult. I need to know more about the medallion. I think it's time I came into my full power before we are overrun with infected shifters." Eloi kept her voice steady.

"I agree with your mother, Eloi. You're not ready." Eyolf flinched at Eloi's scowl. "I can give you some reading, but your mother barely controlled the power when she got it. We need to prepare you more. You're still so young."

"I'm nearly eighteen!" Eloi raised her voice slightly before she caught herself. She cleared her throat. "I'm already better prepared than she was. Didn't your reading say that a younger age was better and easier?"

Eyolf rubbed his chin as he considered. "I don't think there is a set age, it might be that the only reason your mother survived is because she's older. We need to assess your power, put it under strain, and see how you adapt to it. This all takes time, which we don't have with the constant attacks."

Eloi groaned. "It's like a loop. Mom needs my help, but to have it, she needs to train me, but she can't because she doesn't have time with all the attacks, for which she needs my help. So can't you train me?"

"I no longer have the appropriate power." He shook his head.

Eloi sighed. "I do understand; I just don't like it. Are you keeping the medallion safe?"

"Only Aine and I know where it is—actually, Lachlan, too." He touched her arm. "Give it time; you'll be ready when you're ready. Now, how about a cup of tea?"

The girl smiled. "Of course."

~

Eric wandered through the caves and spoke to the shifter refugees. They seemed timid, but from what he could see, they were content, and all insisted that Solus had saved them, that if it wasn't for the Faction, they would have had nowhere to go.

A pit formed in Eric's stomach. They came here to find

Lachlan. Ciara had insisted there were things he needed to know and that she wanted to help him. The urgency to return to his mate pulled at him, but Solus wanted him to make up his own mind. He knew nothing about the packs in America.

Eric looked across as Solus entered the cavern. "So, Eric," the leader spoke. "Are you satisfied?"

"Yes. I don't understand how Ciara could have thought the pack we were going to were friendly. She was looking for Lachlan, but there's no way he would fall in with them if what you say is true. Are you sure they're that corrupt? Maybe it's a misunderstanding."

"Ah, remember what I told you about my daughter? She has a dark power, and she has influence over him. I believe he's no longer in control of his actions. She has corrupted a good man, and there will be no redemption for him. Even if he does recover his wits, how could he live with himself after costing so many shifters their lives?" Solus looked tired, his face drawn and pale.

"When can we leave? Understand I'm grateful for what you've done for me, but I worry about my mate, Ciara." Eric held his breath as Solus opened his mouth to speak. They were interrupted by a harried-looking shifter. He wheezed as he approached Solus, pausing to take huge gulps of air. The leader frowned at the shifter, impatient as the man caught his breath.

"Well?" Solus's voice was rough, and Eric frowned. The shifter approached and whispered in his ear. Anger flashed in the older man's eyes as Eric watched the other shifter cower, then Solus softened his face.

"Go rest; I'll take care of it." His voice was careful, and he turned to Eric. "I believe you must leave immediately. My daughter just discovered one of our safe havens and killed two of the guards. You'll need to lead her out of the village. It will be easy to capture her when there are fewer shifters around for her to influence."

"That's awful. I'm sorry." Eric tried to control his impatience. "I'll do what I can."

"Just one thing. My daughter doesn't know I'm alive. She will kill me if she finds out and everything we've worked for, all these shifters will be in danger." He gestured to the refugees. "Please don't mention me."

Eric nodded.

"When you get the chance...." Solus handed Eric a glass vial filled with a dark, viscous liquid. Eric examined it. "Put this in a drink my daughter has. Just a drop or two will do. But be careful; it'll kill anyone else. And be aware, your mate and her brother may be under my daughter's spell—she can be very charming. Don't be fooled by her."

Eric nodded and put the vial in his pocket. He looked through the crowd, hoping to see Olivia before he left, but she was nowhere in sight. Solus watched him curiously.

"I'll go now. How do I get out of here?" Eric watched Solus pull a hood out from his back pocket.

"I'm sorry, but if you're captured or influenced, I need to know my Faction is safe. You understand?"

Eric swallowed but nodded slowly. "Sure." The hood completely cut out all light, and Eric felt dizziness come over him.

"It won't be for long." Solus led him through the tunnels and helped him walk. Eric found it hard to breathe, and the time it took for them to reach the car Solus had arranged for him felt like ages.

Solus removed the hood. "Thank you, Eric, you're a shifter of honor. I hope you find your mate well and that she hasn't fallen under Aine's spell. Rolan here will take you out into the country, so you won't know our location. He will point you in the right direction once you stop."

The car engine started, and Eric tried to keep his breathing slow and deep as the car started on his journey. It felt like hours, but it couldn't have been more than thirty minutes when they stopped. Rolan, the lean shifter with black hair and deep chocolate eyes, nodded towards the door. Eric opened it eagerly but paused when he felt Rolan touch his arm.

"Head west, you'll come to Sumter in about five miles," Rolan told him.

"Thank you, I appreciate the lift. What's your connection to all this?" Eric felt awkward after they had sat in silence so long.

"Aine is my wife, and she tried to kill me to take my power." Rolan grimaced.

Shock shot through Eric as he looked at the shifter. He couldn't imagine Ciara turning on him like that. He gave Rolan a nod. "I'll do what I can to stop her."

Rolan smiled, and Eric cringed at the sight. There was a gleam in the man's eyes that unnerved him. He quickly left the vehicle and headed in the direction Rolan had pointed him in.

~

AINE COULD FEEL the fatigue and cold through her bones despite the mild weather. She finally relaxed as she entered Sumter, and they parked the cars in the garage they'd built to hide vehicles. Lachlan helped her out of the SUV and supported her weight to the door. She took a deep breath before they left the building, walking under her own power. Lachlan didn't flinch when she pushed him away.

Several pack members waited for them, and she took the time to reassure them that they were all unharmed. There were skeptical glances at the hunters, and she made sure to praise their actions during the attack on the outskirts of Tivaci. There were questions shouted asking after the pack there.

"I need to consult with Eyolf and the other Elders. We will let you all know the details soon." Aine smiled and strolled towards her home, with Lachlan leaving to make sure the hunters were happy with their house.

Once she walked through her front door and closed it behind her, Aine slid down it and sat on the floor. Her head was in her hands, and she tried to breathe deep and slow, her thoughts on Jason.

The back of a cool hand on her forehead made her jump until she scented Eloi.

"I didn't realize you were home." She looked at her daughter. "They're trapped in the village, Eloi. Rolan has imprisoned them and is using them to produce the shackles that bind shifters."

Aine dropped her hands and looked at Eloi, her voice breaking. "I can't imagine if he had taken you or if he imprisoned everyone here."

"He hasn't, Mom. You've protected everyone." The girl pulled her mother up and helped her to the kitchen. "You're tired. Do you want some coffee?"

"I could murder some coffee," Aine laughed.

"You sound more like Lachlan every day," Eloi chuckled at her. Once Aine had the warm mug between her hands, Eloi observed her.

"You can't do this alone, Mom. Let me help you." She sat opposite Aine and waited. Her mother sighed heavily.

"Are you trying to bribe me with coffee?" Aine quirked an eyebrow. "It might work."

Eloi smiled. "Well, it was worth a shot," she said, her voice growing tight. "We've worked for years on my training, and I feel ready. What more do you need from me? Tell me, and I will do it."

Aine could feel her daughter's frustration. "I will work harder with you, even I must admit I can't do this alone. But I worry about you being too young. Eyolf's research shows that the older you are, the more likely it won't kill you. It won't happen overnight, and I don't want to rush this." She took Eloi's hand. "I can't risk losing you."

Eloi's expression changed from triumph to frustration in a second. "Why years? You need my help now."

"I won't be so selfish and put that burden on you."

"It's not a burden!" Eloi shouted, and Aine flinched. "I'm sorry, Mom. I'm just frustrated."

"I know. Can we talk about this tomorrow? I have a headache." Aine took Eloi's hand; the girl squeezed it and nodded. Aine felt energy surge into her, and she scowled at her daughter, who stuck her tongue out. Aine laughed.

"Thank you. You shouldn't have, but I needed that." She smiled.

"See, not so hard to accept help." Eloi grinned, and Aine scoffed. They laughed until the door slammed open in the hallway.

"Aine!" Nyko's voice rang through the house. Aine quickly stood, followed by Eloi.

"What's wrong?"

"It's Jason; it's not good. He's asking for you."

"He asked for me? He's conscious?" Aine's chest tightened.

Eloi cleared her throat. "We found that he is more lucid

than Gary. Tania thinks it's easier to fight the infection if he's conscious. He requested to be moved to somewhere secure where he could be comfortable, so I moved him home, and we've secured the house."

The girl looked into Aine's eyes confidently. Aine smiled and squeezed her daughter's shoulder.

"Well done, I would have done the same." Her mother smiled, and Eloi returned it. "Let's go and see him."

They reached Jason's house, and Aine could hear him cry out from a few houses away. The sound reverberated through her, and she jerked to a stop. Eloi crashed into the back of her.

"Mom?"

"I can't help him. Even if I did have the energy, I couldn't help Gary. What can we do?"

"Let me help." Eloi gritted her teeth.

"I can't risk you." Aine's voice sounded shrill in her own ears.

The girl huffed and crossed her arms. "Stronger together, that's what Eyolf said. Trust me, Mom. Just this once."

Aine's heart hurt when she shook her head. Eloi pulled her inside Jason's house, and Aine shook herself before she stepped through the door. She took a deep breath, bracing herself. Jason smiled at her, his face pale and sweat sheening his brow. He sat on a couch in the living room.

"Pack Leader," he nodded. Aine looked at her warrior and smiled, then glanced around his house, raising her eyebrow.

"This place needs a woman's touch. How are you feeling?" She looked him over.

"It won't be long," Jason grimaced.

Aine opened her mouth to speak, and Jason stopped her.

"Don't try to help me. I saw what it did to you. And you..." Jason looked at Eloi. "Neither of you are indestructible. I'm expendable. There's no replacing you two."

Eloi opened her mouth, and Jason growled; she snarled back, and he laughed. "Yep, I know you're fierce, but this is my choice, and I won't let either of you take it from me."

Aine sat on the couch next to him and leaned into him. Eloi took his other side. Her lip trembled, and they sat in silence for a while. Aine heard Jason draw in a sharp breath.

"What will you let us do?"

"Let me go into the woods and end this on my own terms."

"Jason—"

"Please, Pack Leader." Jason's voice cracked slightly, and Aine's chest tightened. She nodded, and Eloi gave Jason a hug from her side of the couch. Aine nearly smiled at the look of surprise on his face. She stood and offered her hand, which he took.

"You are one of the bravest men I know." She leaned in and gave him a kiss on the cheek. His face reddened, and he looked at the floor.

"Thank you, Pack Leader."

They all walked together to the door. "I said my good-byes to the warriors today," Jason continued. "I'll leave you all in peace now. Just promise me you will end the son of a bitch this time."

Aine nodded. Lachlan stood outside the house, and Jason approached him.

"Let the hunter walk me to the edge. It feels right." Jason turned for one last look at Eloi and Aine. "It has been an honor to serve you both."

Aine kept her face blank as he walked away.

"I KNOW we've never seen eye to eye, Lachlan." Jason gave him a stern look, and Lachlan curled his lip in a half-smile.

"I respect you as a warrior, and your loss will hit Aine and Eloi hard," the hunter replied, glancing at Jason as they walked.

"Aine is a great Pack Leader. I gave you a hard time because I knew you needed it. Plus, I don't trust hunters. But, even I can see you've done your best here. I still don't think mixing hunters and shifters is a great idea, though," Jason said sternly.

"If we don't learn to work together, there will never be peace. There will always be uprisings like the Faction if shifters feel suppressed, and hunters will always hate them if shifters keep fighting." This wasn't the first time they'd had this discussion.

"I just think it's a lost cause." Jason looked out at the woods.

"That's when you know you need to fight the hardest for it." Lachlan held out his hand to Jason.

The man shook it. "Look after my pack."

"I will." Lachlan thoughtfully watched him disappear into the trees.

8

The atmosphere in Sumter had been somber since Jason left the day before. He was a beloved warrior, missed by many in the settlement. Eloi had kept a watch on the villagers. Her mother's voice echoed through their home.

"Catori, I know you think it's for the best to leave, but where would you go? I've told you all that we saw in Tivaci. You will be safer with your grandchildren here!" Aine pleaded with the teacher. "We've been through hardship before."

"Not like this. I don't know what your grandfather would think about bringing hunters into the village. What if they kill the younglings as they sleep?"

Aine sighed. "Lachlan is watching out for them and for us. This needs to happen; otherwise, there will never be peace. We've feared the hunters for generations. What if we were wrong like the histories say? They are a part of our past, and I want to make them a part of our future."

Catori looked unsure, but after a moment, she nodded.

"I promise I will do everything in my power to keep you

safe here. Other packs are suffering under the Faction's attacks, and none of them have anyone like Eloi or myself. It is our responsibility to keep you safe." Aine's voice was calm and reassuring.

"I'm not the only one who wants to leave. You should know others are starting to talk." Catori stood to leave, and a thrill of horror ran through Aine. If any of the pack left, they would be in danger. Catori exited the home, and Eloi entered the kitchen. Aine kept her face blank.

"She's right; I've heard others mention leaving." Eloi sat to face her mother.

"I'm not surprised, but things are bad everywhere." Aine looked at her daughter. "What are your plans today? Training with Lachlan?"

"Yeah, I was just on my way out. I'll be working with Owen and Ian. Lachlan thinks that there's a natural fighting style when a hunter and shifter combine. Like when we fought Rolan at his house. When he mentioned it, I realized how natural it felt to fight beside him."

"If only the others could see that," Aine chuckled. "You better be off. Don't want to be late."

Eloi nodded as she stood and strode to the door. "Let's show these hunters what we are made of!" She pumped her fist in the air, and Aine laughed.

Eloi jogged quickly to the warrior's training area, her elation at being trusted to train with the hunters giving her extra energy. Lachlan waited for her with Owen and Ian; each had a bow staff and looked eager.

"You ready to get your ass kicked?"

Eloi grinned and let her eyes glow amber. Ian flinched, but Owen moved for a closer look.

"Freaky! I've never seen that before." His eyes searched

hers, and she relaxed the color, her eyes returning to chocolate brown.

"As Eloi has just demonstrated, shifters can partially change if they are powerful enough," Lachlan said, gesturing toward the girl. Ian's eyes narrowed, and he looked at her almost with respect. Eloi straightened. "Now, Eloi and I had an experience three years ago where we had to fight several shifters. I barely knew her, yet we naturally fell into a fighting style that complemented each other's weaknesses."

"Did you win?" Owen's eyes were wide.

"No, there were too many, but we held them off long enough to complete a ritual which reconnected Aine back to her pack."

"Back to?" Ian frowned and looked at Lachlan.

"That's another story."

Eloi was curious why Lachlan was telling them so much, and it made her feel uneasy. He put his hand on her shoulder, looking into her eyes, and she could see he'd noticed her concern. He smiled at her and winked. "Let's show them how it's done."

Nyko and Elijah walked into the area, and Owen grinned while Ian tensed. The shifters approached Eloi and Lachlan, the partners facing them and nodding. Nyko and Elijah returned the nod before they shifted.

"This is gonna be cool!" Owen practically bounced up and down.

Eloi remained human, watching Nyko for his tells. A slight twitch gave him away, and she moved. She loved fighting with Lachlan as her partner; they intuitively knew each other's position and how to cover their defense since that first fight. Nyko once described it as an intricate dance without contact.

During a move from Elijah that would have taken

Lachlan out, Eloi leaped and shifted mid-jump. Her trajectory caught Elijah, and Lachlan moved fluidly to cover her exposed flank as Nyko went in for a winning blow. Eloi disabled Elijah, and he conceded; when she turned, she saw Nyko submit to Lachlan. Lachlan's chest heaved with the exertion, and Eloi snorted at him.

"I'm older than you, youngling!" Lachlan laughed when Eloi growled at him.

"Wow, that was awesome. It's like you were one entity!" Owen ran forward eagerly. Ian smiled, causing Eloi to do a double-take.

"Team up. I'd suggest Nyko and Owen, Elijah and Ian. Your personalities probably match the best. Get to know each other first." Lachlan walked over to Eloi, who had shifted back, and laughed.

"Elijah and Owen will barely say two words together." Eloi grinned at Lachlan's raised eyebrow.

"They will have to learn." Lachlan approached her and put a hand on her shoulder. "You did well today; you've come a long way."

"Not far enough, apparently," Eloi huffed and crossed her arms.

Lachlan shook his head slightly. "Your mom giving you a hard time? It's only because she doesn't want to see you hurt. In her mind, you'll always be her baby, and after what you both went through, she's going to be overprotective."

"But this is stupid. I can help. We could have saved Gary and Jason."

"That's not her fault, Eloi. She loves you too much to risk you."

"I know, but I could be so much more. What about the medallion? I know you argue about that; I heard you tell her I was ready."

"When did you hear that?"

"Shifter hearing." Eloi laughed at him.

"I said, 'nearly ready.' I know I can't understand what your mom went through, but I don't think she gives you enough credit. It'll always be hard for her to be objective when it comes to you."

Eloi sighed. "I kind of understand, but I'm frustrated."

Lachlan put his arm around her in a half hug. "Just be patient. I know you teens think everything has to happen now but make the most of the time you have without the world on your shoulders." He lifted his hand, and before she could stop him, he ruffled her hair.

"Hey," Eloi pushed him away.

"Cut your mom some slack. She will come around; just keep showing her you're ready." Lachlan smiled at her. "Want to show these hunters how it's done again?"

"Always." Eloi bared her teeth when she grinned.

Eloi was tired after the session with Owen and Ian. It was a joy to see them work with Nyko and Elijah. As Lachlan thought, they fell in line with each other and immediately found the synchronicity she had found with him years ago, Ian and Elijah even laughing together. The plan for hunters and shifters to come together might just work.

~

THE GIRL GAVE a content sigh as she lowered onto the flat rock next to her pond. The water was clear today, and she took off both her shoes to cool her feet. They throbbed a little after so much exertion. When the rustle came behind her, she didn't immediately jump up. She inhaled deeply.

"Trying to sneak up on me," she chuckled.

"How did you—?" Daniel's face came into view to her left, and she looked towards him.

"You sound like a large animal charging around," she responded with a giggle.

"I do not; you must have exceptional hearing!"

"You could say that." Eloi flinched when Daniel unexpectedly plopped down next to her. He removed his shoes and put his feet in the pond with hers. She tried to relax.

"You seem a bit tense," he noted.

"I don't know who you are." Eloi watched him from the corner of her eye.

"I won't hurt you. I'm just curious."

Eloi blushed. "About me? Why?"

"I've heard a lot about you."

Eloi's head snapped to face him. "What? How?"

"You're legendary with shifters. Yes, I know about shifters. And you know I know because you heard me leave." He grinned at her.

Eloi grimaced. "What do people say about me?"

"That when you were young, you saved your mom and your pack from an evil Faction member." Daniel watched her face, which heated under his scrutiny.

"I didn't do much—my mom did the most to stop my father. I just reconnected her with the pack."

"Exactly. Without you"—he gestured toward her—"no victory."

"What do you know of the Faction?" Eloi turned to face him, and Daniel's face went hard.

"That they need to be stopped."

"Where are you from?"

"Can't tell you." He leaned in close and whispered in her ear, "It's a secret."

Eloi shivered at his closeness, and her stomach flipped.

He carried on watching her, and her blush deepened. Daniel reached his hand up to touch her face, and she quickly leaned back.

"How can I trust you if you keep secrets?"

Daniel laughed, and it melted her insides. "That's a good point, I'll have to think about that." He looked out into the distance.

Eloi had never met anyone like him. He leaned towards her, and his arms briefly touched hers.

"Maybe it can be our little secret." His words tickled her ear, and she shivered again. Then, before she could speak, he swept up onto his feet. Eloi looked over her shoulder and quickly followed.

Lachlan was leaning against a tree ten feet from her pond. His face was hard, and his arms crossed. When she looked at him, he quirked his eyebrow at her in question.

"Daniel, Lachlan. Lachlan, Daniel." She gestured between the two men and blushed harder, wishing the ground would swallow her. Lachlan didn't move.

"Pleased to meet you, sir. The famous hunter who fell for a shifter." Daniel walked forward with his hand outstretched, his smile easy but his eyes sharp. Lachlan didn't take his hand.

"Why are you here?"

"Well, you see... I bumped into Eloi here, and I wanted to get to know her better...." Daniel's voice trailed off. Lachlan looked past Daniel's shoulder at Eloi, eyebrows raised.

"It's true; we've just been talking," she said.

"Are you with Rolan's wolves?" Lachlan stared at the boy pointedly.

"No, they are an abomination."

"Eloi?"

"He's not lying. I'm not sure why he keeps coming around, but that's the truth." Eloi had kept a mental connection open as they spoke. So despite his faint signature, she could tell when he wasn't being truthful.

"I've been coming to see you." Daniel turned to grin at her.

"Oh, brother." Lachlan sighed and pinched the brow of his nose with two fingers. "Aine won't like this."

"Please." Eloi rushed forward. "Does she need to know?"

"Yes, Eloi, and you should know better."

"Can I tell her?" Eloi looked down at her feet and felt Lachlan's gaze pierce her.

"Fine, but if you don't, I will."

"Just give me a bit of time." Eloi swallowed, and Lachlan nodded.

"Okay, but not too long." His gaze flicked to Daniel. "If you're up to no good, you do realize how much trouble you'll be in if the Pack Leader finds out?"

"Cross my heart." Daniel drew a cross with a finger across his chest. He turned to Eloi and took a step toward her. He stopped when Lachlan coughed and cleared his throat. "I better go."

Eloi nodded sadly. "Sure."

"See you soon." Daniel grinned.

"We will see about that." Daniel's grin dropped as Lachlan spoke. "Come on, Eloi, let's get back."

"Fine," she huffed and pulled her shoes on, nearly tripping in the process. She stormed back towards the village, and Daniel's voice followed her.

"Girls, am I right?" She imagined the cheesy grin on his face and thumbs up. It made her smile, and a delicious heat jolted through her.

Aine had spent most of the day speaking to her pack. She had pushed her mental power further than she should to get a feel for their intentions. More than half the pack wanted to leave, and the rest were terrified. After seeing what happened to Jason and Gary, they had lost faith in her ability to protect them. She needed to go on the offensive and push back at Rolan. They couldn't afford any more losses. As Aine wandered home, Lachlan and Eloi approached on the path ahead of her.

"I heard training went well." Aine smiled at Lachlan and took his hand. "I'm glad your idea worked. Some of the other warriors can't wait to meet their hunter."

"Well, at least something is going right." Lachlan looked pale and drawn.

"Are you okay?" Aine spoke quietly but was aware of Eloi's wary gaze. "Did something happen?"

Lachlan glanced at Eloi. "Story for another time. Let's get home." He took her hand, and they left. Eloi stayed behind, and Aine glanced back at her, frowning.

"You coming home?"

"Need to talk to Nyko about something." Eloi waved and turned to find Nyko.

"She needs some sign that she's progressing more," Lachlan said after a moment. "I know you want to protect her, Aine, but she's nearly eighteen. You need to start trusting her a bit more. Maybe introduce her to pack protocol and let her sit on council meetings."

"You're right. If anything, the council meetings will put her off progressing so fast." Aine grinned at him, and Lachlan finally relaxed to laugh with her.

"In all seriousness, you were younger than her when you took Pack Leadership."

"I've already agreed to work more on her power." Aine's voice was sharp. "She can't have the medallion. Not yet. She needs to grow into her power more, and she can't do that if she's fighting a tsunami."

"I know, Aine, I don't mean that. Just let her know it's a possibility." Lachlan drew her into a hug. Aine held him tightly.

"Something is coming, Lachlan. I can feel it, and I can't lose her. I'm scared the power will kill her if she tries too soon." Aine took a deep breath. "You know the odds. We've read the histories. Eyolf thinks she needs to be at least twenty-five for a chance to survive."

Lachlan chuckled. "She won't wait that long. She can see the strain you're under. Catori said some of the pack want to leave."

"It's more than you think."

Lachlan sat her on the bench outside their house and held her tighter. "Always together, Aine, we are in this as a family. Eloi will see that. Give her a chance. You need to tell her about the age thing."

Aine sighed but didn't speak. They held each other like that until the sun sank below the horizon. A cry near the edge of the village broke their silence.

They looked at each other before both sprinted towards the sound. Ciara sat on the ground, holding on to the shifter that had been taken by Rolan's wolves. He was filthy and looked exhausted. The woman sobbed as she held him tight.

"Have you been bitten?" Aine's voice came out cold and harsh. Lachlan squeezed her arm, and she turned to him.

"We can't risk the village," she whispered harshly. He nodded.

"No," the wolf replied.

"Elijah!" Aine shouted. "Take him to the infirmary and get Tania to check him over. Now."

Ciara looked up at Aine's tone. "Can I go with him?"

"Let's make sure he's safe first." Aine turned to Elijah and watched him haul the shifter to his feet. Ciara still clung to him. Lachlan approached and pried her grip away.

"It'll be okay, we just need to make sure he's alright, and then you can see him." Lachlan smiled at Ciara. Her legs gave way, so he helped her over to Conor, then walked up to Aine.

"Don't you think you're overreacting a little?"

"No, we need to make sure he's safe. I don't think I can lose any more shifters." She left for the medical building, and Lachlan followed. Tania hurried about, checking the shifter while Aine and Lachlan stood near the entrance.

"Eric is fine, no bites. Just tired and in need of a shower." She smiled. "Nice to have some good news for a change." Aine nodded.

"I'll get Ciara." Lachlan left and quickly returned.

"Eric!" Ciara ran across the room and threw herself on her mate. He held her, and Aine looked away when they both started to sob. She took a step towards them, but Lachlan stopped her.

"Give them a minute," he laughed when she huffed.

Eventually, Eric spotted them and froze. Ciara looked over her shoulder and grinned at them, but Eric's expression was cold and closed. Aine frowned as she took Lachlan's hand and walked forward.

"I'm glad you're safe." Lachlan grinned at the shifter and

held out his hand. Eric eyed it warily and clung to Ciara. She looked at him, puzzled.

"What can you tell me about where you were taken?" Aine took a step closer. "We need to stop the Faction taking or killing any more shifters."

Eric cleared his throat. "I need to shower and spend some time with my mate. But if you give me until morning, then I'll take you there."

Aine's eyes widened, and she turned to Lachlan. "This is the break we needed. I'll take a small group, and we can scout the area. See if we can end this, once and for all."

Eric narrowed his eyes and watched them. Aine gave him a smile and tried to relax. "I'm sorry, it's been a stressful few days, and we are all on edge. I'll leave you to settle in, and we can talk in the morning. I'll arrange a small team to go with us." Eric watched them leave, and Aine gripped Lachlan's hand as they walked to the area the warriors were trained in. She turned to him and smiled, but Lachlan kept his face blank.

"Are we sure this is a good idea? Leaving again so soon?" He lifted his hand to her face. "You've only just recovered."

"Yes, we need to know where he is and what his plans are. Let's go put a team together."

~

ELOI SAW Daniel on the rock as she approached the pond. He was relaxed as he watched her approach. Her mother would leave in a couple of hours, and she needed some peace before she was left behind. Again.

"Hey, Eloi."

"How did you know I'd be here?" She came to sit down next to him.

"Just a hunch. So, listen. Seems like your parents are giving you a hard time. Want to run away with me, we could have our own pack?" Daniel smiled in a way that made her insides melt.

Eloi laughed. "Yeah, right. Like I could just pick up and go."

"I can take you somewhere special. A secret place. You'll be safe there, and you'll like it. I promise."

"I bet you say that to all the girls." Eloi had heard some women from town use the phrase and hadn't realized what they meant until that moment. It made her laugh out loud.

Daniel scowled. "Only the ones named Eloi. What do you say?"

Eloi thought about it; leaving her mom and her family, her pack; a pack she'd fought so hard to save and keep safe. It was a real temptation.

"I can't." She shook her head. "I can't leave everyone to be hurt or lost."

Daniel's eyes looked sad, and his mouth turned down. "I understand. Well—I don't, but I won't push you."

Eloi sighed. "It is tempting. How about I think about it?"

"Sooooo." Daniel drew out the word. "What's going on today? You seem sad."

"My mom and Lachlan are leaving again; they're going after Rolan." Eloi gasped as she said it. "I shouldn't have said that… why do I trust you so much? You can't tell anyone; that's dangerous information." She scowled at him.

"Don't worry, I won't tell him you're coming." Daniel grinned when her head turned sharply, and he laughed. "I'm kidding. I don't know him or like him—let's say you and I have a common enemy. I told you and Lachlan—I meant it when I said he needs to be stopped."

Eloi relaxed and blew out a breath. "What is it about

you? It's like you draw me out, even when I don't want you to. Maybe we knew each other in a past life."

"I'm just talented." He leaned into her. "I like being around you; it's peaceful. Do you really believe in past lives?" He quirked an eyebrow at her.

"That's just this place. It's why I'm here and not really. Just always thought it would be cool." She leaned back into him, and they sat in silence.

"What was it like growing up in a pack?"

"Don't you know?" Eloi tilted her head and frowned.

"Not exactly. I actually grew up in the human foster care system. Was a bit of a shock when I turned seventeen—I changed while my parents were out of town. I had no idea what was happening to me."

Eloi's hand flew to her mouth. "I cannot even imagine what that was like. I had my mum to talk me through it, and I still freaked out a little the first time."

"I've actually only known about shifters about three years."

Eloi gasped. "Three years? You can't be serious; you only just found out?"

"Deadly serious." He nodded solemnly, then ruined the effect with a smile. "When my parents came back, I'd trashed the house. They thought I'd had a party—the house was wrecked, and I had to clean it up. I was grounded for weeks."

"Wow, I can't imagine that. I first turned when I was eleven, so seven years ago. That's rare, and we had to keep it a secret. Mom didn't want the pack to treat me differently, and I think even then she didn't trust Rolan."

"That's young. Could you imagine if I shifted at eleven?" He paused. "You don't call him 'Dad.'" Daniel watched her. It was more a statement than a question.

"He stopped being 'Dad' the day he poisoned my mom and stole her title. You should have seen what he did. The way he influenced the crowds—they changed into an angry mob. I was almost glad when I thought he was dead."

"I don't blame you." He lifted his hand, and his knuckle slowly caressed her cheek. Her face heated. "Sorry, I just couldn't help myself."

"That's okay. I like it." Eloi looked up at him through her eyelashes as he leaned closer. Her eyes drifted shut.

Eloi, we are leaving soon. Where are you?

Eloi snapped her eyes open and leaned back a second before Daniel's lips touched hers.

"S–sorry, my mom is calling me!" She quickly got up to leave.

"Did you tell her? Can I still come back here?" Daniel looked hopeful. She grinned at him.

"Not yet, I'm sorry. And, maybe you can come back. I'll think about it." She winked before she shifted and left.

"Think about leaving with me, too. Our own pack, remember?"

Eloi giggled. She wouldn't tell Aine yet; it would have to wait until they got back.

It didn't take her long to return to the village. She could hear Eyolf and Aine arguing as she walked through the front door.

"At least take Elijah!" Eyolf stood near the front door, hands on his hips.

"I'll have Lachlan. I'm worried about taking shifters in case someone else gets bitten. It's bad enough Eric has to come with us to show us the way." Aine sighed and put a hand on her old mentor's shoulder. "We will be fine."

"I still think it's a mistake. You should take more protection."

"If we take too many, then we can't be stealthy. It'll be fine, we just want a quick look, and then we will be back," Aine said.

"I could come." Eloi pushed through the door, careful not to knock it into Eyolf in her haste. Aine sighed and put her hands on her hips.

"I know you want to, Eloi, but you need to stay here. I'm making you temporary Pack Leader while I'm gone." Aine smiled brightly.

"What?" Eloi froze and she gulped.

"If you want to grow into your power, you need to be ready to accept the responsibility that goes with it." Aine put a hand on Eloi's shoulder, and the girl flinched it off.

"That's not what I meant!" Eloi whined. "I want to be ready for the medallion, not taking over from you. That's years and years away."

"At your age, I'd been Pack Leader a year. You need to be ready in case anything happens to me." Aine smiled sadly.

"But I want to come with you, leave the leadership to Eyolf!" Eloi gestured to him, and Eyolf shook his head at her.

"Enough, Eloi." Aine let a growl lace into her voice. "You need to earn the power. This is how you will start. I know you want to advance your power, but I need to know you're ready for it."

Eloi crossed her arms and scowled. "That's not fair." Eyolf put a hand on her shoulder and gave it a squeeze.

"You'll be a great leader one day, youngling, but you'll have to learn first. There's more to leadership than power." He smiled at her, and Eloi pushed his hand away. She let out a frustrated growl, storming out the front door. Nyko bumped into her as she turned a corner, his smile dropping.

"What's up with you?" He fell into step beside her.

"I'm being left behind...again?" Eloi continued to walk, and Nyko quickened his pace to keep up.

"I'm being left behind too." He shrugged. "No big deal."

"But you got to go last time!" Eloi whirled on him, and Nyko put up his hands to ward her off.

"Okay, but I can see why this time. We can't afford to lose anyone else if they're bitten. Stop being so whiny."

Eloi growled and continued to stride towards the training area. Ciara and Eric stood off to one side, separate from the other groups. Eloi frowned. They stood rigid and wouldn't look at each other. When Aine walked into the area, Eric strode straight up to her.

"Please, can Ciara and Conor come with us?" Eric's voice was tight.

"We've had this discussion. The fewer shifters, the better, and we don't want to be detected," Aine snapped. Eloi scowled at her mother's tone; she was obviously still annoyed.

"I don't understand why." Eric crossed his arms.

"Don't argue with me, Eric; the decision is made. Ciara and Conor will be safer here." Aine held up her hand and walked over to Lachlan.

Eric's frown deepened, but he didn't push further. Lachlan stood next to Phil, and Eloi squealed. She raced forward and threw herself on the big guy.

"I didn't know you were visiting, Phil!"

He twirled her around and put her down. "I think yer getting far too big for that, little wolf. How have ya been? Ya haven't been to the diner recently."

Eloi shrugged. "Too much training. Did you just call me fat?" She cocked a hip and crossed her arms. Phil laughed at her scowl, and she grinned. She had missed him.

"Nope, not going there." He held his hands up in defeat and shook his head violently.

"How have things been in the town? Liam hasn't been giving you a hard time?"

"Nah, he's a big softy when you get to know him. Cillian and I have been talking to the town folks. Keeping the peace. I think they like having the hunters around to keep the nuisance animals at bay."

"Diner doing okay?"

"Yeah, hunters come and meet with Liam from other areas. Business has been good, as they usually meet in the diner." Phil grinned. "I've never had to work so hard."

"Maybe I'll take up that offer of giving you a hand," she said with a smile.

"Not sure your mom will appreciate that; heard you're acting commander while she's gone." He pulled her in for another hug and whispered in her ear, "You'll do great."

Eloi let him go and watched Aine and Lachlan with the young hunters. They argued with Lachlan gesturing toward the trees. The leader scowled at them but didn't say anything. Eventually, Owen nodded, and Ian followed his agreement. Lachlan clapped both on the shoulder before he turned to Aine.

Nyko shifted next to Eloi, but she kept her eyes on her mom next to Lachlan. They had packs beside them and opened them to check the contents. Eyolf handed them some water bottles, which Aine passed over to Eric to pack into his satchel. Aine saw Eloi and met her gaze, then walked over to pull her into a hug; Eloi stiffened but hugged her back.

"We won't be long, a couple of days at most." Aine smiled, but Eloi scowled at her. Aine sighed and hugged Nyko. "Behave while I'm gone."

Aine spoke to each pack member that had come to see her off before she met Lachlan with Eric at the edge of the village. Eloi pouted as she watched them go, and Nyko gave her a nudge.

"Cheer up, I'm sure she will take you next time," he laughed when she continued to scowl at her mom's back.

"She better, or I'll leave myself." She whirled and headed back toward their house.

~

AINE WATCHED Eric's back as they continued to walk. They trekked for about half a day, causing her to breathe hard. Her chest was tight, and it was difficult to take a deep breath.

"Why couldn't Rolan have made his evil lair easy to access so we could have taken a car?" Aine huffed, and Lachlan put an arm around her; she leaned into him.

"We need a break, Eric," Lachlan called after him. Eric stopped and turned to look at them. He slowly worked his way back.

"Shouldn't we keep going? Don't want to waste the daylight."

"Just a quick break." Aine sat down on a rock to rest. Her muscles quivered, and she started to doubt she'd make it to Rolan's base.

"Who is Rolan?" Eric's brow drew together. "You've mentioned him a few times."

Aine shivered involuntarily. "My evil ex-husband, who thought my leadership should have been his because women aren't fit to rule." She curled her lip. "He poisoned me to take my power, stripped my connection to the pack, beat the shit out of me, and then left me for dead." She chuckled, then added, "I should thank him, really. I wouldn't have met Lachlan otherwise."

Eric continued to frown at her, and Aine swallowed. "I know it's not funny, but I have to joke about it. I had no memory when Lachlan found me, and I was fortunate I wasn't found by the wrong people." She moaned when Lachlan rubbed her back. "Why am I so tired?"

"Maybe it's the stress of everything. You haven't stopped recently, and the attacks are happening more often." Lachlan kissed her temple, and she felt him push energy into their connection.

"Here." Eric handed her a water bottle, and she took it gratefully.

"Thanks." Aine drank deeply, and the water settled her stomach.

Lachlan cupped her face and looked into her eyes. "Maybe we should head back. You don't look well."

"No," Aine replied sharply. "This is the closest we've been to finding him. I need to know where they are. They have to be stopped."

"Aine..." He continued to gaze at her.

"Lachlan, we can't lose any more shifters. I can't take it. Trying to save Gary nearly killed me, and I couldn't help Jason. The least we could do is stop Rolan from making any more abominations to infect our pack."

"What are you talking about?" Eric stood over her, his face pale.

Lachlan moved to stand behind her and rubbed her shoulders. Aine gestured toward Sumter. "Rolan has used dark magic to create an army of dark wolves. The ones that took you, they bit Gary. Once infected, a shifter will turn rabid and attack other shifters. We think they join the other dark wolves and can be influenced by their creator." She took a shaky breath. "I tried to save Gary, tried to draw the darkness out of him, but it was too strong. It nearly killed me. I'm so sorry about your friend."

Eric flinched when she reached out to grab his hand. His face paled further. "I don't understand."

"Didn't Ciara tell you?" Lachlan asked. Aine felt his warmth against her.

"We argued." Eric looked at the ground. "I wanted her to leave. I thought...how could I have got this so wrong?" He started to pace the area, and Aine watched him.

She flinched as a shot cracked through the air, sounding like it came from a rifle. She looked at Eric; all the blood drained from his face, but he wasn't hurt.

Lachlan's hand on her shoulder dropped. Pain, which wasn't hers, lanced through her chest. She whipped her head around and watched in horror as red blossomed from the center of Lachlan's torso. Blood drained from her hunter's face; his jaw was slack as he dropped to the ground. His eyes closed.

"LACHLAN!" Aine's scream echoed through the trees. Eric came into view and crouched beside the man as she lunged for him, pushing him away and falling beside Lachlan. His chest was still. Frantic, she felt for a pulse; it was there but weak. She froze when a laugh from her nightmares sounded behind her.

"Thanks for coming to me, wife—saves me the trouble of coming to get you," Rolan smirked next to Eric, who had turned a sickening shade of green.

Aine stood quickly and gathered her power. He deserved to die for everything that he did three years ago and for what he'd just done. But nothing happened. The well of power within her pulsed, but she couldn't access it. She threw her hands out again desperately. Rolan's laugh was cold.

"Performance issues?" He quirked a brow and clapped Eric on the shoulder. "You have your new friend here to thank for that. Surely you should have learned by now not to drink anything another shifter offers you."

"I don't...." Eric looked at her helplessly, his eyes pleading with her. His gaze dropped to Lachlan, and he put his head in his hands, his shoulders sagging. "I didn't know."

Rolan's eyes sparkled with glee. "What a mess, Aine." He held the rifle and aimed it at her.

"I can still take you, Rolan." Her fists clenched, and Aine pulled herself into a fighting stance.

"Not if I shoot you first. Can you take them too? Just one bite and you're dead."

Growls surrounded them, and fifty wolves appeared in the trees. "Now, come along quietly, and I won't go and fetch our daughter instead."

Aine swallowed hard, looking down at Lachlan. "Let me get him some help first."

"He'll be dead soon enough," Rolan said darkly, and she blanched.

"What about me?" Eric's face was still green. "I need to make sure my family is safe."

Aine glared at him, and Eric recoiled. His eyes pleaded with her to understand, and he looked at the direction they'd come from Sumter.

"You can go." Rolan dismissed him. "You played your part, and they'll need to know their fearless leader was too weak to defend herself."

"Go and get help," Aine begged. Eric didn't look back as he sprinted into the trees, and Aine's heart sank. "Let me bring him with us; he needs to be healed."

"No chance, that filth can rot where he is." Rolan grinned at her.

Aine cried out as he grabbed her arm and dragged her away. Lachlan didn't move, and she tried to connect to him —their connection there but faint. She pulled at her power again and cried out in frustration.

"Now, now. None of that." Rolan pulled her so hard she landed on her knees. She swiftly spun and knocked his legs out from under him. The growls around her were nearly deafening, and she froze.

"Don't try anything like that again." Rolan caught her around the waist and pulled her away from Lachlan. Aine felt a tear fall down her cheek, and a sob tightened her chest. She reached out to their connection one last time and pushed as hard as she could at her power.

Lachlan!

9

Eloi felt a pain rip through her chest and fell to her knees. Her weapon clattered to the floor in front of her. Nyko immediately stopped his attack and dropped the bow staff he'd been working with. He gripped her shoulders as Eloi let out a heart-wrenching scream. She felt the whole pack fall silent around her, eyes all turned in her direction. Her chest ached, and it was hard to breathe. She reached out to feel for Aine, but it felt like someone had sliced her heart out. Aine was there but very faint.

"Something's wrong." Eloi tried to stand, and her legs gave out again. Nyko caught her and helped her to her feet. Aine's mental voice echoed through the pack, and they both collapsed to the ground.

Lachlan!

"No!" Eloi managed to stand. "Did you hear that?"

Nyko nodded, his face pale. She looked around; every pack member had fallen to their knees. Eloi trembled as she came to her feet, turning in the direction of pounding feet.

Owen and Ian ran up to her. "What happened?" Owen said frantically.

"I don't know, but my mom is in a lot of pain. I think she's okay physically, but something must have happened to Lachlan." Eloi managed not to sway as she took a step towards the edge of the training area. "Call the warriors together. We need a plan of action until we know more."

Ian and Owen glanced at each other with worried frowns.

It took time to round up pack members; everyone was shell-shocked. The warriors gathered in the training area, and Eloi stood before them, butterflies in her stomach. She looked around at the faces before her and held her head high.

"You all know as much as I. My mother reached out mentally and is in pain. I can only guess that something happened to Lachlan on their journey. I've tried to reach my mother, but there's a block on her. Something like this has only happened once before, and it involved Rolan. I think it's likely that he has something to do with this. Any suggestions?" Eloi looked around at her warriors, but blank faces stared back at her. She turned to Eyolf at her side.

"This will be your choice, Eloi. You need to think as a leader and not with your heart." His voice was quiet next to her, and she nodded. Every fiber of her being wanted to shift and run out after her mother. But she couldn't leave the rest of the pack unprotected.

Owen and Ian stood on the edges of the group, Nyko next to Owen, and Elijah stood by Ian.

"Hunters, do you think Liam would be open to helping on this?" Eloi looked at the men who had willingly joined their pack and fought beside shifters. Ian coughed, and Owen looked thoughtful.

"It took a lot of faith for us to come and join you. We can see what you have in this pack, and we can see why Lachlan insists we work together," Ian spoke up. "We've been reporting back, and I think Liam is curious to see how this relationship can develop. But there are older hunters that I don't think will come around." He looked at the floor.

"What about his brothers?"

"Cillian would help, but his older brother has left the hunters. Once Liam confirmed Lachlan would be his heir, Finn disappeared." Ian kept his face blank, but he squirmed under Eloi's gaze.

A disturbance on the edge of the area caught Eloi's attention, and a dark brown wolf sprinted into the back of one of the warriors. They were both sprawled out on the edge of the group. The wolf looked exhausted, and his chest heaved.

"Eric!" Ciara cried out and ran to his side. Eloi hadn't seen her with the warriors at the back. She helped lift Eric in his human form, and he limped to the front with Eloi.

"What happened?" Eloi demanded.

"I'm so sorry; it's all my fault," Eric panted. "I didn't know; I thought I was doing the right thing!"

He turned to Ciara. "I just wanted you safe."

"What did you do?" Ciara stepped back when Eric reached for her.

"He told me that she was dangerous and that this pack was being controlled. That I would be helping to release them from an oppressive leader. There were rumors that the refugees told me. That Aine controlled the hunter with dark magic and threatened everyone with death to keep them in line." Eric took a shaky breath. Ciara just stared at him.

"I put something in Aine's drink; I think it stifled her power. Rolan took her, but Lachlan...." Eric's head drooped, and Ciara's eyes widened. "Rolan shot Lachlan with a rifle. He wasn't moving when I left."

A growl rent the air, and before she could stop him, Eyolf launched himself at Eric, who didn't react. Eyolf shifted and pinned Eric down. He snarled in his face, his jaws inches from his neck.

"Please don't!" Ciara knelt beside them both. "He didn't know. He was trying to protect me!"

Eyolf growled at her.

"Stand down. We might need more information. Take them both. Get Conor and place a guard outside their house. They aren't to leave." Eloi pinched her brow. "We need to find out what Rolan wants with Mom, and we need to get to Lachlan."

Eric stood up slowly, mouth downturned and his face pale. "It's not Rolan who wanted her."

Eloi snapped her head to him. "What do you mean?"

"Rolan isn't the one giving the orders; there's another shifter. His name is Solus and—"

"Solus!" Eloi grabbed Eric's arms. "It can't be. Are you sure?"

"He called himself Solus. There was tension between them, but Rolan took orders from him." Eric's eyes darted between the group.

"It can't be," Nyko whispered.

"Who is Solus?" Owen threw his hands up. "What's going on?"

Eloi glanced at Eyolf, who had paled. She took a deep breath and turned back to the hunters, "Solus is my mother's father, my grandfather. He died on the same day as Conrad, my great grandfather. My mother told me they were killed by hunters, but it looks like more happened that day than we know."

"That's messed up." Owen put a hand on her shoulder. "Don't worry, we will get your ma back. Liam has been coming around. He's stubborn, but he will do anything to help Lachlan."

Eloi shrugged and sighed. "I hope so. We will need all the help we can get."

AINE LOOKED around the cave Rolan left her in. It had a bed and furniture, but there were no decorations on the wall, and the bars on the entrance looked newly embedded into the rock. She sat on the single bed and plucked at the sheets. They were light blue and familiar, reminding her of her childhood.

She squeezed her eyes shut and desperately reached for her power again. With distance, the weak connection to Lachlan had dulled, and she couldn't feel him anymore. She reached out for Eloi, the link to her daughter and pack muffled somehow. She frowned. How had Rolan convinced Eric to betray them? A wave of exhaustion pulled at her, and she lay her head on the pillow.

The smell in the cave made her stomach feel queasy. She tried to fight the fatigue but must have dozed; movement near the cave entrance had her springing from the bed and crouching to face the shifter there. The sudden movement made her dizzy, but she held her balance. A petite woman stood at the entryway holding a tray of food.

"Hi, I'm Olivia." She gently placed the tray on the floor and pushed it under the door.

"I'm not eating that," Aine scoffed.

"Why? The master is being very generous, considering your crimes." The woman scowled at her.

"My crimes? What the hell are you talking about?" Aine

ran to the bars and gripped them. "Are you insane? Rolan tried to kill me and corrupt my pack."

The woman stumbled away from the bars. "You tried to kill him and control his pack with dark magic. You've even got a hunter under your control to kill any shifters that defy you."

Aine laughed darkly. "Sure I did. You're stupid to believe that."

"They've been nothing but kind to us here, sheltering us from your attacks!"

"Our attacks? The Faction has been a menace for generations. Now that Rolan is in charge, they've created abominations and enslaved packs. That's not us. You need to open your eyes and really look around you." Aine slumped against the bars and frowned. "Is that why Eric betrayed us?"

"Eric, is he okay? They said you captured him again."

Aine shook her head. "No, he came back to us and was going to lead us here. Olivia, you're being lied to. You need to help me out of here. I have a daughter—" Her words cut off when a large shifter appeared down the corridor. He cleared his throat, and Olivia quickly moved away.

"Hey!" Aine tried to catch the shifter's attention. "Let me out of here!" she screamed at him and shook the bars. The shifter moved away, and she shook them harder. She turned and kicked the tray of food, which flew at the wall and clattered on the floor. Aine smiled in satisfaction before she sat down heavily on the bed.

When the shifter returned, he approached the door, and black manacles swung in his hands. "Now, are you going to behave, or do I need to make you behave?" His eyes narrowed at her.

Aine swallowed and stood slowly; the tantrum earlier no

longer made her feel better. Needless to say, she scowled at the shifter.

"Hard way it is." He unlocked the door and came at her with the manacles. Aine dodged easily and delivered a swift kick to his kidney. The shifter sprawled on her floor, and the manacles clanked into the corner. As she leaped for them, he caught her foot, then blood flooded her mouth as her chin hit the stone, her hands barely breaking her fall.

Dazed, she lifted herself to her knees and retched. When she'd finished vomiting, she saw one wrist chained by the manacle, and the shifter roughly grabbed the other to pull her up. Once she was secured, the shifter held the chain and pulled her down the corridor. She could feel blood trickle down her chin and a sour taste in her mouth. She spat as they walked and was reprimanded with a sharp tug on the chain.

"Where are you taking me?"

"To the master," the shifter grunted. He didn't turn to look at her, just continued to drag her through the caves. The tunnel ahead opened into a large cavern, which they crossed. Shifters stopped to stare at her, and she looked at the floor to keep her head down. With blood and dirt on her face, she must look a sight.

There were hundreds of shifters in this area; they all appeared to have a purpose and seemed to move freely. Aine frowned and stopped. She stumbled when the large shifter tugged on the chain.

"Keep moving."

"Well, I'll give Rolan a piece of my mind about how he treats guests." Aine tugged on the chain herself and laughed when the shifter nearly tripped. Then, as they entered another tunnel, she tried to keep track of the twists and turns until they reached a large room with an altar and bowl as its centerpiece.

The shifter grabbed her arm and jerked her forward.

"Hey!" Aine tried to smack him but proceeded to fall over his foot. She sat down hard on the floor. A dark shadow fell over her, and she felt like a bucket of water had been thrown over her body when she heard the newcomer speak.

"What did you do to her?" growled a familiar voice. Aine looked up to see the large shifter slammed into the wall.

"M-Master, please!" There was a crack, and the shifter dropped to the floor.

Aine blinked at her father. She squeezed her eyes shut and shook her head. But when her eyes opened, he still stood before her. Solus crouched and touched his hands to the cuffs. They dropped from her wrists.

"Father?" She sat on the floor and looked up at the man she hadn't seen in nearly twenty years.

"I'm here now; everything will be okay." He reached down to help her up and used a handkerchief to wipe her face. Aine just stared at him, eyes wide and mouth open.

"Come, let's take a seat." He led Aine through to another cave where there were two couches.

She sat down heavily. "But how—how are you alive? Rolan said..." Aine stopped abruptly. How could she have been so stupid? Rolan was the only one to return from the hunting trip; both her father and grandfather had never returned. She frowned at her father. "Why are you here?"

Solus looked up at her and smiled softly. "That doesn't matter now; what matters is that we are together."

"But Rolan...are you his captive?" Aine watched her father, and he chuckled.

"No, of course not; he's my protégé." Solus patted her on the knee, and she lurched up from the couch.

"But he tried to kill me, he—" Aine closed her eyes. "He hurt my mate."

"But Rolan is your mate." Solus frowned at her. It was then she saw the swirl of darkness around him. The smoke curled, and his eyes darkened; she gasped softly as she stepped back. "You have been married to Rolan for years. The hunter took you from him!"

Dark tendrils curled towards Aine, and she shook her head; the power within her swelled, but she still couldn't reach it. She fled from the room and stopped abruptly as she collided with a hard body. Rolan gripped her arms, turning her to face Solus again. The dark smoke continued to float towards her. She shook her head violently and screamed when it touched her skin.

Pain exploded behind her eyes, and she gritted her teeth. Rolan held her firm, and his words tickled her ear. "You will be mine once more and under my control."

A sick feeling coiled within Aine, and she pushed as hard as she could against him. Rolan fell to the floor, but Solus stood before her and gripped her forearm.

"We need to work together!"

"I won't help you! Why are you doing this?" Aine cried.

"We need to take the power we deserve. Humans are destroying this planet." Solus's voice was thick with power. "We need to correct the balance."

"This is not the way!" Aine collapsed to her knees as she felt his power try to influence her. "I will never bow before you."

Aine stood and took a step forward. She felt her eyes glow amber, and she pushed what power she could behind the stare. Solus blanched and took a step back. His hands came up, and the smoke became denser, the color a deep black. An impossible wind whooshed past her ears, but she held her ground.

Solus dropped to a knee, and Aine grinned in triumph. She heard a slight noise behind her and turned in time to see Rolan's fist smash into the side of her head.

Everything went black.

ELOI CONNECTED with Nyko when she felt a mental nudge from him. She was sitting in Eyolf's kitchen and had been waiting to hear.

What did you find?

Eric led us to where Aine was taken, and we've found a lot of blood, but there's no Lachlan. Nyko's emotions whirled with his words, his sorrow palpable.

Eloi put her head in her hands. She could feel him prowling around the area, trying to suppress his panic.

There's too much blood, Eloi; there's no way he survived. It looks like he was dragged and then lifted. Rolan probably took him to make sure we couldn't help. The hunters found a trail and followed it about half a mile, but it just...stopped. Do you want us to keep looking?

Eloi pinched her nose and blew out a long breath. *No, we can't risk you being taken too or bitten. Return to Sumter. We will just have to hope that whatever is restricting my mom weakens and she contacts us.* She cut the connection.

"It's the right decision, youngling." Eyolf took her hand and squeezed.

"I told you not to call me that." Eloi's voice came out weary.

"I'm sorry—you'll always be a youngling to me."

Eloi snorted. "That's 'cause you're so old." She paused. "What now?"

"As you said yourself, we wait. Aine is strong. She will push to contact you for help if she needs it." Eyolf fell quiet.

"You've not mentioned my grandfather." Eloi kept her face blank. Eyolf sighed and put his head in his hands.

"I'm not going to lie, Eloi; I'm shaken." Eyolf scrubbed his hands down his face. "I'm beginning to wonder if he was the reason that no one came back from that hunting trip."

"You never talk about him." Eloi shifted to face Eyolf. He leaned on the table, his shoulders curled in and face drawn.

"After your grandmother died, he seemed to go mad with grief. He locked himself away and refused to see everyone. Even Aine." Eyolf swallowed. "Conrad eventually dragged him out on the hunting trip, and neither of them came back."

"I don't understand why he wouldn't just come back with Rolan. Why stay hidden?" Eloi brushed her hand through her hair and pulled a face when her fingers snagged in it.

"I don't know, Eloi." Eyolf sighed and sagged in his seat. Eloi shook her head and gazed out the window. She needed to get away. She rose from her seat and clasped Eyolf's shoulder, then departed.

The cool breeze was welcome as she left his house. She surveyed the village, noticing everyone had taken shelter in their homes. She glanced toward the house she'd sent Ciara and Eric to, took a step forward, then stopped. She couldn't face them right now.

Her heart ached. She jogged toward the edges of the village and shifted. The run to her place felt good, and her heart pounded by the time she got there. She lay down on her rock and shifted back to human form. She marveled at how little energy it took for her to change.

"Daniel!" Eloi heard her voice carry through the woods but couldn't sense anyone there.

"Daniel..." she tried again, but there was no answer. Sadly, she sat down on her rock, pulled off her shoes, and left her feet to dangle in the cold water. She stared out at the gushing waterfall, the sound calming her rapid heartbeat, and sighed. She would give it an hour to see if Daniel came, then return. She watched the sun fall behind the trees and welcomed the dark night around her.

10

Lachlan felt like someone stood on his chest, the pressure pushing down and suffocating him. He struggled to take a deep breath, but his lungs would not expand beyond a shallow one. Lachlan groaned and coughed, his throat feeling like sandpaper. He tried to open his eyes, but they were too heavy. He sagged into the mattress he was laid on. He didn't have the energy to flinch when ice touched his lips and slid into his mouth.

"Careful, now, don't move too much. You need rest." A gentle, feminine voice soothed his mind. "You were shot, and we've done all we can. You'll need to heal yourself the rest of the way, and that will take time." The voice was like a lullaby, soothing him as he let the blackness take him away from the discomfort and pain.

When he woke again, the pressure on his chest had lifted; it was a relief to draw in a deep breath. He blinked at a bright light several times before he managed to keep his eyes open, though they still watered. He looked at a plain white ceiling, a bare bulb hanging down, and the walls bare brick. He shifted to sit up and groaned at the pain in his chest. A white bandage was wrapped around his upper torso, and he wore grey sweats.

On his elbows, he surveyed the bare room, his stomach flexed. He appeared to be in a hospital bed, a glass of water on the table next to him with an IV hooked up to his arm. He pulled at the tubes connected to his arm and flinched as he pulled it out. The door in front of him was metal and slightly ajar; he looked around. The room looked like a prison cell, but he wasn't bolted in.

The sound of voices had his gaze on the door. A familiar male voice carried into the room, and Lachlan shook his head, which felt like cotton. He pushed himself into a sitting position and tried to swing his legs around, but they wouldn't move. Finally, with a jerk, he was able to shift them, and he knocked the glass off the table next to him in the process. The shatter made him wince, and the voices stopped. Heavy footsteps approached the door; it creaked slightly as it slowly opened.

"Daniel?" Lachlan coughed and clutched his chest. The boy rushed forward and clapped him on the back. Lachlan spluttered. "Thanks."

"Surprise, Woah...don't get up. You're still healing." Daniel put a hand on Lachlan's shoulder and firmly held him down. Then, the boy gently helped him back into his bed, although more upright than laid down.

"What happened? Where's Aine?" Lachlan groaned. He reached for their bond and took a sharp intake of breath at its absence. Frantically, he said, "She was with me in the woods. I can't feel her."

"You took a rifle shot to the chest. Aine wasn't with you. Her trail led away with another shifter, a third shifter headed in the opposite direction back to Sumter. We didn't have time to look for her; we needed to get you back here."

Daniel gripped his shoulder. “You were in terrible shape. It’s a miracle you survived.”

“How *am* I still alive?” Lachlan stirred. His chest felt tight, but there wasn’t as much pain as he expected. “I don’t feel like I was shot.”

“We have some very skilled healers here. With a bit of rest, you’ll be as good as new by tomorrow.” Daniel had to push Lachlan back down as he tried to get out of bed again. The hunter shook his head.

“I can’t stay here; I need to get to Aine. Rolan must have taken her. There’s no other explanation.”

“You are in no condition to go anywhere yet. We are looking for her, I promise. The healers said you need to rest, or you will undo what they did.” Daniel shook his head.

“Shifter healers?” Lachlan coughed.

“Yes, they’re very gifted.” Daniel grinned at him.

Lachlan continued to cough, and a woman walked into the room with another glass of water. She had short auburn hair, an athletic build, and familiar blue eyes.

“I know you,” Lachlan croaked.

“Yep, though you looked better last time I saw you,” she said with a thick Irish accent.

“You look like your ma.” Lachlan stared at her. “Though you have the O’Reilly eyes.”

“I get that a lot. Especially around here.” She rolled her eyes and laughed.

“Shauna.” Lachlan’s eyes widened.

“Wow, good memory. It’s been a while, cousin,” she said with a wink.

He looked at her in astonishment. “You must have been fourteen when I left!”

“Fifteen, more like,” she huffed.

"Did you come across with Liam?" He frowned. Why hadn't he seen her in Burntwood Falls?

Shauna snorted. "Nope, though I only just found out they were here. I'm guessing my dear uncle came for you?" She passed him the water, and he drank gratefully.

"Yep. As expected, Finn was getting out of hand. He's asked me to be his heir." Lachlan shrugged, then winced at a flash of pain.

"Liam should have got a handle on him years ago. He was bad when I left, had a thing for the younger girls." She shuddered. "It was creepy."

"When did you leave?" Lachlan placed the glass on the side table.

"About two years ago. It took me a while to realize I was on the wrong side; your ma used to talk about a balance that needed to be found." She looked at him apologetically. "I'm sorry about what happened. I tried to find you after, but you'd already left. In the end, so did I, and went looking for my ma."

Lachlan frowned. Shauna's ma had gone missing when she was twelve. They'd always suspected shifters had taken her. "Thanks, but wasn't she taken by shifters?"

"It's not what you think, Lachlan." Shauna sighed. "Briana knew where she was. Ma had been writing to me for years. After you left, I stayed as long as I could, but I stopped believing in the cause."

"Ma knew?"

"Yeah, they were pretty close. Ma couldn't take me with her—she thought she was doing the right thing after my dad died. Liam got worse after that, losing a brother and then his wife. Things got worse after you left, and it meant I could make up my own mind."

"Your own mind about what?" Lachlan's eyes shifted to Daniel. "What's going on here?"

"It's a long story, and you still need to rest." Shauna turned to leave.

"Wait, he's a shifter." Lachlan smiled when Daniel held out his hand, which Lachlan ignored, "Aw, come on, I'm not stupid. I knew what you were as soon as I saw you. Eloi isn't stupid either." He raised an eyebrow at the boy.

"Actually, it's more complicated than that." Daniel grimaced. "I guess you'll find out soon enough…I'm a hybrid."

Lachlan's eyes widened. "A hybrid?" He barely stopped himself lurching forward.

"Part shifter and part hunter. Shauna got more than she bargained for when she went looking for her mom—she's my half-sister. Though don't call me cousin because Shauna said you're related on her dad's side."

"Briana and Ma were best friends. Lachlan, here is still your family." Shauna nudged Daniel and winked at Lachlan.

Daniel's head turned sharply to Shauna, and he stuck his tongue out.

"Seems we have a lot to talk about." Lachlan relaxed back into the bed.

"Yes, it does, 'Kind Warrior.'" Shauna laughed when Lachlan frowned at her. "I know all about that, too. There are a few people here who want to meet you. You set a lot in motion when you freed that shifter and left your father all those years ago."

Lachlan grumbled. "What about Aine?"

"We are doing everything we can, but it looks like the Faction did indeed take her. She's tough—she'll be okay, Lachlan. We won't stop until we've found her." Daniel patted his shoulder. "Rest. We will be back later, and you can meet the rest of the pack."

Lachlan sagged back into the pillow and stared at the wall. He wondered how many other hunters they thought taken by shifters had left of their own free will. Finally, he closed his eyes and dozed.

A few hours later, a healer, a beautiful woman with a large scar running down her face, came and checked on him. Lachlan grumbled while she examined his injuries but was relieved when she said he could move around freely. He thanked Daniel when he came to fetch him, and they wandered through the corridors of an underground bunker.

"So, how many of you are there down here?"

"About a hundred, a mixture of shifters, hunters, and hybrids. All one big happy family." Daniel nodded toward the door ahead.

"It sounds like a good place. How long have you been here?" Lachlan followed slowly.

"Three years. Something happened to my mom, she left me at a diner. When the police were called and came to collect me, I went into the human foster care system." Daniel's eyes darkened, and Lachlan decided not to push.

"So, how did everyone come together?" Lachlan walked into the open area through the door ahead. The room was spacious; it looked like a cafeteria, with tables lined up and people—shifters and hunters—all sat together talking. Their voices echoed around the room and created a pleasant atmosphere.

"We are various outcasts; we've picked up a lot of strays. From packs that don't tolerate mating with humans or hunters that don't tolerate mating with shifters. You'll know a bit about that." Daniel gave Lachlan a sly grin and bumped his arm. "Though things are obviously easier when you mate the Pack Leader with incredible powers."

"It was hard to start with, but once I proved myself, it got easier. There's still some that think I'll betray them. However, Liam is coming around; he's sent some of the younger hunters to join us to see how it goes."

Daniel stopped, eyes wide. "Hunters are volunteering to mingle with shifters? Maybe the prophecy is true."

"You mean the 'Kind Warrior' prophecy. I never really believed in all that, a Kind Warrior helping to unite shifters and hunters. At least not until I met Aine." Lachlan cleared his throat and shifted. He looked around at the ease with which everyone interacted. "It's good to see that it's possible. Aine and I have talked about a world where hunters and shifters come together to keep those in line that would harm either side. Or even humans."

"Lachlan!" an older woman exclaimed and quickly walked toward him. Her red hair was greyer than he remembered; she looked identical to Shauna but older. Almost the same as when he'd last seen her.

"Vivienne? Shauna didn't mention you were here!" Lachlan hugged her hard.

"I wanted to surprise you." She smiled at him "I was so sorry to hear about your mother. We kept in touch, and when I didn't hear from her, I got scared. When Shauna told me what happened, it nearly broke my heart. She had always supported the choice I made."

Lachlan sighed. "It explains why she encouraged me to take a side. I just wish I'd been there when...." His voice cracked and trailed off. He looked between Vivienne and Daniel, reaching up to rub the back of his head.

"I left Ireland because I fell in love with a shifter. I fell pregnant, and we didn't know what to expect, and when

Derek was killed by hunters in New York, I gave Daniel up. I was being hunted by them and thought he would be safer. I never dreamed he would be a shifter since I'm not one. Though it did help me find him again." She smiled at Daniel brightly. He returned the smile, though Lachlan noticed a shadow behind his eyes. "Shauna turned up looking for me a couple of years ago."

"How did you find the hybrids?" Lachlan gestured toward the tables in the room.

"They found me." Vivienne shrugged. "Michael has been bringing hybrids into the fold for years. This pack has existed for generations since the original shifter families started to fail."

Lachlan shook his head; Vivienne talked fast. "Generations?"

"Yes," Vivienne said enthusiastically.

"Who is Michael?" Lachlan looked around the room, but no one stood out.

"Pack Leader. His parents were killed by hunters when he was in his teens. Turns out that some hunters think the same as us and don't believe in killing for the sake of killing."

"Do you think it's possible to bring balance?" Lachlan stared out at the groups in front of him, a pang making him realize how much he wanted that.

"Absolutely. It's what we have been trying to do." Vivienne's eyes sparkled. "Come and meet Michael!" she grabbed Lachlan's arm and guided him to the back of the cafeteria.

They entered an office filled with shelves and books; some overflowed and were stacked on the floor. Lachlan stared at the large man before him, who was tall and muscular with prominent features. Michael stood from behind a modest desk and reached out his hand to Lachlan.

"Nice to meet you, Lachlan. I've heard a lot about you." He smiled warmly.

"Thanks. I wish I knew more about this place...." Lachlan paused. "Is there any news on my mate? Daniel said she was taken by the Faction."

"Yes, you must be worried. We've been looking for her. Daniel wanted to make sure you were okay before he let your pack know where you were. I'm guessing you're anxious to get back to them." Michael tilted his head. "For now, I need you to stay here. You need to heal, and we have a lot to discuss. I think we could be great allies. Another day won't hurt."

Lachlan frowned. "How long have I been here?"

Michael shifted and didn't look him in the eye. "About a week."

"A week?!" Lachlan's voice came out high-pitched, and he coughed.

"I'm sorry, my healer had to put you into a healing sleep. She's very gifted. She's of the Tivaci bloodline."

"I didn't think there was anyone from that bloodline left." Lachlan watched Michael nod.

"There is none of the bloodline in the pack, but some of the original families split off when mating with humans was no longer accepted. My guess is the original bloodline died off in the pack, and the ones mated with other shifters struggled to produce offspring." Michael rubbed his chin.

"Our historian has mentioned the fertility issues and that it's easier with true mates. Usually a shifter and hunter partnership." Lachlan smiled sadly.

"Yes, I've heard of true mates." Michael scratched his

chin, a few days' stubble shadowing his face. "Never really believed it, though."

"I didn't know what was happening, but it's incredible. I can't feel Aine anymore, and I'm worried." Lachlan shifted and looked Michael in the face. "I don't mind staying, but I need to find my mate and at least let my pack know I'm alive."

"We have a rough idea of where the Faction is based. We were already working out a plan of attack. I'm pretty sure I know the answer to this, but...can we count on you being with us?"

"Absolutely." Lachlan's shoulders relaxed. "I think we should reach out to the hunters too."

Michael frowned. "We have survived this long by keeping our existence a secret from hunters."

"So did the Aoibhan pack." Lachlan spread his hands. "But they have thrived since they came out of the shadows. I have maintained that shifters and hunters should work together. My father has been coming around to the idea."

Michael sighed. "I don't think we can risk it. We've been hated by both sides when they've found out about our existence."

"You also have hunters in your pack. If you don't take the risk, then we will never find the balance everyone wants. Think it over—you might find it's worth the risk, and you have my word that you will not be harmed by my pack or my family." Lachlan clasped Michael's shoulder.

"I'll think on it. In the meantime, I think there's someone you should see." Michael stood from his desk and led Lachlan down the corridor. It was lined with doors, and Michael stopped in front of one and knocked. A deep voice indicated the door was open. Lachlan took a deep breath and blew it out when he walked into the room.

Inside, Jason groaned as he stood. "Aw, of all the humans you bring in here, why did it have to be him?" he sneered, then his face broke into a grin.

Lachlan clasped his arm; his face hurt from the huge grin on it. "How?" he asked, grinning at the warrior.

"Daniel found me, hanging around waiting for Eloi, I think. We might have to have a heart-to-heart with him." Jason quirked an eyebrow and continued. "The healers here are unreal. They can link in a way we've never thought of, let alone seen before. They spread the burden of power and managed to draw out the poison. Aine could never have done it by herself. I have a theory, each original family brought a unique power to their pack. The Aoibhan have strong communication and warrior abilities, and the Tivaci are healers." Jason sat down heavily, his face pale.

"You're still healing?" Lachlan sat next to him. Jason nodded and sighed.

"I get tired very quickly, and they won't let me leave. I tried to get back. Especially after I heard Aine had been taken. Can you feel her?"

"No, but the bond sometimes doesn't work when one of us is weak. Unless she's being blocked…it's happened before," Lachlan huffed.

Michael stirred near the door. "From what we can gather, one of the new shifters betrayed you. The one that was taken, we found poison in one of the water bottles."

"Eric? But I've known him for years; he's a good man." Lachlan turned his head and frowned. "I need to get back to the pack. Daniel said a shifter returned to Sumter."

"Not yet; you're both still healing. Guess you will have to keep each other company until you're strong enough," Michael said dismissively.

"Can you at least get word to them that we're okay? Eloi will be worried about us."

"I don't want to expose us. Daniel tried to get Eloi to come here before Aine was taken. I'll ask him to pass on a message to her—she might come if she knows you're here. He seemed to think she was open to the idea."

"He what?!" Lachlan stood too quickly and stumbled forward. He shook his head. "You had no right. She has a family in Sumter."

"The boy is smitten—he thought it would be a way to reach out to your pack. Guess we won't need to now."

"I'll definitely be having a word with that boy." Lachlan scowled.

11

"Phil?" Eloi entered the diner and looked around. It was busy, considering the lunch rush was normally finished by now. She quickly realized he wasn't out front and approached the kitchen to check there.

"Hey, Eloi!" Emily brought coffee over to refill a man's cup. "What brings you here?"

"I need to see Phil." Eloi glanced toward the kitchen.

"He's not in today; he went to see Liam in town." She cocked her head toward Burntwood Falls.

"Thanks, I'll head that way. How are you doing?" She liked Emily; the woman was always kind.

"I'm good, thanks for asking. Got another camping trip next week," she said chirpily.

"I bet Phil loves that," Eloi laughed.

"Yeah, he can never find the coverage. Can't put my life on hold, though." Emily gave her a wink and moved on to her next customer.

Eloi waved as she left again, blowing out a breath when she walked toward the road. She had hoped Phil would give her a lift. She looked toward the trees and thought about shifting. It would get her to the town quicker, but she didn't want to spook any of the hunters on patrol. Groaning, she resigned herself to the walk into town.

Her mind churned as she walked, going over what she would say to Liam, and grimaced. It took her half an hour to get there, but when she finally started seeing the houses and approached the town center, she thought she knew what to say. She paused when she recognized a woman approaching her. Caroline was a retired nurse who helped with medical emergencies for the town.

"Caroline, it's good to see you." Eloi's smile was genuine.

"You've grown up so beautiful, Eloi, just like your mother. What brings you here? Fancy a rendezvous with one of the boys in town here?" The older woman winked at her and pushed a hair behind her ear. It was up in her signature messy bun.

"No, not really." She shifted and looked over Caroline's shoulder. "I'm sorry, I can't really stay and chat. Have you seen Phil or Liam?"

Caroline's brow creased, and she looked over her shoulder. "Not today, though Liam is usually hanging around the center. I've got to say it's gotten very exciting around here since we found out about your shifter pack in Sumter. A lot less dull than it used to be."

"I bet there are a lot who wouldn't agree with you." Eloi nodded toward the town.

"They will come around—now that there have been some attacks by other shifters, they will appreciate your protection."

"The attacks have made it here?" Eloi gasped, and Caroline put a hand on her shoulder.

"Lachlan has told us how you've been keeping them at bay. It's only recently the hunters have had to sort out the ones who made it through." Caroline squeezed her shoulder. "Aine has protected us so far. Hopefully, the town will realize just how much now."

Eloi shuddered. "I'm so sorry; we thought we'd kept them away."

Caroline shook her head. "Nonsense, we know it would be worse if your pack wasn't there to stop them. The town knows your efforts and how much you're doing, don't worry."

"We do everything we can, but I think things will get worse before they get better. The attacks are more frequent and—" Eloi stopped herself and pulled Caroline into a hug. "You don't need to know the ins and outs. We will do our best to keep them from the town. Now you stay safe."

"I will, my dear. Get on with your business so you *can* start chasing some boys." She winked and gave Eloi a wave as she left.

Eloi continued toward the center and watched the town, grateful the hunters had moved in. She didn't know what she would have done if she'd found out anyone here had been killed because they'd not defended them well enough. She squeezed her hands into fists and walked quicker, more determined than ever, to convince Liam it was time they combined their efforts.

She breathed a sigh of relief when she saw Phil's parked truck and quickly made her way to it. He wasn't within sight, but she probably wouldn't have to wait long; she looked around at the shops nearby and saw the hardware store. Heading that way, she wasn't surprised to see Phil walk out the door.

"Eloi!" Phil shouted and waved. She ran toward him, and

he opened his arms, crushing her with a hug. "Where have you been hiding? I swear ya've grown up more since I last saw you. How's ya mom and Lachlan?"

Eloi's lip trembled, and he held her at arm's length to look at her, the grin falling from his face. "What's wrong? Has something happened?"

She didn't trust herself to speak, so she nodded. Phil waited patiently. Taking a deep breath and fighting back the tears, she finally managed, "I need to find Liam. Can you take me to him?"

"Of course, but where is Lachlan?" Phil said shakily.

Eloi took a shaky breath. "My mom has been taken by the Faction. There was a lot of blood and...." Her voice broke, and she shuddered. "Lachlan is missing—it smelled like his blood."

Phil swore. "Come on, he's at the town hall with Cillian. Maybe this is the boot up the ass he needs to finally work with Sumter. Let's go."

"What if Lachlan's dead? When I say a lot of blood, I mean *a lot* of blood." Eloi paused as she let her fear out and looked at the ground.

"Lachlan is tough. Have faith in him, little wolf." Phil put a finger under her chin and tilted her head so he could look her in the eye. "I promise, all will be okay. It always is with ya family. Ya've been through worse, remember?"

Eloi nodded and had to jog to keep up as she followed him toward the town hall. She looked up at the building the town used for meetings. She had never been in the modest building and was curious as to what the inside looked like. The foyer was simply decorated, with double doors directly across from the main entrance. Loud voices carried through them, and Eloi looked at Phil.

"Cillian and Liam, they're always like that." He winked at

her. Eloi gulped as she walked toward the doors and pushed them open. She spotted Cillian as she walked in, and he did a double-take when he noticed her, his mouth open.

"We won't change generations of indoctrination overnight; it's not that simp—" Liam stopped when he saw Eloi, his brow creased.

"Eloi, what are you doing here?" Cillian looked past her shoulder. "Phil? Where's Lachlan?"

Eloi glanced at Liam and held her head high; a cold sweat broke out on her back, but she held her ground. Resisting the urge to wring her hands and fidget, she wondered if she should have brought Eyolf. She managed to sneak out without him noticing and dreaded his reaction upon her return. Liam watched her as she entered, and she couldn't help her grin.

"Gramps." She nodded and smirked at him.

"Don't call me that," Liam growled. He had softened to her, but she couldn't help teasing him. "I don't see you here often. What's wrong?"

Eloi cleared her throat. "Something has happened. I know you've been picking up the strays that have got too close to town, and for that, we are grateful." She took a deep breath. "Lachlan and my mom thought they knew where the Faction was hiding. So they went to see if they could scout the area. We don't know exactly what happened, but there is a lot of blood, and Lachlan is missing. We believe Rolan had my mom taken. I need your help…the pack needs your help." It all came out in a rush, but she stood straight and tried not to tremble. She looked at Phil, who had stepped into view, his gaze on Liam.

Liam paled. "What do you mean Lachlan is missing?"

Eloi looked down, shook her head, and lifted her head

to look him in the eye. "From what we can tell, the blood is his. There is a lot of blood at the scene, too much." She glanced at Phil. "But I haven't given up hope. Two shifters went in a direction away from Sumter, and a third shifter returned. We can't figure out what happened to Lachlan. The Faction is the enemy, and you have the best trackers." She hoped flattery would win him over.

Liam rubbed his chin. "When did this happen?" His eyes flashed.

"Two days ago, I will admit that I wasn't sure whether to trust you, but we've searched the area and can't do this alone. I have experience with hunting, as does most of the pack, but we know you are exceptional." Eloi sighed. "Lachlan wants us to work together. I come here, as an ally, looking for help. Will you?" She hardened her gaze and held her breath.

Liam's expression hardened, and he blew a breath out his nose. "We need to end them; they've gone too far by hurting my son." He kicked his chair and stormed out. Cillian reached out as if to touch her shoulder, then pulled his hand back quickly, watching his father leave.

"I think that's a yes. Are you sure about Lachlan? Surely you'd have been able to tell if he walked away?" Cillian's face looked hopeful.

"He definitely didn't walk away. There's some evidence of someone there, but they've covered their tracks really well." She touched his arm. "He's tough. I'd like to think I'd feel it if he was gone. He's part of my pack." She gave him a slight nod, then approached Phil.

The big guy looked green, and she took his hand. "Like you said, he's tough." Eloi smiled at him, and he nodded. His eyes glistened, and she pulled him into a hug. A loud bang made her jerk away, and she looked at the door that had crashed into the wall. Liam was loaded to the teeth with weapons. Eloi had never seen so many, especially all on one person. She grinned and narrowed her eyes at him.

"Think you can keep up, old man?"

Liam scoffed. "I'll see you in Sumter, little wolf." His eyes gleamed. "I am going to find my son and make the son of a bitch pay. Give me an hour to get some men together, and we will join you."

Eloi walked over, lifted onto the balls of her feet, and gave him a kiss on the cheek. Liam froze. "We can both make them pay," she told him before she walked out of the hall and toward the edge of town.

She let out the breath she'd subconsciously held since walking into town and relaxed. She had done it.

She wasn't far from the edge of the village when the hair on the back of her neck rose and tingled. She froze and looked around the street, straining her ears and eyes. Then, not seeing anything, she turned back in the direction she had been going and started, jerking back a step. Finn casually leaned against a wall a few feet from her. Lachlan's older brother had always felt wrong to her; she avoided him as much as possible.

"Well, hello. I don't often see you here, little shifter. What has brought you into town without Mommy and big bad Lachlan to look after you?" He held a knife in his hand and used it to pick at his nails. Eloi eyed him carefully.

"I needed to speak to your father. If you head toward the town hall, I'm sure he will update you." She took a step to walk past him and involuntarily flinched when he pushed off the wall toward her.

"Why ask my father when you're here already?" He smiled, but it didn't reach his eyes.

"My mother has been taken by the Faction, and Lachlan is missing." Eloi clenched her now clammy fists.

Finn tutted. "So sad, Lachlan in trouble again...I guess it'll be the hunters to the rescue."

Eloi kept her face blank. "We would do the same for the hunters—you should be preparing with the rest of them. I'm sure your father will want to speak to you. Don't let me keep you." She gestured back toward the town.

"I've got better things to do than prepare. I'll be ready when they need me." He took an intimidating step toward her, but she held her ground. "You're all grown up. I'll have to stop calling you 'little shifter.'" He'd adopted the nickname after hearing Liam use it.

"You know you sound creepy when you say things like that." She crossed her arms and glared at him. Slowly he circled her, and she resisted the urge to cringe.

"That's not very nice. How can you expect to meet a nice man to marry if you talk to them like that?" Finn grimaced.

"I don't need to find a man to marry; I've got better things to do," she said, mimicking his face.

"How do you feel about older men?" He picked up a few strands of her hair and sniffed them. She slapped his hand away and whirled to face him. His eyes looked at her coldly.

"Don't be disgusting! What's wrong with you? I am your niece by marriage, and you're older than Lachlan!" She balked at his expression.

He quickly stepped forward before she could react, and he pushed her against the wall, one hand around her throat, the other on her hip. He inhaled deeply, and she leaned away. His hold wasn't tight, so she fought the panic and adjusted her position. With a quick thrust, she brought her knee up between his legs; his eyes bulged as he released her, and he bent over. She coughed and took a breath of fresh air. Finn held his balls with one hand and reached for her.

"You little bitch," he groaned and stumbled. She sidestepped him and walked backward toward the trees. "You'll pay for that!" He sounded strained as he coughed, his face bright red; his eyes burned into her. He stumbled again and collapsed to the ground.

Before he could recover, Eloi sprinted toward the trees, her chest heaving as she breathed quickly. Her stomach churned, and she stopped to retch as she reached the trees. Liam had said she would be safe to leave and shift once she reached the trees. She shuddered and shook off the feel of Finn's hands on her body.

She shifted and relished the power of her wolf form; her strides stretched as she raced through the woods. She couldn't believe how creepy Finn was or that Liam allowed such behavior. Her surroundings blurred as she moved faster toward her home. A mental call from Eyolf gave her pause, but she answered and let him know to expect her.

She headed straight to Eyolf's house. His face did not show any amusement when she arrived. Her shift was seamless mid-stride. Once in human form, she looked him in the eye, her head held high.

"Where have you been? I told you it would be a bad idea to leave the pack," he fretted.

"I met with Liam in Burntwood Falls. It needed to be done." She walked up to him and took his arm. "Come with me."

She led him out of his house and to the training area, where Ian and Owen sparred in pairs with Elijah and Nyko. She paused to admire their tactics; they worked well together and had chosen excellent partners. Eyolf cleared his throat and they turned to face her as she approached.

"Hey, where did you go?" Nyko frowned at her.

"I went to meet with the hunters. Liam is on his way, so we will need to prepare ourselves. You'll be joining us. We are going to the area where my parents disappeared." Eloi looked at each of them. Owen looked a little sick, Ian stoic as usual, and Nyko grinned. Elijah sighed and nudged him.

"Yes, Pack Leader." Elijah gave her a stiff nod.

"I'm not Pack Leader, Elijah. Just call me Eloi," she sighed.

"It's about time we joined forces." Nyko couldn't contain his glee, and he looked at Eloi. "You still think he's alive."

Eloi smiled. "I have no doubt. Lachlan is part of our pack and we've not felt his death. We need to find him. If he's injured, then he will need help."

"What do you need from us?" Ian asked.

"Liam will bring more hunters. You've been fighting with Elijah a while now, and you work well together. I know that there will be some skepticism on both sides." She looked him firmly in the eye. "I need you to show the hunters how well you work together. Lachlan thinks bonds will naturally form because of the history of hunters and shifters working together. So, between the four of you, find willing shifters, and let's hope some natural pairs form."

The four of them nodded, and she walked away, Eyolf following her. She turned to look at him as she caught him up.

"Well done, youngling," he said.

"Eyolf, I'm not a youngling," she huffed.

He smiled proudly. "You're right, Eloi, you're not."

"There's something else." She told him about Finn. "Should I be worried?"

"Liam has kept him on a leash—I wonder if he's pushing his boundaries. I would let Liam know, though I doubt he will be surprised." Eyolf frowned. "Just make sure you're never alone with him."

"I can handle him. I just don't know what he will do next." Eloi ran a hand through her hair and shuddered as she remembered him sniffing it. "I can't worry about this now. We have a lot to do."

12

Aine stared at the ceiling. Her prison was reasonably comfortable, which surprised her. She had a bed and a couch in the corner, but the walls were bare rock, with water trickling down. The moss and damp smell made her feel nauseous. Though that may have been because she refused any food brought to her.

She sniffed the water she was given and couldn't smell any poison, but she didn't risk a drink anyway. The trickles of water kept the cave walls damp, so she had used her hands to capture it and quench her thirst. Her hunger, however, was becoming a problem. Her empty stomach gnawed at her, and she felt sick and dizzy. She tried to rise from the bed to stretch her legs and swayed as she stood. Aine turned at the movement near the door and stumbled.

Olivia sighed. "You need to eat. I can see you're weak, and you're making yourself sick for no reason."

"I can't trust anything I'm given, not since Eric poisoned me." She turned her back on the petite woman.

"Eric didn't poison you—he went to find his mate. He's a

good male. What makes you think you were poisoned?" Olivia scoffed.

"The fact that he told me the water he had given me had something in to block my power. I can't even shift! How would you feel?" Aine didn't look at her.

"If he did, then I'm sure he had a very good reason. Come on. It's been three days; you'll waste away." She pushed the tray under the door. "Here, it's good."

"I'm not stupid. As soon as I eat something, then I will be asked for. There will be something in the food to weaken me. See if I'm wrong." The smell of sausage and potato made her mouth water as she stared longingly at the tray. Her eyes stung, and she swallowed.

Her power had started to stir when she woke; she pulled, and tendrils reached for her. She reluctantly pushed the tray away. One more day, and she would have access to it again. She frowned at the food when Olivia pushed the tray back toward her.

"You have to eat something. At least drink the water. That's what will get you first." Olivia's eyes pleaded with her.

Aine huffed and picked up the tray as Olivia watched her; she took it to her bed and dropped onto the thin mattress.

"Fine." She picked up a piece of sausage, popped it in her mouth, and pretended to chew under Olivia's gaze.

Olivia grinned. "See, it's fine. You'll feel better after you've eaten. I'll leave you to it."

She turned when the guard called her back, and Aine spat the food into her hand as they left her. Her mouth watered, and she cupped her hand for a trickle of water to rinse her mouth. She spat water out a second time, then groaned. She tipped the rest of the food into the corner behind the couch and left the empty tray near the door.

Even that small task left her drained, so she lay down again, a dull headache throbbing behind her eyes and her stomach growling. She let her eyes close and blew out a breath; she tried to relax each muscle in her body and counted her breaths to calm her thoughts.

Aine jerked when she heard the door open. Rolan entered the room and smirked at her; she glared back at him.

"I heard you've finally eaten. I knew you'd cave," he sneered, holding out his hand for her. She slapped it away, and he chuckled.

"Fine, be that way." He walked out the door. She followed him if only to get some respite from the room she'd been in for three days.

"Prisoner is a good look on you, Aine." He sniffed and shook his head. "Shame about the stench."

Aine growled at him. "It would help if you let me wash."

His laugh was sinister as they walked through the cave system. Aine tried to feel the minds around her. Puzzled, she pushed a little harder; most of the shifters were content. They felt safe, though there was an underlying tension. There was no fear from what she could tell, which surprised her. She frowned and stopped to watch a group of shifters to their left. Rolan stopped when he realized she no longer followed.

"Keep moving," Rolan growled and reached back for her; Aine flinched from him. He scowled and waited until she started to walk again, then led her to Solus's rooms, gesturing to the couch. "He wants to talk to you; now you've eaten, that will be easier."

The sneer on his face made her want to vomit; she had been right about the food. "You mean try to pry into my mind again? No thanks." Aine crossed her arms and narrowed her eyes at Rolan.

"Just talk to him, Aine. You'll see you're on the wrong side of this war. Solus wants to bring harmony to the packs." Rolan mirrored her posture.

"That's rich, coming from the man that took my power, then tried to kill me," she sneered back.

"That was a mistake, one I'm still paying for. I underestimated his attachment for you. I won't make the same mistake again." Rolan's eyes burned into her as he stared her down.

"Now, now, you two. I can recommend someone for marriage counseling if you'd like." Solus smiled at them as he walked into the room. "It's good to see you together."

"I'm not married to this monster. He died, which nullified any connection we have," Aine spat.

"I wouldn't want to be married to you, anyway. You're tainted goods. No decent shifter will touch you after you slept with a human, a *hunter* of all things." Rolan lunged toward her. She didn't react fast enough, her limbs sluggish. Rolan backhanded her, snapping her head to the right.

A deep growl rent the air, and Rolan was thrown back by a thick smoke tendril. Solus followed and pinned Rolan to the wall.

"Do not touch her," Solus growled in Rolan's face. He paled and dropped his gaze.

"Looks like you don't learn after all," Aine taunted.

"Aine, be nice to your husband." Solus looked over his shoulder at her.

"Not my husband," she mumbled and crossed her arms. Her cheek throbbed, and she tried to ignore it. Solus let Rolan drop to the floor; he still held Rolan's shirt and flung him toward the cave entrance.

"If you're not going to behave, Rolan, then you can leave." Solus's face was hard, and Aine looked between the two of them. Her eyes widened when Rolan stood meekly and limped from the room.

"He's always been a handful." Her father reached a hand to her, and she gaped at him. He smiled at her, and suddenly all she could see was the father she had loved when she was a child. She took his hand, and he led her to the couch. She shook her head as he sat down next to her.

"You suffer needlessly. Why haven't you eaten before today?"

"I know you're putting something in the food. I won't eat poison or anything that will lessen my power," she said weakly. She put her head in her hands and rubbed her eyes as the pressure behind them caused a dull pain.

Solus scoffed, his voice silky. "Don't be silly; there was nothing in your food." Aine felt a tendril of his power caress her; it rolled across her mind pleasantly. She shut out the feel of it and shook her head again.

"Where is my husband, my mate?" Aine asked.

"Rolan is outside." Solus gestured to the door.

"Not Rolan. He's the worst excuse for a shifter I've ever seen," Aine snarled. She grasped some of her power, and her head cleared slightly. Her vision swam, and she blinked to clear it. "Where is Lachlan?"

Solus growled. "He is not worthy for you to call mate." He swept up on his feet and paced the room. "How could you betray our kind in that way?"

"It's not a betrayal—we are stronger together, which is better for the pack. You don't understand; we've been researching and found that hunters worked with shifters in our history. They were always supposed to mate if there was hope for more than one child." Aine squeezed her eyes shut and shook her head.

Solus's growl was deep and rumbled through him. "That is a sore spot, and you know it." He glared at her. "We are supposed to be powerful and rule them all. I want to bring back the old traditions, the ones the Royal families upheld. The Royal families rule and are governed by a single shifter, the strongest of us."

Aine scoffed. "You're dreaming—it was never like that. We were never ruled by a single shifter. The families worked together, and the original families worked with hunters. I have records that show—"

"Your records are wrong!" Solus interrupted. "You have been brainwashed, and I can help with that if you let me."

"You are not the strongest; no one will follow you. You won't be able to take control by force and keep control. You won't get loyal followers that way. We will stop you, if not now, then in the future." Aine rose to leave and flinched when he appeared in front of her.

Solus grabbed her, his hands positioned on each side of her head. She tried to push him back but was physically too weak. Dark tendrils stabbed into her mind, and she screamed. She gripped his hands and gritted her teeth. Then, with every ounce of energy she had, she pushed back with her power. She felt it as it poured into him, and her vision went white.

Aine stood next to Solus; they stared at each other. Solus frowned and looked around.

They were in their family home, and Solus sat next to his mate, Arwen. She was beautiful, and Aine felt the sorrow she always felt when she thought of her mother. Arwen's belly was round, and Solus's hand caressed her, his face full of awe. Aine stared at the happiness which radiated from her parents before her.

"It was the happiest day of my life when you were born...she gave me the most perfect, beautiful baby girl. I wish it had been enough for her, but she wanted a second child." Solus's voice was quiet. He watched the scene unfold. "How are you doing this?" He whirled to face Aine.

"I don't know." Aine looked back at the scene; her parents now held a newborn baby. "You both look so happy."

"Your mother was one of a kind. Strong, stubborn, with a beautiful soul and mind." Solus gritted his teeth and clenched his fists.

"She insisted she could survive another birth, even though we'd been warned," he went on. "She never would have been taken from me if your grandfather had allowed the use of dark magic. I could have saved her."

The scene changed, and Aine saw the day her grandfather died. She couldn't contain her horror as she watched her father kill him. She looked at him, and his face was blank. She turned back to the scene, and Solus lay broken at the cave entrance. An old shifter approached him. Aine shivered when she saw him; his eyes were completely black, and his mannerisms manic.

"If it wasn't for Vernon, not only would I have died, but I never would have walked again. It took years to recover from the injury." Solus scowled at Aine. "By then, you were Pack Leader, and I couldn't return without raising suspicion. I couldn't think of an excuse as to why I was away so long."

"I was fooled by Rolan. He told me that you had all been killed by hunters." She felt her heart ache for the boy she thought he was and the relationship she believed she had with him. "I

thought he loved me; I thought you were dead. It nearly broke me."

Solus smiled at her with pride. "But it didn't. You would have been a great leader with my guidance." His face changed. "I will never understand why you let humans into the pack."

"What do you have against humans?" Aine huffed when she looked at him.

"Everything. They have so much, and we are left with nothing. We have the most power; we should rule them. Human society flourishes, yet we live in hovels. It's time we took what is rightfully ours!" Solus growled and tried to storm away. Aine jerked away from his anger, and her connection slipped.

AINE OPENED HER EYES. She was slumped on the couch, and her father stared at her.

"You have so much power, despite the draught. How did you do that?" His brow furrowed.

"I'm stronger than you think." Aine stood swiftly and tried to leave the room. Solus rubbed his face and sat on the couch opposite her. He lifted his hand, and smoke curled around it; Aine could feel the power. He watched the smoke, mesmerized, his face cold and his eyes gleaming.

Aine watched in horror at the mania behind his eyes. She thought about Eyolf's comments about anyone without her blood, how the dark power drove them mad. She slowly stood and approached him, reaching out to touch the smoke. It jumped from his hand to hers, like static, and she felt it flow into her. Solus jerked away from her and growled, crouching low.

"Father, I..." Aine paused; the madness in his eyes had

subsided. His eyes looked clearer, but his words made her flinch.

"Get out!" He grabbed Aine's arm and thrust her through the door.

She stumbled and fell to her knees. Rolan entered from the tunnel and roughly pulled Aine to her feet. She scowled at him as he dragged her away, and she was once more returned to her room.

She slept fitfully to fill the time confined to her room, and it was a few days later when she could smell the spoiled food she'd disposed of in the corner. It made her feel even more nauseous. She pretended to eat each time the food was brought and felt physically weaker each day. She could connect to her power, but now she didn't feel strong enough to use it. So she spent all day in bed to preserve her energy.

"What is that smell?" Olivia's voice was right next to her, the gasp that escaped her loud in Aine's ear. Aine opened her eyes and looked into Olivia's face; she groaned and tried to sit up but fell back onto the bed.

"I can't risk the food," Aine said weakly, her own voice sounding far away.

Olivia frowned and looked toward the corner of the room. Aine looked to the guard at the door and saw him shake his head. She scowled at him; there was no chance of escape while Olivia was distracted. Olivia used the empty tray to scoop the food up from the corner, wrinkling her nose. Aine retched at the smell.

"Bring her with us." Oliva gestured to the guard and glanced at Aine. "I don't know why you don't trust us, but I'll prove to you that the food here isn't poisoned."

Aine didn't resist the guard as she was dragged to the main cavern. Shifters milled around and were collecting stew from a huge cooking pot over a fire. Aine sniffed, and her mouth watered at the stew. She could smell beef, pepper, and oregano. The guard stopped her in front of the pot, and Olivia spooned some stew into a bowl.

"Here, we've all eaten from here today. No chance to poison you, you stupid woman. Eat before you pass out." Olivia narrowed her eyes at Aine.

Aine took the bowl and smiled weakly. "Thank you. I just can't risk it."

She sat next to a young shifter and ate slowly. The guard stood vigilant behind her. Each mouthful soothed her stomachache, but she forced herself to take her time. She savored each bite.

The boy next to her stared as she ate. She offered him a smile. "How did you come to be here?" she asked. She watched his face change from curious to fearful.

"Hunters drove our pack south—they picked us off one by one. The Faction found me and took me in. I was all alone." He spoke quietly, and Aine could feel his pain. She reached out a hand and stroked his back.

"I'm sorry, youngling. No one should have to go through that."

"But you work with the hunters, Rolan told us so." His tone was accusatory.

"The hunters I know don't hunt innocent shifters," she replied with a smile.

"But they did!" the boy yelled at her and stormed away. Tears streaked his face when he glanced back and left the cavern. Aine sighed and looked at her bowl, now empty. Olivia handed her a second bowl, and she thanked her.

The wounds on both sides were deep, and the hate ingrained. Lachlan thought hunters and shifters should work together. She closed her eyes and let a breath out through her nose. When she opened her eyes, Olivia sat in front of her and eyed the second empty bowl.

"Better?" Her concern seemed genuine.

"Much, thank you." Aine handed over the bowl. "Can I stay here and talk to the shifters? I've been alone for so long." She smiled meekly at Olivia. The woman bit her lip and looked around.

"Five minutes, and you'll be with the guard and me the whole time." Olivia watched Aine's face intently as she nodded.

Thirty minutes passed, and Olivia hadn't taken her back to her room. Aine spoke to every shifter she could. They all had the same story—driven from their homes, forced underground, saved by the Faction. Some by the dark wolves, but most by hunters. Aine's heart ached with each story; she tried to comfort them as much as she was able. She found herself defending her pack more than once. Rolan had obviously spread rumors that the dark wolves were hers. She wasn't sure how many believed her when she talked about her pack and their relationship with the hunters but hoped it was more than that morning. If her power had been stronger, she may have been able to show them. But she didn't want to risk Solus knowing how much strength she had already regained.

When Olivia returned Aine to her room, she paused before she left. "You aren't what I expected," the young wolf said hesitantly.

"What did you expect?" Aine asked.

"Solus said you've been driving shifters out of their homes and forcing them to work with the hunters." She bit her lip. "You're either very good, or you had no idea of what has been happening."

"I have some idea, but I didn't realize the extent. As for

driving shifters from their home, I can't be sure, but I think the Faction is more to blame than we are. The hunters came from Europe to stop them; they have been attacking humans, which hunters can't allow. Surely you can understand that?"

Olivia sighed and shook her head. "I don't know; it doesn't sound right."

"I understand; you don't know me." She touched Olivia's arm. "If you get the chance, go to Sumter. My daughter Eloi is there. She will help you."

Aine caught Olivia's gaze and continued. "Rolan can be charming. He fooled me for over twenty years." She lifted the side of her mouth. "Be careful, Olivia. Things here aren't as they seem." She looked at the guard, and Olivia followed the direction of her gaze, nodding. Aine reached out and squeezed her hand.

When Aine lay on the bed, weariness took over her body, and it wasn't long before she slept.

13

Eloi watched Liam, Finn and Cillian as they examined the area. She had taken them, along with Nyko, Elijah and Owen, to where they had found the blood.

"No way Lachlan survived this, Liam. There's too much blood." Cillian spoke quietly, but Eloi could hear. He shifted some leaves with his foot, examined the soil, and then headed in the direction the pack had thought Lachlan was dragged. "His body was pulled and then lifted—the footprints here are deeper." He followed the trail and lost it at the same point Elijah had before. Eloi sighed.

"I can't believe he's gone. I would have felt it." She thought back to the despair in her mother's last call and swallowed hard, her throat tight. Then, rubbing her arms, she waited for the hunters to finish. Finn watched her from the side, and she shivered under his cruel gaze. He smirked at her.

"It's a dead-end; I can't track further. Whoever took the body knew how to hide their tracks." Cillian rose from a crouch and looked at Eloi. "I'm sorry, but we may never know what happened."

"Looks like you're wrong, and he's dead after all."

"Finn, shut up," Liam scolded.

Eloi shook her head, her eyes stinging. "He's alive; I know it." She clenched a fist to her chest and turned from them, taking a deep breath.

Nyko reached out and put his arm on her shoulder. "We will find him."

Liam leaned against a tree and heaved a sigh. "I think we need to assume the worst for now. I just..." The hunter stopped, and Eloi looked at him; his eyes were closed and his face pale.

"Liam, you okay?" Cillian stood before him and held the older man up. Finn's gaze flicked to his father, and his lip twitched as if he resisted a smile.

"I'm fine," Liam growled and pushed him away. Eloi approached him and put an arm on his shoulder. Weariness seeped into her from the touch, and she pushed a small amount of power into him. Liam looked up sharply at her and opened his mouth.

"What the...what did you just do?" he barked.

"I gave you some energy; it's a hard walk back." She walked back to Nyko and Elijah.

"Handy trick," Finn commented.

Nyko looked stunned, and Elijah frowned. Owen grinned at her, and she returned the smile. "Let's get back," she said. "We need a plan if we are going to take on the Faction."

Eloi could hear the hunters discuss the scene and how Lachlan had disappeared as they walked back to Sumter. They all concluded that Lachlan couldn't have survived, and Liam snapped at Finn.

"No need to look so pleased with yourself—you're half the man he was." Liam glared at his eldest son.

"Stop bickering," Eloi shouted over her shoulder. "There may be scouts in the area, and you all sound like elephants tromping through the trees."

They fell silent until they reached the edge of Sumter. Eloi left Liam, Finn, and Cillian with Owen and Ian in their home after they briefly discussed various plans, between a stealth operation to invade Rolan's base and an all-out attack. Finn's sporadic glances had worn her down, and she needed to get away for a while. When she got up to leave, Finn moved to the door as if to follow her.

"Come near me, and I will kill you." Eloi's snarl turned into a growl, and she felt her eyes shift.

"Such fire," he whispered and laughed at her. Then, he turned back and entered the room where the hunters were. Eloi quickly left and breathed a sigh as she crossed the settlement. She hoped Finn wouldn't follow.

~

SHE HAD BEEN to her place a few times over the last few days, and there had been no sign of Daniel. So when she arrived today, she was surprised to see his silhouette sitting on her rock. She froze as he turned to look at her. His gaze was wary, but he lifted one side of his mouth in a cocky smile.

"Miss me?"

She frowned at him and approached with caution. "Where have you been?" she asked sharply.

Daniel frowned and swallowed. "I needed to help a friend." He wouldn't meet her eyes, and she scowled.

"Did you have anything to do with my mom's disappearance? Because if you did...." She strode towards him as her threat trailed off.

Daniel stood quickly, his hands out, "Woah, wait! I had nothing to do with that!"

"Am I supposed to just believe it was a coincidence that you disappear right after her and Lachlan—" Eloi tried to fight a sob, but it escaped her lips.

"Hey, it's going to be okay." Daniel grabbed and held her tightly in a hug. Eloi hammered her fists weakly against his chest, letting her tears flow. He lifted a hand to her face and ran his thumb across a tear on her cheek. "I know you've barely been holding on, but just keep going a little bit longer."

Eloi looked up into his face, eyes swollen and red. Daniel's face was so close to hers; her eyes darted to his mouth and back to his gaze. Then, slowly, as if to let her move back, he leaned down and pressed his lips softly over hers. Eloi moaned, and electricity sparked within her. She gasped and pulled away.

"Did you feel that?" She touched her lips.

Daniel frowned and looked into the trees. "Yeah, I did." He shook himself. "I have to go."

"Now?" Eloi took a step to follow him.

"Yes, but I'll be back soon. I'll explain everything, Eloi." He put out a hand and caressed her face. She leaned into him. "One thing before I go. Lachlan is alive—we will return him as soon as he's fully healed."

Eloi gasped, but Daniel was too fast. He shifted, his wolf, a brown with a white underbelly, and was gone before she could react. Joy surged through her, and she ran halfway back to Sumter before she realized she had moved.

Liam leaped to his feet, and Cillian lunged for a weapon

when she burst through the door. Finn was nowhere to be seen.

"Lachlan's alive!" Eloi was breathless, and her chest heaved.

"What? How do you know?" Owen quickly strode toward her and gripped her shoulders.

Eloi still breathing heavily. "There's a shifter from another pack—I get the impression they are a pack of outcasts or misfits. He said that they would return him when he's fully healed." She beamed at the group.

"We need to go and get him now!" Liam strode to the door.

"I can try to connect with him. I've managed before, but my connection isn't as strong as it is to Mom. I can find out where he is."

"You trust this other shifter?" Liam's eyes were wide.

Eloi blushed. "Yes, I do. Lachlan knows him."

Liam blinked at her and looked at Cillian, who smiled. "Someone is a bit smitten," Cillian laughed. Finn entered from the other room.

"Who's smitten?" He grinned at her, but they ignored him.

"This is good news. If we can get this other pack to join us, then we will have larger numbers." Eloi spoke quickly, and Liam nodded.

"Get some rest, Eloi," he said. "You've been working hard recently. I need some too, and if we have to wait until Lachlan is healed...." Liam collapsed into the chair and put his head in his hands. His shoulders shook, and Eloi looked at Ian and Owen, eyes wide.

"He okay?" she mouthed, and they shrugged.

"Don't talk about me like I'm not here," Liam growled at them.

Eloi backed from the room slowly and left them. She spoke to Eyolf, Nyko, and Elijah next, spreading the good news. Nyko grabbed her in a big hug and swung her around while she slapped at his arms until he eventually put her down. Eyolf sighed and hugged her.

"Well, at least one of them is okay." He looked her up and down. "Now, tell me about this boy?"

Eloi rolled her eyes.

~

AINE SLEPT FITFULLY. With no sunlight, she had no idea how long she had been imprisoned. For the past few days—at least she thought it was days—Olivia had taken her to eat in the cavern. She confided in Aine and told her she'd been disposing of the food prepared for her, just in case it was poisoned.

Aine spoke at length to all the shifters; she eventually found out the old and the weak were usually taken for a "special" task on the first day and never seen again. She frowned, wondering if that was how Rolan made his dark wolves. Or was it Solus making the dark wolves? Rolan does call him master. Aine sighed, thinking of the madness in her father's eyes.

She rolled onto her side and closed her eyes. She hadn't been asleep long when she jolted awake, haunted by dreams of her father and grandfather. She thought about Lachlan—they had never been apart this long, and her body ached for him. When she drifted off again, she imagined waking in his arms.

~

"Aine? Can you hear me?" Lachlan was quiet, and Aine held onto his voice with all her strength.

"I'm here." She looked around wildly. Everywhere was dark, but she could feel him near and reached out with her mind. A sharp pain forced her to cry out, and strong arms wrapped around her. She sighed into them. "I miss you."

"I miss you too. Where are you?"

"In some caves. Am I dreaming? I thought you were dead," she sobbed.

"Dreaming, yes, but in your special way."

Aine kept her eyes closed and clung to the arms around her. Even if they were only in a dream, she would make the most of the time with him.

"You're alive?" she cried.

"I'm alive and with Daniel's pack."

"Daniel?"

"Eloi didn't...." Aine felt the equivalent of a mental sigh from him. "Of course she didn't."

"Who is Daniel?" Aine's voice was stern.

"A shifter. Eloi has been seeing him. I'm with his pack—they healed me."

Aine felt her shock reverberate into him, and he chuckled. "Healed you how?" she demanded.

"It's a long story. I'll explain when I see you. I can feel our bond is weak. Let's fix that."

"How? I've been poisoned again."

"Remember last time? I'm going to send you energy. You'll need to purge yourself."

Aine grimaced. "Urgh, I was hoping never to have to remember that, let alone do it again."

"I'll see you soon, my love." Lachlan pushed energy toward her.

"Wait, I need time—" The connection faltered, and she could

barely feel Lachlan. His confusion bled into the bond with his energy but quickly faded as his presence left her. Aine growled in frustration.

AINE GATHERED the energy Lachlan had sent her. She smiled, her heart no longer aching, and she was filled with new purpose. She sat up in bed and crossed her legs, then thought better, lowering herself to the floor.

Once she had purged the black, oily sludge from her system, she felt the muffle around her power disappear, and she reveled in the feel of it. The putrid smell in her room made her gag; fortunately, Olivia had come to get her, and she smiled at the petite woman.

"What is that smell?" Olivia held her nose and retched.

"You don't want to know." Aine quickly followed Olivia out. They were halfway to the cavern when Rolan stepped out from another tunnel and grabbed her.

"What is she doing out?"

Olivia cringed away from Rolan's demand. Aine stepped in front of him and pushed Olivia behind her.

"She was bringing me to see you. I need to talk to my father." Aine held her breath as Rolan looked at her.

"She should have come to get me, not bring you out." He grabbed Aine's arm and dragged her down the tunnel. She pulled back on his grip, and his hand tightened.

"Let me go; I can walk." Aine stumbled.

"I can see that." Rolan glared at her and didn't let go. Instead, he threw her forward as he entered a room. It took Aine a moment to realize it wasn't her father's.

"Why couldn't you have just died when you should

have? I would have had your pack and taken my rightful place as their leader."

Aine scoffed. "I'm not having this argument with you again—it's like you're stuck. It is *my* birthright, Rolan, and *my* power. You're a parasite; you expect everything for nothing!" She shouted it in his face, and Rolan raised his hand. Aine dodged quickly but didn't engage.

"What are you doing, Rolan?" Solus's voice boomed around the room. His eyes burned into Rolan's, and Aine shrank back. Black smoke surrounded her father; Rolan cowered before him. She smiled at his pathetic form as Solus stared at Rolan and smirked.

"Aine, come with me. I needed to see you anyway." Solus held his hand out, and Aine watched him pull the power back into himself. She watched him and sighed when she saw the mad gleam back in his eyes. "Let's take a walk. I want to explain some of the work we do here."

She slowly followed him out the room, pausing to grin wickedly at Rolan, who still crouched in the corner. He wouldn't meet her eyes and quivered slightly.

Once in the main cavern, Solus slowed. "I heard you've been talking with our refugees."

"Yes, I wanted to get a feel of what was going on here, why they blamed our pack for the attacks. Hunters, I can understand, and I'm working to bring hunters and shifters together, but why blame the Aoibhan?" Aine spoke quickly.

Solus frowned. "I never blamed your pack." He looked back towards Rolan's room. His lips thinned, and he looked around at the shifters before him.

"Well, if they don't blame the hunters, they blame me." Aine crossed her arms. "It's taken some convincing that we are victims just as much as them. But they don't believe me about your dark wolves." She scowled at him, but Solus carried on forward and didn't speak. Aine sighed and followed.

After leaving the cavern, Aine felt fresh air on her face from down the tunnel they entered. Solus brought her out onto a ledge, a massive opening out into the surrounding area that showed a stunning view. Aine gasped and walked to the edge.

She looked around and marveled at the distance she could see. With her back to Solus, she hid a smile as she drank in the view, memorizing every detail. Solus placed a hand on her shoulder, and her power surged. Before she could control it, her power connected to her father's and started to pull it into her, just as it had before but on a much larger scale now that she had purged herself. Aine gasped as the feel of his power was swarmed by her own. Solus jumped back with a cry, stumbling to the ground. He panted and shook his head.

"Father!" Aine lurched forward and knelt next to him. She reached for him, and he scrambled backward. His eyes were clear of the madness, and she held her breath. In a second, his eyes flashed with anger, and he quickly stood over her.

"Don't do that again." He took a step back and rubbed his brow. His voice held less darkness, and Aine let her breath out. He walked back inside, and she had no choice but to follow.

LACHLAN WOKE from a shallow doze at the sound of his name being called in his head.

I'm here, Aine.

I know where I am.

Lachlan jolted up in his bed and groaned. The pain in his chest had lessened, almost to the point that he couldn't believe he'd been shot. But the sudden movement pulled at something inside, and he grimaced. *Where?!*

I can send you an image of the view from the caves. You can use it to pinpoint my location. Aine sent a pulse of love through their bond with an image of the landscape view from a ledge in a cave, and Lachlan could feel her smile.

It will take us time to prepare and get there. I think it's time I spoke to Eloi. We can maybe persuade my father to finally help.

I tried to reach Eloi, but something happened, and I didn't have the energy. Our bond is easier to reach, but I don't have much left.

Then rest, my love. I'll be with you soon. Lachlan grinned when he thought about seeing her again. He carefully got up from the bed and walked to Jason's room. When he explained the image Aine had sent him, Jason lurched and nearly fell out of bed. Lachlan just managed to catch him before he hit the floor. Jason insisted on Lachlan taking him to see Michael.

"We can use this information to finally pinpoint their base," Jason spoke animatedly. "This is what we've been waiting for."

Michael sighed. "I can't just get everyone ready in an hour; it takes time to prepare. We also haven't decided if we want to reveal ourselves."

"I think it's time." Lachlan shifted impatiently. "You've seen the changes we've made in Sumter. The hunters are coming around, and I think showing them what you've built and what is possible will help. The older generation will know some of the hunters here."

Michael scratched his chin. "Let me think about it and discuss it with the pack. I can't make this decision myself. I think we need more information about the area around it. Has anyone gotten close?"

"I understand. Eric led us as far as we got when we were attacked. I didn't even think to ask after him. Was he okay?"

"You were alone when Daniel found you. We didn't see another in the area." Michael frowned.

Lachlan strode to the door. "I need to get to my pack, explain what's happening, and see if Eric can help us." He hesitated near the door and looked back. Jason immediately stood.

"I'm coming with you. It's time we finished this...sir." Jason took a step forward, and Lachlan held the door for him; he stared wide-eyed at the shifter before he followed.

Daniel brought them provisions and hefted a backpack himself. "We will have to take it slow with both your injuries." He smirked at Lachlan and cocked his head.

"Fine." Lachlan sighed and lifted a bag. Jason looked for one as well, and Daniel shook his head. Jason grunted but didn't argue.

It took them half a day to reach Sumter. Lachlan's legs felt like lead, and his chest ached. As they entered the outskirts, Lachlan felt eyes on him and searched the area ahead. Jason stopped next to him and sniffed loudly. Daniel tensed on Lachlan's other side.

"Well, well, well...look who finally decided to show up." A scruffy, red-headed man emerged from the trees in front of them, a massive grin on his face.

"Girvan? What are you doing here?" Lachlan frowned, but a smile reached his lips.

"You always say that when I show up. I'm going to start taking offense." Girvan clasped Lachlan's wrist and pulled him into a hug. He let go when Lachlan flinched and coughed.

"Not one hundred percent, huh?"

"Could say that."

"Well, you're in for a treat! That Eloi of yours has charmed your father so completely. It's been hilarious to watch." Girvan laughed heartily. "I think half the hunters are in love with her."

Daniel growled next to Lachlan, who held his hand out to the boy. "He's joking."

"No, I'm not." Girvan looked Daniel up and down. "You're new." He quirked his brow at the shifter. Daniel huffed and adjusted his pack.

"We going to stand here all day?" Jason nudged Lachlan, and they started walking. Daniel followed slightly behind, his gaze on the ground.

"You knew I was alive?" Lachlan looked at his cousin.

"Yep, this one here told Eloi last time he saw her. Said he would bring you back; looks like he kept his word." Girvan glanced at Jason. "Wasn't expecting this one, though."

"Surprise." Jason kept his face straight and watched ahead. His posture was slouched, weary, and Lachlan kept an eye on him the rest of the way.

As they entered Sumter, people stopped to stare, and Lachlan froze. Hunters among the shifters. He gaped as he saw them converse easily. Jason tensed next to him and looked around.

"How long were we gone?" Jason whispered. Daniel gaped at the crowd, eyes wide and mouth open.

"I've never seen this outside our pack," he exclaimed.

Eloi came into view, her face lighting up when she saw Lachlan; she quickly approached. Lachlan felt a mental touch brush against his mind. Her joy and shock bled into him, and he sighed with relief.

"I tried to connect with you and Mom, but something blocked me!" She gently hugged him, and he held her.

"Jason?!" Eloi next threw herself at Jason and laughed. "How are you alive?"

"Long story," Jason groaned, and she released him. Her face shifted back to Lachlan.

"I'm sorry I failed to protect her." Lachlan closed his eyes.

"From what Eric told us, there wasn't much you could do. He thinks you're dead, by the way." Eloi shifted to Jason's side and leaned into him.

"I'll let him know it wasn't his fault. How did he escape?" Lachlan frowned at the scowl on her face.

"It is absolutely the arsehole's fault. Ciara, Conor, and Eric have been restricted to their house until I decide what to do with them."

"What? Why?" Lachlan watched her.

"We have a lot to catch up on." Eloi gestured toward the settlement and grinned. "Change is good."

"Where is he?" Liam's voice carried through the air, and Lachlan smiled as his father came into view. "Not even bullets can get you now!" He gripped his son's shoulders and searched his face.

"Got our new friends to thank for that," Lachlan replied.

Liam noticed Daniel, who gulped. He took a step forward and held out his hand.

"I'm Vivienne's lad, she said not to get too comfortable." Daniel paused. "She will still give you a run for your money."

Liam gaped at him, his mouth dropping open. "You're a shifter; I can sense it."

"Lots to catch up on," Lachlan muttered.

14

Aine felt joy surge through her bond with Lachlan and Eloi. She closed her eyes and basked in their reunion. If she concentrated hard enough, she could almost feel their embrace.

She tensed when Solus returned to the couch beside her. After the ledge incident, he'd returned her to the cavern, where she spent the afternoon with the other shifters. She had expected Olivia to return her to her room, but Solus had come to collect her. They now sat in his caves, the silence stretching between them awkwardly.

She waited for him to speak, and he handed her a cup of tea. A citrus scent rose with the steam from the cup. She sniffed it before she set it aside.

"Still don't trust us?" he asked.

"Let's just say I'm a lot warier of poison after I failed to learn my lesson the first time." She rolled her eyes and looked around the room. There were no decorations on the wall, just the two couches.

Solus sighed. "Why do you always have to be so difficult?"

"Speaking my own mind, having an opinion other than yours, is not difficult. I have been leading how I see fit. Just because it isn't how you would do it does not mean it is wrong." Aine huffed and folded her arms.

She felt like a teenager again, with her father standing over her in disappointment. She snarled restlessly and leaped up from the couch to pace.

"Why are you doing all this? I don't understand!" She threw her hands up in the air.

"You have no idea how suppressed shifters have been," Solus lectured.

"Yes, I do. I lived it for over thirty years before I met Lachlan. I know what it is like to be a shifter," she snarled.

"That hunter was unworthy of you—you don't even seem upset he's gone. It just shows how you weren't meant for each other. I'm willing to look past this dalliance. Rolan is your perfect match." Solus sipped his tea.

"Rolan?!" Aine threw back her head as she laughed. "He is weak and twisted. You both are if you think I could ever mate him again."

Solus's face turned red, and he leaped to his feet. "We are forging a world where shifters can rule. Humans should be our slaves—"

"Slaves? We aren't better than them. I don't get it. Why do you feel this way? Where is it coming from?" Aine marched toward him, her face inches from his, her rage just as evident. "Why are we better? Why are they better? Why can't we be equals? Lachlan and I are building a future where no one is hunted. Hunters and shifters together."

"It is a dream; they are worthless." Solus stood so fast his cup dropped to the ground.

"Just like the shifters you turned into dark wolves? Aren't

they worthy enough for your pack?" she demanded, pushing him.

Solus growled, his eyes dark. "A necessary evil to secure our pack's future."

"All you've done is attack other packs," she accused.

He glared at her. "To build our numbers, so we can take on the humans."

"With the weapons they have, you could never defeat *all* humans, Father." Aine spat the last word. "How did you become this?" She threw her hands up in the air and gestured around the room.

"I did it so you wouldn't be held back!" Solus yelled and breathed hard. Aine gaped at him.

"What does that even mean?" she sighed.

"I saw your potential when you were young. Even at ten, you were more powerful than any shifter there. The elders wouldn't let me take your training to the next level. Your mother agreed with me, and we fought with them for years. Your grandfather even dampened your power, but you broke through." Solus ran his hand through his hair and watched her. "The last thing your mother did was push her power into me as she died. She thought it would help you."

"But those who aren't of our bloodline, they go crazy with the power," Aine said quietly.

"No, I kept my sanity!" Solus threw his arms out, and smoke curled around them.

"Obviously," she said, her voice dripping with sarcasm. "Your first act after my mother died was to kill my grandfather and abandon me."

Solus growled, and Aine felt her eyes change. She stared him down and pushed her full power into him. Solus took a step back, but she grabbed him before he could move further and pulled at the darkness within. Pain spread through her with the darkness inside him, but she held on. Solus's cry wrenched her heart, but she continued anyway. Her power overwhelmed his, and she trembled; her energy drained quickly, and her knees almost buckled.

"No," Solus gasped and pushed at her. Aine stumbled back and fell against the wall. Her head throbbed, and she groaned. Solus was before her in a second; he reached for her head, and she flinched, slumping against the wall, closing her eyes. They darted open when Solus caressed her cheek.

"What did you just do?" he asked gently.

"I don't know." Aine's gaze pierced his eyes, and she saw no sign of the madness that previously plagued them.

"I feel different." Solus held out a hand to help her up. Slowly, Aine lifted herself to her feet.

"I'm going back to my room." She thought of the oily sludge and hoped Olivia had got someone to clear it up. Solus nodded, his expression dazed.

"I'll take you." He shook his head and led her from the room.

~

ELOI WATCHED DANIEL. He stood on the edge of the group that had moved to the medical building and shifted uncomfortably.

"I do not need to be put in a bed. Can't I at least go home?" Jason moaned. Tania looked over him and Lachlan, who sat at his side with a mirrored scowl, crossing his arms.

Eloi laughed. "You should see your faces right now."

Lachlan grumbled incoherently, and Jason agreed with him. Tania fussed over them both until she was happy with their condition.

"It's impossible, but you both seem nearly at full health." Her eyes glistened, and Nyko lurked behind her. "How did this happen?"

"It's not our story to tell," Lachlan said firmly but glanced toward Daniel. Eloi looked at him herself, and his face reddened.

"Is there something on my face?" His eyes flicked between Eloi and Lachlan. He pushed off from the wall he leaned against and walked to the door.

"Where are you going?" Eloi demanded.

"Places to be." He looked at Lachlan pointedly and raised an eyebrow. "We will be in touch."

Lachlan nodded. "Don't think too long."

"What was that about?" Eloi glared at Lachlan.

"It's a long story." Lachlan sighed wearily. "I've heard from Aine."

Eloi froze and crouched in front of him. "And?"

"She was poisoned. I think she's purged it, but she's still weak. I don't have much more than that." Lachlan stared at Eloi. "I don't know how you've done it, but it's great to see hunters here. How is the pack coping?"

Eloi sighed. "It's not been easy. Some have left; I tried to talk them out of it," She shrugged. "I can understand, but I know what you and Mom are building and that it will change everything. Mom will be upset, but nothing will change their minds if they're set in their ways. I just gave the hunters a nudge, Ian and Owen helped. When the hunters saw them fight alongside Nyko and Elijah, it made a huge difference."

"I always thought that if they saw the connection and how natural it is to fight with a shifter, that it would shake their beliefs." Lachlan rose slowly, and Eloi put her hands out as if to catch him. "I'm okay. I need to talk to Eric, and I'll need your help."

Eloi moved aside and followed him; Jason shifted as if to stand.

"Jason, sit down. I'm not done with you yet." Tania pushed down on his shoulder, and he scowled at her.

"I'm fine; let me go with them." Jason looked at Lachlan longingly.

"I know you want to throw yourself back in, but the hike will have taken it out of you, and I'll need you at one hundred percent." Lachlan gripped the shifter's shoulder, and Eloi looked between them quizzically. Jason grumbled but didn't move again. Lachlan looked around the village as they walked to where Ciara, Conor, and Eric were housed.

"Since when have you two been best buds?" she asked.

"Oh, you know, near-death experiences and all that. Have you spoken to them?" Lachlan put his arm around Eloi, and she laughed.

"No, I was too angry." She thought back to how she'd locked them away and growled.

"Don't forget how charming Rolan can be. Plus, he had that dark influence thing." Lachlan waved his free hand in front of him and felt Eloi stiffen under his arm. "What's wrong?"

"Rolan isn't the problem. It turns out he's not the shifter in charge." Eloi looked past Lachlan and sighed. "Turns out my grandfather is alive. Solus has been behind this all along."

"Aine's father? But he died in the hunting trip." His brow furrowed.

"The one where Rolan was the only survivor," Eloi elaborated.

"Motherf—" Lachlan caught himself and cleared his

throat. Eloi smirked at him. "Why didn't we think of this before?"

"I guess it happened so long ago?" Eloi shrugged and led Lachlan toward the house.

"We need to get to Aine; she didn't have enough energy each time she contacted me. I'm guessing she didn't have enough to tell me everything that had happened." Lachlan strode faster to the house. Two warriors stood outside.

"No trouble, sir. Good to see you back." The guard on the right nodded at them, and he returned the nod.

"Thanks." Lachlan lifted a hand and knocked; Eloi nodded at him awkwardly. He shook his head and gently pushed the door open. Looking around, he saw Ciara sitting at the table through the kitchen door. Her head was on her hand, elbow on the table, and she looked utterly miserable. Eloi stirred and looked at the floor; she should have spoken to them before now.

Ciara's head lifted, and she jerked out of the chair when she saw Lachlan. As he approached, she threw her arms around him and let out a sob.

"I thought you were dead," she sniffled. Eloi glared at her.

"All fine, just a bit sore." He pushed her back gently.

Ciara backed away, her face tear-streaked and her eyes tinged red. "I should never have come here."

"Not your fault. We will get Aine back, and it'll all work out." Lachlan smiled at her, and Eloi frowned. She shook her head and looked through to the other room. Conor put down the book he'd been reading when he saw her.

"Everything okay?" He got up from the chair and froze when he saw Lachlan. Then he grinned and reached out his arm. Lachlan gripped it back.

"Man, there is no killing you. I don't know how you do it,

but I shouldn't be surprised at this point." Conor touched a hand to Lachlan's chest.

Lachlan clasped his shoulder. "I think I just used up my last life."

"Is Eric here?" Eloi asked sharply, looking around. Ciara glanced at the closed bedroom door.

"Please," Ciara said, standing before her. "He didn't know; he was worried about us, and—"

"I'm sorry, I should have come sooner." Eloi looked between them. "I was angry, but I forgot what Rolan is capable of. Lachlan thinks Eric can help us find them. We need him."

"He said they put a bag over him—he didn't see anything."

"I think we can help with that." Eloi gestured toward Lachlan.

"Eric, get your ass in here!" Ciara yelled. A noise behind the door indicated he was in there. "I mean it, stop moping and come and help. Now!"

The door slowly opened, and Eric looked out at the group. When he saw Lachlan, the blood drained from his face. "How?"

"Question of the day," Eloi grumbled. "Come on, let's fix this. Follow me, all of you."

Eloi held the door open for them, and they paused, looking at her. "I haven't got all day," she said loudly.

They left the house, and by the time they returned to the medical building, Eyolf had joined Jason. His face crumpled when he saw Lachlan, and he reached out to touch the hunter as if he wasn't real.

"This is all a bit too much." Eyolf sat heavily in a chair and covered his face with his hands.

Lachlan put a hand on his shoulder and laughed. "I

agree, but don't tell anyone." He winked and sat next to the elder wolf.

Liam walked through the door and nodded at each of them, then smiled at Lachlan. The smile turned into a frown when he saw Eric, but he didn't say anything. Cillian and Girvan joined them next, also scowling at Eric.

Eloi waited until everyone was seated before she questioned Eric.

"From the beginning. I should have asked before, but everything you can remember." She looked at him expectantly, and it all flowed out of him. He told them everything he could from his time in the caves. They listened, and Liam asked questions as Eric gave them all the information he could.

"When Rolan took the bag off, how far out from here were you?" Liam still scowled at him.

"He said about five miles. It was difficult terrain, so it took me some time to get here, but it felt about right," Eric replied.

"So, when you led my son and the Pack Leader away from here, you took them in the wrong direction?" Liam glared.

"No, I led them to where I'd been left." Eric looked at the group. "I know what I did was wrong; I don't know what I was thinking. But the way Rolan talked, he was believable, and it made so much sense and the other shifters... They all believe you're the enemy."

Liam grunted and scowled at Eric, who shrank under the hunter's gaze. Eloi got up, full of nervous energy, and paced as Liam continued his questions. Lachlan then described the image Aine had sent him. Maps were called for, and they studied the area around Sumter.

"Son of a bitch," Liam exclaimed. "They're less than ten

miles from here." He pointed at the mountain, which must contain the hidden cave system between Sumter and the Tivaci pack. Eloi stared at the settlement and rubbed her chin.

"We can't go for Mom yet." Eloi pointed at the Tivaci pack's location. "They have been making the cuffs that take away our abilities. We must free them first while Rolan and Solus are distracted by Aine's presence." She felt a sharp pain in her chest as she realized this was the responsible, right decision, no matter how her heart ached for her mother.

Lachlan froze, and she watched the same emotions flicker across his face. Eventually, he swallowed and nodded, his jaw clenched. Liam put a hand on his son.

"She's lasted this long. She's strong; a little longer won't kill her, and it looks like they want her alive for something," he conceded. "I know someone who might be able to help."

There was a heavy silence, and Lachlan ran his hands through his hair, looking at the group before he locked eyes with Jason. "But it's not our story to tell."

Liam laughed. "I think we can pretty much guess where this is going. If that really is Vivienne's boy, then there's a pack out there with hunters and shifters together already." He quirked an eyebrow at them, and Eloi watched Lachlan squirm. She had never seen him look so uncomfortable.

Liam took his silence as agreement. He kicked a chair and walked toward the other end of the room, running both hands through his hair.

"Wow, he does that a lot," Eloi commented. Jason frowned at her. "He kicks chairs," she clarified with a wink.

"He had a thing for Vivienne before he married Lachlan's ma," Girvan whispered. "Vivienne and Briana were like sisters. Hit him hard when Viv left. Come to think of it, Briana didn't seem that upset...." His voice trailed off.

Lachlan looked across at his father. "They kept in touch after she left. Viv fell in love with a shifter. They moved here and were hunted by both sides. They had a son, but she left him with humans after her shifter was killed to save him from being hunted. He ended up in foster care."

"She could have come back," Liam growled. "He would have been safe with us."

"Not the way your views were back then." Girvan glanced at Lachlan before he continued. "You told your own son never to come back because he freed a shifter. What would you have done to a half-shifter boy?"

Liam shook his head. "So much hate, and for what?" He threw his hands in the air and strode out of the building.

"Let him go." Cillian put a hand on Lachlan's arm. "He will calm down."

Eloi watched the exchange with interest, then shuddered. "Is Daniel any relation to you?"

Lachlan laughed. "No, don't worry. His ma and mine were best friends. Shauna, Daniel's sister, is my cousin through her dad's side. Daniel is no relation."

"Okay, because that would have been weird." Eloi shuddered again. "It's still a bit weird, to be honest. I'm going to try and forget that, and I'm going to gather the warriors, see who is up for freeing some prisoners. Do you guys have any way to get in touch with Daniel?" She tried to hide her disappointment when they shook their heads.

After she organized the warriors and left them to prepare, she went to the one place she thought Daniel might be. When she got to her place and looked around, her shoulders slumped. She sat down on her rock and watched the water.

"Miss me?"

Her neck tingled at the words whispered in her ear. She turned slowly to look at Daniel, their lips a hair apart. She stared into his dark eyes.

"Thank you for saving them both." Her words came out breathy and sultry.

"No problem," he whispered. His eyes dropped to her lips, and she closed her eyes as he closed the distance between them. Electricity flooded through her with the contact from his lips, and she gasped. He took advantage and deepened the kiss, his tongue brushing over hers. He pulled back too soon and cupped her cheek with his hand. Briefly, he touched his forehead to hers and slowly took a seat beside her. He watched her closely and waited.

"Part-hunter then?" She quirked a brow at him. She had never seen him look so unsure.

"Yes." He dragged the word out slowly and scratched the back of his head. "So much for keeping our secret, guys."

"Lachlan didn't tell us. Liam figured it out from what you said about your mom."

"Ah, damn, so it's my fault the cat is out the bag? Figures." He sighed and looked out toward the small waterfall in front of him. "What now?"

"We need your help." She shuffled closer to him.

"It's not up to me what the pack does, but I'll help in any way I can." Daniel took her hand and brought it to his mouth. He placed a sweet kiss on her knuckle and held her hand to his chest.

"We are going to Tivaci first," Eloi said.

Daniel jerked his gaze toward her and frowned. "Not after your mom? That doesn't really make much sense."

"The Faction has imprisoned them and are forcing them to make cuffs which will cut us off from our powers. While they're distracted, we thought it would be better to put an end to that situation first." Eloi sighed. "If they attack us with those cuffs, then we won't have a way to defend ourselves."

"The Tivaci were captured." Daniel went very still.

Eloi continued, "Lachlan thought you ought to know."

Daniel grinned at her. "Well, *this* changes everything." He winked and quickly stood.

"Hey, where are you going?" Eloi yelled after him.

"I'll be back." He smiled at her as he left.

"We leave in the morning!" Eloi cupped her hands as she saw him shift, then smiled, running back to Sumter to tell the others.

15

The following morning, half the warriors and all the hunters gathered in the training area. Eloi looked around. There was still a division between the groups, but the animosity she usually felt wasn't there.

"Why aren't I coming with you again?" Nyko grumbled next to Eloi. He stared at the groups with longing.

"I need you here. Elijah is coming with Ian to show how shifters and hunters work together. It makes no sense to send everyone. What if they attack Sumter while we aren't here? I'm only taking half the warriors, and I need either you or Elijah to stay. One shifter hunter pair with us, and one remains behind," she explained for what felt like the tenth time. "Now you know how it feels."

Eloi dodged the punch to her arm. "It still sucks," Nyko said.

"Hey, I'm acting Pack Leader!" she groaned.

"You keep telling us to call you 'Eloi'—that's what you said. That you were just Eloi, so no, not to me you're not. God, you're annoying." Nyko scowled at her, and she ignored him. "Why can't Elijah stay?"

"You drew straws and lost; suck it up." She enunciated the last three words. Silence fell between them, and she caught Owen's eye. He came over and smirked between the two of them.

"Do we have enough vehicles?" she asked him.

"Burntwood loaned us the school bus, and we have a few SUVs," Owen smirked at her. "If you ever get fed up with the wolf boy you meet in the woods, let me know." He winked, and Eloi laughed.

"In your dreams!" she shouted after him.

"From what I hear about your powers, that's actually possible!" Owen yelled back.

Lachlan cleared his throat. "Shouldn't take us too long to get there." He came up beside her. He was dressed in the hunter clothes his family wore. Khaki pants with plenty of pockets, a loose shirt, and a leather vest stretched tightly across his chest. She plucked at his shirt, and he smiled. "I'm showing solidarity."

"What are we waiting for?" Liam approached, and she smiled widely.

"A few more minutes, Gramps, you'll see. We have some special guests making an appearance." She cast out her mental net to check and nodded.

"Don't call me 'Gramps,'" he grumbled, but she saw him smile and winked at him.

Movement from the trees caught their attention, and Eloi watched the hunters' faces as a group of tall, muscular men emerged from the trees. Fifty in total joined them from Daniel's pack. Each had broad shoulders and was packed with muscle. She heard someone whistle next to Lachlan.

"Now that's one hell of an army. Please tell me they are on our side?" she heard Girvan whisper to his cousin. Cillian grinned as his eyes caught the size of the group.

Eloi watched Lachlan walk up to the most significant guy at the front, who was taller and broader than him. Eloi stared at the stranger when he grinned, showing all his teeth. The shifters of Sumter looked on in wonder at the giants before them. Eloi followed Lachlan, gazing shyly at Daniel next to the leader.

"Welcome. We are pleased to have you." Lachlan clasped the leader's arm and grinned back.

"Most of them are descendants of the Royal Tivaci." Jason nudged Eloi. "Good job."

Eloi looked at him, stunned. "They're descendants? I thought the bloodline died out! I only mentioned the prisoners because I thought they would want to help free them."

"No, they mated with hunters and have been in hiding. They had the same fertility issues the Aoibhan had with shifters. The original Tivaci bloodline began to mate with hunters and were shunned. They've been hunted by both sides ever since and chose to stay hidden. This is a big deal —Michael was reluctant to reveal them." He nodded towards the man Lachlan had greeted.

Eloi couldn't help but glance at Daniel again. He met her gaze and gave her a cheeky grin and a wink, cocking his head to one side as if in question when she didn't look away. She nodded coolly and resisted the urge to wave like a lunatic. Instead, she turned back to Liam, who was standing tensely next to Girvan.

"What do you think, Gramps? Hunters and shifters living in harmony." She smirked at him. "You said it will never happen, and it has been happening for generations."

Liam looked stunned, his eyes scanning the men before him. Suddenly he stiffened when a figure broke away from the group and strode right up to him. Eloi watched the woman move toward them. She had deep red hair streaked with grey and appeared close to Liam's age.

"Uh oh." Girvan covered his eyes in mock fear. The woman walked right up to Liam and prodded him hard with a finger. Eloi laughed at the expression on Liam's face. She had never seen him look so stricken.

"Liam O'Reilly, it's about god damn time you came to your senses and dropped all the stupid nonsense you used to spew. It amazed me Briana put up with you." She slapped him up the back of his head, then pulled him in for a hug. "I was sorry to hear about Briana—we kept in touch after I left. I miss her too."

Liam carefully wrapped his arms around the woman and crushed her to his chest. The shifters looked away awkwardly, and Eloi chuckled. She had heard about Briana and her friend with the smart mouth from Lachlan when he'd explained about Vivienne and Daniel. They had gotten into a lot of trouble when they lived with the hunters. Eloi felt a pang that she would never know Lachlan's mother. He talked about her all the time.

It was then Eloi noticed Finn, and she cringed as his eyes followed her. He stood separately from the group and blew her a kiss when she looked his way. She scoffed and tried not to heave.

"What's with Finn? He keeps looking at you, and it's creepy," Nyko whispered.

Eloi rolled her eyes. "I've got it under control." She approached the red-haired woman and smiled.

"Hello, I'm Eloi, Lachlan's daughter. He's told me a lot about you." She held out her hand but wasn't at all surprised when the woman pulled her in for a hug.

"He's told me all about you too. I'm Vivienne, but call me

Viv. My daughter Shauna can't wait to meet you and your mother." Viv gave her a squeeze.

"Thank you for coming." Eloi squeezed her back.

"I'm glad Michael came to his senses. I've been waiting for this day!" She grinned, and her eyes sparkled as she looked around at the hunters. "Excuse me, there are some familiar faces I must go and see."

Eloi laughed as Viv raced off. "She makes me tired just watching her."

Lachlan put an arm around her. "She never was able to sit still too long."

Eloi looked back out at the group and caught Lachlan's eye. "We better make a move then."

He looked back at her, and they exchanged nods. Eloi clapped her hands and let the concussion of air drift over the group to catch their attention.

"The Tivaci are being held against their will. Who is ready to go and free some shifters?" she shouted, and a cheer rang up amongst the groups before her. "Let's go change the world."

~

AINE WATCHED Olivia as they entered the main cavern. Olivia brought her from her cell every day, and she exchanged stories with the shifters; she immensely enjoyed her time with them. At first, they didn't believe her, but she slowly began to earn their trust. They listened to stories about Sumter and Burntwood, but they still weren't convinced about the dark wolves.

"Can we walk a bit today? I need to stretch my legs a bit more than normal." Aine touched Olivia's arm, who turned, looking unsure.

"I promise to behave myself. I won't get you in trouble, I promise—I just want to see the rest of the cave system." She smiled.

Olivia's lip twitched. "Okay, I can't imagine staring at one wall all day is much fun." She led Aine to the other side of the cavern. Aine slyly asked Olivia pertinent questions, requesting to see where she was first brought when the Faction took her in. There were a few new refugees huddled in that area. Some guards spoke to them, and Olivia frowned at how terse they were.

"It's okay," she said to a woman near the entrance. "They're a bit gruff, but there is food and shelter here. You will be safe."

Aine watched the interaction and saw the group relax in Olivia's presence. Then, one of the guards spotted them.

"You shouldn't be here," he barked at them. "Get back to the cavern, now."

Olivia gulped and nodded quickly. She took Aine's arm and led her further down the tunnels. She showed her the storage areas and where they kept the children, even the living quarters for the refugees. Aine noticed there were comfortable but simple arrangements.

As they got close to Solus's tunnel, Aine noticed another one past his. It had a funny smell and looked darker than the other tunnels. It made the hairs instinctively stand up on Aine's arms and neck.

"What's down there?" Aine pointed.

"I don't know; I've never been this far." Olivia's voice was small, and Aine squeezed her hand.

"Come on, quick look." Aine darted forward and away from Olivia before the petite woman could react.

"Aine, wait!" Olivia whispered harshly.

She didn't stop, and Olivia was forced to follow, her footsteps quick behind Aine. The tunnel angled downward, leading them deeper underground. As they descended, Aine wrinkled her nose as the smell of wet dog met them. Stale sweat and the image of many bodies in close quarters came to her as she got closer to the source of the smell.

Olivia cringed when Aine looked back behind her. "We should go back," the small woman said, her eyes wide.

"You can wait for me if you want; I'll be really quick. I need to know what's down here." Aine continued down the tunnel. There was very little light, but she shifted her eyes to see deeper. She'd never thought to do that before and shook her head at the simple solution. Oliva marveled at the animal glow when Aine turned back to face her.

"How do you do that?" she asked with wonder. "I can't shift outside the full moon."

"I'm powerful and have been taught great control. Come on, there's something ahead." Aine pulled Olivia with her as the tunnel opened into a large cavern. There was no light source here, but Aine could see row upon row of shifters standing before them.

Olivia gasped, and Aine observed them in their human forms. They stared, unmoving, at nothing, appearing vacant like empty vessels. Dark veins lined their skin and spider-webbed out over each of them. They looked clammy with a sickly pallor to their skin.

"What are they?" Olivia whispered.

"These are the dark wolves I've been telling you about. They've been attacking my pack for years." Aine took a step forward, and Olivia grabbed her arm. "It'll be okay; just wait near the entrance for me." She heard a noise up the tunnel and looked wide-eyed at Olivia.

"Quick, hide here." Aine pushed her into a crevice in the wall and went to stand on the edge of the wolves. Her heart raced as footsteps echoed down the tunnel, and she stifled a groan when Rolan appeared at the entrance. She registered surprise on his face before he glared at her. Vibrations pushed through the air when he growled, and the wolves around her echoed the sound.

"What have we here? How did you get out?" Rolan stalked up to her slowly, and Aine held her ground as he stalked her.

She shrugged. "I'm exploring."

Rolan's grin was wicked. "How did you get out of your cell?"

"The guards let me out, not like I can find my way out of here anyway." Aine crossed her arms and matched his glare.

"You found our soldiers then; how inconvenient." Rolan scratched his chin.

"What do you want, Rolan?" Aine sighed. "I'm bored of you."

"Well, we can't have that. I'll make sure you won't be bored anymore." His eyes gleamed with malice.

Aine jerked as two hands grabbed her from behind. A strong, elongated jaw ripped into the flesh between her shoulder and neck; one of the dark wolves behind her had shifted. She screamed as the pain ripped into her collar bone, and the wolf's paws on her shoulders held her firmly in place. The sharp teeth deepened as the jaws closed around her and bit deeper, black saliva running down her white shirt. As the dark wolf shook her, the pain worsened. She tried to struggle away, but the weight of the wolf pushed her to her knees.

"At least we will have some use for you when you turn." Rolan's grin was wicked, and he put up his hand. The wolf dropped her, and Rolan's laughter echoed down the tunnel as he walked away, a loud clank indicating he'd locked her in. She could feel the poison coursing through her and drew on her power to fight it. Her vision swam, bile rising in her throat.

"Aine!" Small hands shook her. "Aine, please answer me!" Olivia begged.

Aine slumped into her and closed her eyes.

~

THE VEHICLES PULLED to a stop where Lachlan had parked the last time they entered the Tivaci territory. His chest still had a dull ache, but he ignored it and went to meet Michael, Eloi, and his father. Finn glared at him behind their father as he approached, but Lachlan ignored him. He could feel the buzz of excitement among each group; the hunters had been working with the Aoibhan shifters, but the hybrids brought in a whole new element.

"So, what is the play here?" Liam looked at Lachlan, but his eyes occasionally flicked to Michael and Vivienne, who stood at her leader's back.

"Since we haven't worked together before, or very long, I think we each take the side of a triangle. Hit them at the same time and meet in the middle. If one group struggles, you'll at least have the distraction of what is happening behind the enemy." Lachlan picked up a stick and drew a rough view of the settlement in the dirt. After a quick explanation of the layout, Michael spoke.

"What if all three groups struggle?"

"From what I could tell, we vastly outnumber the dark wolves." He grinned at Michael. "Your hybrids make this a game-changer. If we can start freeing prisoners, then our numbers will increase, but we can't rely on the Tivaci to be able to fight. We don't know how long they've been imprisoned."

"So pretty much we charge in and hope for the best," Liam grumbled. "That's no plan."

"We won't be going in completely blind. I'm going to send some scouts up to the ridge. Eloi, will you feel out the area? I don't want any surprises." Lachlan looked at Michael. "You've seen what their bite can do. We don't know how it affects the hybrids. Best not to get bitten to be safe."

"Liam said that his hunters have been bitten and not been affected," Eloi remarked, Michael glanced at Liam who shrugged.

"Yeah, we've had some injuries. Hard not to; those wolves are really aggressive. The injuries were superficial and we heal fast. Eloi checked them over, and they were fine."

While they waited for the scouts, he checked in with each group. They took longer than expected, and by the time they came back to report, he could barely keep still with anticipation.

"What do you have for us?" he asked Elijah and Ian.

"Looks the same as before, but with additional guards. Some of them don't have the veins like the dark wolves. That must be how they are kept under control. Otherwise, they would have attacked the prisoners by now, I would assume," Ian spoke.

"Good, hopefully, our numbers will make up for the increased presence of the enemy." Lachlan nodded and turned to where Eloi sat, concentrating on her mental map, as she called it. She grimaced while searching through the settlement.

"The dark wolves...taste funny."

"Taste funny?" Lachlan chuckled.

"I don't know how else to describe it, like a mental taste, I guess?" She opened her eyes and shook her head. "As far as I can tell, we still outnumber them, but there's more here than you described."

"How many do you think?"

"Nearly as many as us, but we've always fought well against them. They usually swarm and overpower us with sheer numbers. We should be able to handle it."

Lachlan pulled Eloi into a hug. "Look after yourself. I don't want to get your mom back only to tell her I lost you."

"We going to get moving? I hate standing around." Girvan bumped Lachlan with his shoulder, and he scowled at his cousin.

"Waiting on the last of the scouts." Lachlan bumped him back. Girvan grumbled and walked away, muttering about waiting around. When the scouts finally returned, the buzz of anticipation had started to wear on Lachlan. They confirmed what Eloi had felt, and Lachlan passed the information to Liam and Michael.

"Ready?" Lachlan had maneuvered his team into position, and Eloi crouched beside him.

"Nearly. The hybrids are harder to link with; I'm working with Daniel." She blushed.

"Already have a connection with him, do you?" he teased, and Eloi shrugged.

"Do you have any concerns?" Lachlan asked.

"Nah, we got this. We have the numbers, the element of surprise, and I'm pretty sure my mom will be causing enough trouble to distract the Faction while she's their prisoner." Eloi winked at him.

He laughed. "You're probably right."

16

Lachlan turned to face the group of warriors behind him. They had always fought defensively, and this would be their first attack of another settlement; the whole experience would be new for them. The older warriors appeared unphased, and Lachlan smiled at the younger warriors. Each held a look of determination and anticipation; he felt their trust and settled himself into his role.

"I know that you had your doubts about me in the past." He raised an eyebrow and heard a few chuckles. "But I am here as your Pack Leader today. Aine can't be here and would not want us to prioritize her over the prisoners here. They need our help, and they deserve to be freed. We have some unlikely allies with us today. Including the hybrids you've all just met. I know that every shifter here will do their best, and that is all I can ask of you."

Lachlan turned to leave, but his face heated as a cheer went up from the group of shifters. He turned and smiled at them, grateful for their presence. He approached Eloi, and she nudged him.

"Think you've finally won them over. I've spoken to Michael and Liam, and we are waiting for your signal, Lachlan." Eloi looked up at him, and he nodded. Eloi closed her eyes; she would signal the hybrids, and the hunters would listen for the shifters to move.

"Stay safe," he whispered to her and stepped forward. He grabbed his battle-ax from the sheath on his back and slid his dagger free. He started to quicken his pace, the sounds of the warrior's shift accompanying his steps. Eloi's paws thudded next to him as he broke into a run. His heart raced with the rhythm of the pounding paws around him.

Eloi yipped next to him, and he looked ahead for the first dark wolf on the perimeter. The air around them seemed to crackle with energy; a howl broke the quiet ahead of them, and shouts sounded from the direction the hunters had chosen to enter. He grinned as he saw the dark human figure ahead, the man's black veins and dark eyes stark against his pale skin.

One efficient strike and the man dropped to the ground. The group continued forward as snarls rent the air ahead. Lachlan quickly fell into a rhythm with Eloi, their usual connection blooming within him. He would disarm or subdue an enemy, and Eloi would finish them off once they were on the ground while watching his back. He instinctively always knew where she was, their connection strong. The dark wolves swarmed before them, surging from the settlement, and Lachlan glanced back to check that no warriors were bitten, continuing to pull them into the fray.

He was careful never to be swarmed and moved amongst the shifters, the wolves intent on them rather than him. As they gained ground, the wolves became more aggressive; he blocked and was pushed back. The shifters on his flank leaped to his defense, and the wolf in front fell. When the dark wolves shifted, he took the lead and blocked the jaws from his comrades. Eloi leaped next to him, her jaws mercilessly fixed around another wolf that fell dead at her feet.

A rifle shot cracked the air, and the dark wolf in front of Lachlan dropped before his ax could connect. He looked up to see a line of hunters ready to fire. Spinning, he dodged the snarling jaws on his right; he turned the dodge into a turn and sliced along the wolf's flank with his dagger. The shifters and hunters surrounded the dark wolves ahead and pushed them towards the center of the settlement. Cillian knocked Lachlan aside and plunged his dagger into a wolf's flank.

"Thanks, bro," Lachlan panted.

"Anytime." Cillian disappeared back into the fight. Lachlan saw Liam wrestle with the jaws of a wolf at his throat, laughing as he fought. Lachlan rolled his eyes when he saw his father's dagger enter the wolf's eyes.

"Where are these hybrids then? A bit late to the party, aren't they?" Liam surged forward to face another wolf. When he'd dispatched that one, he froze and stared agape at the scene ahead. Lachlan could understand why. The hybrids ahead had shifted, but not in the way the shifters in Sumter did. They remained humanoid on two feet, but that's where the similarities ended. The head of each hybrid was a wolf, and the bodies were covered in fur. Each appeared to have grown over a foot and put on a hundred pounds of muscle.

The beasts tore through the dark wolves in front of them using giant clawed hands; they threw wolves aside as if they weighed nothing. Lachlan shook himself and continued to fight. The enemy was unorganized and mindless; it was no effort to get past their guard and take them down. Eventually, Lachlan pulled his ax back from a wolf he'd just killed and turned to find the next, but there were none left. The hunters, shifters, and hybrids faced each other with no enemy between, just the bodies on the ground.

"Holy shit!" Girvan's voice rang clear through the silence. Lachlan saw him elbow Cillian, and both gaped at the hybrids. Lachlan walked up to Michael, or at least the massive beast in the same clothes Michael had been wearing. Fortunately, he shifted into human form as Lachlan approached.

"Well, that was something. Anyone bitten?" He looked among the group, and his eyes fell on a young hybrid holding his arm. He groaned.

"Eloi!" Lachlan shouted, and she appeared at his side. He gestured toward the hybrid, who grumbled at Eloi's approach with a frown on her face. She looked over his wound and closed her eyes; when she opened them, she looked puzzled.

"Are you sure that was a dark wolf bite?"

"Yeah, stung like hell at first but feels okay now." The man shrugged.

"I can't sense an infection in him. I did with Gary and Jason." Eloi looked over her shoulder at Lachlan, her hands still on the man's wound. Lachlan came over and looked. Besides being a nasty bite, there was no sign of the usual tar-like saliva or dark veins spidering away from the bite.

"Are the hybrids immune?" Lachlan watched Eloi shrug.

"I'll have to keep an eye on them," she replied, "but I can't sense any infection." At least the hybrids had the ability to heal the bites. But they would need to get the young man back to their base.Lachlan sighed and turned to Michael.

"You certainly made that easier for us. Now, let's get your

kinsmen free." He gripped Michael's forearm, and the man smiled back.

"That was almost too easy," Girvan commented.

"Shut up, Girvan." Cillian punched him in the shoulder and walked over to help free the prisoners.

The Tivaci were all huddled in the cave entrance. The chains that linked them carried on deeper into the caves, where more shifters were being kept.

"Who is your Pack Leader?" Lachlan asked the first shifter he freed. The man's eyes were wide, and he looked around wildly. He didn't speak, and Lachlan looked at each of the shifters before him. They seemed dazed, more like trapped animals than humans. Like they'd just woken and realized they weren't beasts.

He remembered the trance they appeared to be in when he was here with Aine. Anger shot through him as he saw how the shifters had been held, barely able to move, and subdued by the trance.

Eloi moved among the shifters and tried to speak to them. She made contact with every one of the prisoners, and once she had spoken to each, they appeared less dazed. Lachlan watched as she moved among them; after reaching the last in this group, she approached Lachlan and breathed a weary sigh.

"I've done what I can; they need rest and to feel safe," she said.

"Your mom would be so proud of you." Lachlan put an arm around her. "Don't tire yourself too much, though."

Eloi returned his smile. "I won't, but you can't stop me from helping!" She walked over to the warriors and checked in with each one. She was a marvel, and Lachlan was proud to call her his daughter. She might not be his blood, but she was his.

Vivienne approached to take the spot Eloi had just vacated, and Lachlan raised an eyebrow.

"Well, if her mother is anything like her, I can understand why she melted your heart. They both must be special." Viv cocked her head. "Your pack is different from the others."

"So is yours," Lachlan laughed.

"Ever get the feeling we are part of something?" Viv looked around at the groups before them. "Like something is on the horizon that will change everything?"

Lachlan shifted. "Is this about prophecies and fairytales? I'm not sure what to believe anymore. I don't like the idea that I don't have control over my own life." He ran his hand through his hair. "Shauna not here?"

"No, she stayed behind. We couldn't bring everyone." Viv looked out at the hunters. "I can't believe how much they've changed."

"Don't look at me; I worked on them for years. Eloi did more in a few days than I ever did."

Viv watched Eloi move among the warriors and then the hunters. "I dream of the next generation living in peace." She turned to face him. "We need to stop the Faction from ruining that dream."

Lachlan smiled weakly at her and looked over to the hybrids. "I know, and this is a good start." They fell silent and watched the scene before them.

"Excuse me?" A young female shifter from the Tivaci approached meekly. "Are you from Sumter?"

Lachlan softened his features and looked at her; she couldn't have been more than five. "Yes, we saw you had been captured and came to help." He smiled at her and looked around. The adults still seemed dazed, but the children appeared to be coming out of the stupor.

"Are you hurt?" he asked.

"No, I'm okay." She looked up at him curiously. "Are you going to help us?"

Lachlan nodded. "What's your name? Can you take me to your Pack Leader?"

The girl frowned. "I'm Annie. He's gone. They killed him first. But I can take you to Rosa," she said eagerly. Lachlan nodded at her and followed.

He spotted Tania on the way and touched her arm. "Have you checked the prisoners?"

"Most of them, but I hear there are more in the caves. I was just about to head that way." Tania followed Lachlan to the group at the entrance to the cave; he could see the slope down into the ground disappear into blackness. Annie led them to a small alcove, the light from the entrance still lighting the area and reflecting off the pale stone. The young shifter sat in front of an older female; her dark grey hair streaked with lighter greys was pulled up into a neat bun. She wore a simple dress and still seemed to be in a stupor.

Tania dropped down beside her and looked her over. "She's still in some sort of trance. I'll need Eloi."

Eloi appeared next to Lachlan, and he laughed. "Following me, are you?"

"Looked important," she laughed and touched her fingers to Rosa's head.

Rosa shook her head as Eloi took a step back, and her eyes slowly came into focus. Rosa looked around and shrunk away slightly. Lachlan took a step back so as not to crowd her while Tania and Eloi spoke gently to her.

Lachlan left to see if others in the pack had recovered to help with the ones in the cave. He caught sight of his father and walked over; Michael and Viv were with him.

"Any casualties?" Lachlan asked.

"A few bites, but Eloi checked them over, and they don't seem to be infected. It looks like she was right about humans being immune. It is just shifters that are affected by the dark wolves; the hybrids are fine too. Are we really calling them dark wolves?" Liam cringed, and Lachlan laughed.

"That's something, I guess. At least there are fewer that can be infected, and I can't think of another way to describe them." Lachlan clapped his father on the back, and Vivienne laughed at Liam's expression.

"Lachlan!" Eloi shouted from the entrance to the cave. Lachlan frowned as he went to her; she seemed giddy. "You need to talk to Rosa! She's a historian like Eyolf."

"Okay." Lachlan followed her back into the cave and greeted the old woman. She looked up at him, her eyes wide.

"And you're sure he's the Kind Warrior in the prophecies?" Rosa looked up at Eloi.

"Ciara said that everything in their prophecies to describe him has happened." Eloi nodded at the woman. Lachlan sighed.

Rosa looked startled. "I never thought I'd see this play out. It seems all the prophecies are starting to converge." She tried to stand, and her legs shook. Eloi put out a hand to help her, and she took her arm. "I need some fresh air. We've been stuck down here too long."

Lachlan took her other arm and helped her out. "I've tried to avoid that prophecy."

"There's no avoiding fate, young man." Rosa's lips thinned, and he laughed.

"Not that young." Lachlan scowled at her.

"Nonsense." Rosa froze as she looked around at the

devastation of the dark wolves; she spat on one as she passed. "Good riddance."

"Grandma!" Annie trotted up beside her, and Rosa let go of Eloi's arm to hug her granddaughter to her side. Michael approached, and Lachlan shook his head slightly. Introductions would have to wait for now. Once Rosa was settled on a bench, her granddaughter in her lap, she looked up at the group again.

"Have the hybrids revealed themselves?" Rosa chuckled at Lachlan's stunned face. "Thought so."

"How did you...?" Michael stared at the woman and looked around his pack. His eyes betrayed his sorrow. "We are descendants of the Tivaci bloodline, the ones that left to mate with hunters."

"I figured." Rosa nodded curtly.

"Get the feeling this is going to turn into one of Eyolf's revelations about our history," Eloi leaned in and muttered to Lachlan. He huffed and scowled; it most certainly did. Rosa grumbled about younglings.

"So let me get this straight." The old woman shifted and looked around. "The hybrids are out, the fearsome hunters from Ireland have joined with the Aoibhan, and a powerful shifter has emerged and mated with the Kind Warrior."

"If you're talking about Aine, then yes, but she's been taken by the Faction." Lachlan shifted with impatience.

"That's...not good." Rosa pushed a wisp of hair behind her ear and her brow creased.

"Please explain," Lachlan said wearily and rubbed his jaw.

"I know bits and pieces from what we've gathered through history. What do you know of the shifter wars and the original families?"

"I think we need to have this conversation with our

elder, Eyolf. He reveals what he wants when it suits him," he said gruffly, turning to Eloi. "Can you reach him from here?"

"Pfft." She huffed and stalked off. Lachlan shook his head.

"Teenagers," Rosa chuckled. "There is usually a reason we don't tell you everything. We have to be careful what we reveal or risk corrupting the prophecies."

"I'm still not sure I believe all this." Lachlan sat down next to Rosa, and Michael stood speechless.

"You don't have to." Rosa shrugged, and they sat in silence.

ELOI HAD ONLY EVER FELT this exhausted once before in her life—the days when she had left Sumter to search for her mom. She stifled a yawn but continued to check each person for bites and make sure the prisoners were comfortable. They had managed to get most of them settled back into their own homes. She realized they would have to head back to Sumter; a few of the buildings had been torn down or were too trashed for the families to move back into. There would be no space for them here tonight.

"Hey, Eloi, you should get some rest." Cillian reached her and held out a hand to help her up from the floor. She had sat down out of sight to do just that.

"I was just taking a quick breather." She couldn't stop her yawn this time.

"We have enough bodies here to help out. Maybe you should get back to Sumter" Cillian nodded in the direction of the vehicles. "Some of the others are heading back now. The Tivaci are grateful, but I think they would be more comfortable if they could recoup without strangers hanging around."

"We could do with leaving a few people here to protect them, just in case." Eloi gestured toward the cave.

"I believe the hybrids are staying—they are part Tivaci, after all." Cillian shrugged. Eloi looked over his shoulder and frowned. She glanced at each group of hunters and narrowed her eyes.

"Cillian, where's Finn? I don't remember seeing him after the battle. I haven't had that uneasy feeling that someone is watching me." Eloi continued her search.

Cillian's brow furrowed, and he searched the crowds. "Huh, I don't know. I don't actually remember seeing him fight."

A cold feeling washed over Eloi. "Let's make sure no one else is missing, especially any of the prisoners."

Eloi went house to house and directed Cillian to ask the hunters if anyone had seen him. When she was sure the Tivaci were all accounted for, she found Cillian again; he stood with Lachlan and Liam.

"Well?" Eloi said, trying to keep her voice calm. "Anything?"

Cillian shook his head. "He was supposed to join the battle with Liam's group, but none of the hunters have seen him since we left the vehicles."

Liam sighed. "It's not like him to miss a fight. There's more to this; he's been cagey recently. I should have expected it." His shoulders sagged, and Vivienne rubbed his arm.

"He's always done what he wanted. Did you expect him to stick around once you found Lachlan? Good riddance, I say," Viv huffed. "He's a nasty piece of work. No offense."

"I don't like this." Lachlan scanned the trees. "Like you

said, any chance to kill, he's there. He must have something planned."

Cillian shrugged. "Maybe it's for the best he's gone." Eloi couldn't help but nod her agreement.

Michael approached. "Heard you lost a hunter."

Cillian unsuccessfully turned a laugh into a cough. "Not an important one."

"I asked my hybrids. One of them saw a hunter take one of the SUVs at the back and leave. He thought he was a messenger."

"I guess he's had enough of us then. Let him go, Pa. All he's done recently is cause trouble." Cillian clasped Liam's shoulder. "You've got two better sons to worry about anyway. Can see why you didn't stop at the first one." He winked.

Eloi smirked. "You're better off, Gramps."

"Don't call me 'Gramps,'" he groaned.

"Gramps?" Vivienne grinned.

"Don't you start." He pointed at her. "She's got a thing going on with your son, by the sounds of it. Won't be long until you're a granny if you're not careful."

Eloi felt the blood drain from her face as realization dawned. "That's my cue to leave." She turned to Cillian. "Did you say some vehicles were leaving?"

Cillian nodded. "I'll come with you—once these two get started, there's no stopping them." They took the quickest route back to the vehicles.

"Do you really think Finn is gone?" Eloi watched him.

"He was mouthing off about leaving a while back. It wouldn't surprise me, to be honest. I feel better with him gone."

"Me too," Eloi agreed.

17

"Enough, Rolan, we have been over this. Aine is my daughter; I need her to rule over all shifters." Solus growled at Rolan, who threw up his hands.

"You promised me that if I brought you Aine, then I would be able to raise Eloi. She's my daughter, and I must be able to undo what she's been taught by yours. I don't care what you do with Aine, but I'll never follow her. She's weak," Rolan sneered.

"She is the most powerful shifter in existence. We will need that power to take over all the other packs. Eloi isn't important right now!" Solus waved his hand dismissively.

"That is not what we agreed." Rolan gritted his teeth. "I will have Eloi, even if I have to go and get her myself. You can't control Aine; I've learned that mistake. She's better off dead. Besides, Eloi will be just as powerful."

Solus glared at him. "Do not speak of my daughter that way, or I will no longer have a use for you. Now leave; I need to rest." He turned his back on Rolan, who smirked.

"It's only a matter of time," Rolan mumbled, turning to the cave entrance. He left Solus's caves and sauntered to the nearest exit. Once, he escaped from the caves and shifted and felt more relaxed. The cold air breezed over him as he raced away. The walls made him feel claustrophobic, and he needed to run off his nervous energy. His wolf paws pounded through the trees and raced miles from the prison he'd built for himself.

Solus had promised that once they had Aine secured, Rolan would be able to have Eloi. Solus was too obsessed with Aine to think of anything else; he raved about how Aine needed protection in his madness. Rolan thought she needed to be put down. Every time he thought of her with the hunter, he felt nausea burn through him.

He reached a lake and shifted back to human form. The area was peaceful and far from his master. He stared at the moon, pleased that it no longer dictated when he could shift. The openness of this place calmed him, and he thought about his return to the caves. Did he need to return? Could he leave the Faction? The answer was no. Solus would hunt him down with some delusion about what Rolan owed him.

Rolan didn't react when a knife slid under his chin, and he felt the cold metal press against his flesh.

"Not paying attention now, are we?" a cold voice whispered in his ear. "I could slit your throat here, and I know there won't be many to cry over you, Rolan." The stranger cackled behind him.

He resisted the urge to swallow and kept silent. The man kept the knife in place and came into view. Rolan's eyes widened at the hunter that held him at knifepoint. His features were familiar; he smirked down at Rolan and licked his lips.

"Now, should I play with you some more, or would you rather get down to business? Oh, that's right, you can't answer because of the knife over your carotid. I'm going to remove the knife, and we are going to have a chat. Blink once for yes." The man nodded as Rolan did so and flipped the knife away. He took a quick step back, holding the knife out before him.

Rolan didn't move and watched the hunter take a few steps back. "Who are you?"

"Let's just say I'm not an enemy at the moment." His eyes gleamed.

Rolan swallowed. "What do you want?"

"The same as you, to see the end of the pack in Sumter and my self-righteous brother. My father is a fool to think Lachlan can lead the hunters. I don't particularly care for the position; I just don't want my brother to have it," he snarled.

"Brother? You were there in Sumter three years ago with the hunters." The realization made Rolan cringe. "You're that scum's brother? The one that violated my wife?"

"Scum? I like it, looks like we will get on very well. And can you blame him? That woman of yours is a fine-looking lady. The daughter, however, is more to my liking. My name is Finn." Finn grinned at Rolan.

"I still don't understand why you're here. What do you want with me?" Rolan watched Finn twirl the knife between his fingers.

"Well, I thought we could help each other. Heard you're a puppet and that the real guy in charge is Aine's father. That shocker caused a stir back in Sumter. I managed to sneak into the caves of yours and have a poke around. Seems you've lost your dark wolves in Tivaci. With their new allies, all your dark wolves will be defeated. Your ace in the hole gone." Finn spread his hands in front of him. "Poof."

Rolan glared at him. "They should have annihilated them. I don't see how—"

Finn cut him off. "I'll leave that surprise for later, shall I. The hunters and shifters have made some new friends. Now for the important part. I heard you're good at escaping death. Well, the packs aren't far from going after Aine, and I have a feeling the odds are against you on that one. They're all working together, and it makes me sick. Right now, you don't stand a chance. You *will* lose. You seem smarter than that."

Rolan kept his face blank. "So what you're saying is, I need to be prepared to leave?"

"Exactly, and I wouldn't warn your master when you do if I were you. Sounds like he doesn't treat you well. I'll find you, and we can plan a way to bring them all down. Deal?" Finn held his hand out, but Rolan ignored it. He figured that Finn could have killed him by now if he wanted to but didn't want to risk it.

"Why would you help me? What is in it for you?" Rolan stood and faced the hunter, his hands clenched into fists.

"Well, I also heard that you want to take your daughter from Aine. So let's just say I like her and don't want her around the crowd she's with anymore." Finn smiled, but it didn't reach his eyes.

Rolan gulped and shook his head. "Why do I feel like I'm making a deal with the devil?"

Finn threw his head back and laughed. "Good one, I like that. So, you in? You must be tempted by having a hunter of your own. It'll even the odds up a bit." He raised an eyebrow at Rolan.

"Can I think about it?" Rolan stalled.

"When you make your big escape, hopefully with your daughter if you're clever enough. There's a motel in the nearest town from here; when you reach it, ask at the desk for Reginald. They will pass on details of your next destination. I'll find you along the way." Finn stepped away and gave him some space.

"Fine, find me after they attack. If they win, that is." Rolan turned his back and shifted as fast as he could. He took a few strides and looked back to Finn, who had vanished.

~

AINE COUGHED AS SHE WOKE. She was laid on a mattress on a cave floor. It wasn't comfortable, but it was better than being trapped in a cave with dark wolves on the hard ground. Her entire body felt on fire; she trembled, and sweat stung her eyes when she tried to open them.

"She can't stay here; Solus expects her to be in that cell!" Taylor sounded loud in the small room.

"Look at her; she's sick. Rolan is a nasty piece of work, and I'm beginning to wonder if Solus is any better. We've been lied to from the start. You saw the dark wolf things in the cavern. Rolan told us they belonged to Sumter." Olivia paused. "The Faction isn't what any of us thought it was; they might even be responsible for the attacks on our families."

Taylor scoffed. "They've kept us safe; why would they attack us only to feed us?" He crossed his arms.

"Where do you think the dark wolves came from? I recognized them!" Her voice was shrill.

Taylor shook his head and closed his eyes. "Why, though? Why all this death?" he asked wearily.

"I don't know." Olivia sagged. Taylor looked over at Aine and nodded towards her. Olivia raced over.

"Don't move; you're very sick!" Olivia laid a cold cloth on her head, and Aine sighed.

"What happened?" she croaked.

"We were lucky. After Rolan locked us in, I managed to drag you to the cave entrance; not like you weigh much after starving yourself. Taylor heard me shouting." Olivia gestured to the entrance, and Aine saw the guard that had brought Olivia to Aine each day.

"We managed to get you here, but your fever hasn't broken. You've been really out of it," she fretted. Olivia bit her lip. "How could we have been so wrong? I always thought the Faction were the good ones."

Aine's smile was weak. "Survival isn't easy, nor is figuring out who to trust." She squeezed Olivia's hand. "Thank you, you saved my life."

Olivia blushed and fidgeted. "It's fine. How are you feeling? You don't look so good."

Taylor shifted behind her. "She can't stay here, Liv."

Aine grimaced and tried to move; she touched the tender spot on her shoulder. The poison spiderwebbed away from the bite. Aine's hand tingled when she touched it, so she pushed power through. Her head spun, and she swayed, but when she stopped, the poison had drawn back to the bitten area almost entirely.

"How did you do that?" Olivia had paled and gaped at her.

"I don't know." Aine stared at the wound. "I've never been able to do that before with my power." She frowned and tried to stand but swayed as she slowly got to her feet.

"You should rest." Olivia gently pushed her back down and left with a bowl of water. "I'll go and fetch some food for you."

"You're right." Aine glanced at Taylor. "If they find me

here, then it's a death sentence for you both. You should let me leave."

"She's too stubborn to let me at the moment. Eat fast, and then I'll get you back to your cell." He crossed his arms and frowned. "Why did you go down there anyway?"

"I wanted to prove a point; it was a risk." Aine shivered.

"Some risk, you could have been turned." Taylor raised an eyebrow in question.

"I don't know. Probably some other nuance of my power I'm yet to learn about; our historian will probably reveal the information knowing it all along but not having the decency to tell me." She shook her head.

"Sounds tedious," he chuckled.

"You have no idea," she grumbled.

Olivia returned at that moment, and Aine tried to eat the thin soup she brought, but her stomach roiled. She eventually pushed it away after a few mouthfuls.

Olivia looked at her thoughtfully. "What is your family like? You mentioned a daughter."

"Well, you've met my father." Aine's lips twitched. "Solus."

"He's your father? I don't understand why he captured you and blamed you for the attacks." Olivia tried to push the bowl toward Aine again.

"Neither do I." Aine coughed again, and Olivia handed her some water; she took a small sip and relaxed again.

"My daughter, Eloi, she's incredible. Strong, stubborn, a typical teenager, but I couldn't be prouder of her. She will make a great leader one day."

"And your mate?" Olivia asked.

"Lachlan is human, a hunter." Aine frowned at Olivia's expression.

"How can you be with our enemy? They hunt our kind!"

Her face turned red, and her eyes sparkled with unshed tears. "They killed my family; we were hunted by them and dark wolves."

"If dark wolves were there, then it wasn't hunters who attacked you. And it was not my Lachlan; he's a good man. He left his family when he was twenty. Eventually, we found each other, and he saved me when Rolan tried to kill me. We've been working to change the relationship between shifters and hunters. We work together with the humans. We are close to peace with his family, the O'Reillys."

Olivia gasped. "But they are monsters; they have killed more of us than any other family!"

"Not in the last three years. They've been living in a town near us. Do you want that to continue into the next generation?" Aine hardened her voice, and Olivia's brows pinched together. "Something has to change, Olivia. Compromises have to be made, or we will be stuck in this pointless battle forever. No one wins when everyone fights."

Olivia frowned, her face still pale. "Is your daughter half-hunter then? How is it possible to mate with them?"

"No." Aine pulled a face. "Rolan is her father." She scowled, and Olivia didn't push further. "What about your family, Olivia?"

"I'm alone. My family was killed when we were forced to leave our home." Full of disdain, Olivia dropped a cloth into a bowl too hard, and cold water splashed them. "Sorry, just knowing it was the Faction all along, and I've been fooled. It all seems so pointless," she mumbled.

"I'm sorry about your family. I can't imagine what you've been through." Aine looked around. "Or believe that you're helping me after what I've just told you. I know you don't have to and have little reason to believe me."

Olivia didn't say anything, and weariness flooded Aine's body. Her shoulder started to ache again. Aine put her hand to it and instinctively applied more power. Tiredness dragged at her, and Olivia lifted her hand to stroke Aine's hair.

"Sleep, I'll take care of you." Olivia wet the cloth in her hand and dabbed Aine's forehead.

"I won't stay long, I promise," Aine mumbled. She felt herself relax into a shallow doze.

~

Eloi watched Eyolf greet Rosa. She crossed her arms and scowled at them, fully expecting this discussion to be cryptic half-truths about the history of the packs. Lachlan sat with them while they discussed what Eyolf had told them over the years. Eloi had heard it all before, and she sighed.

"Bored?" Daniel appeared next to her.

Eloi jumped. "Stop doing that! How are you so quiet?" She grinned at him.

"Not my fault you don't pay attention." He smirked at her, one side of his mouth lifted. He looked across at the group before them. "What are they talking about?"

"Mistakes of packs long since dead." Eloi shrugged. "I have a bad feeling."

Daniel didn't say anything, and they watched as Rosa and Eyolf started arguing. Eloi huffed and walked over. "Enough! Both of you, stop bickering; we don't have time for this. What's the problem?"

"We both have a different take on how this all started." Eyolf looked at Rosa. "Apparently, the Aoibhan were corrupted by the darkness, and that's what caused the shifter war. Our records say that the other royal lines started kidnapping our female shifters...."

"Preposterous," Rosa chimed in. "That makes no sense."

"It does when you think about the fact that our females could make and breed more shifters," Eyolf argued.

"Well, everyone who can tell us is dead." Eloi looked at Rosa. "I know our history. Why don't you tell me yours?"

Rosa nodded. "There were four original bloodlines, each has different abilities related to the elements. Aoibhan, Air; Tivaci, Earth; Xerxes, Water; and Torak, Fire."

"I didn't know that." Eloi's brow puckered. "I thought all the Royals were like our pack. They could communicate."

"No, just the Aoibhan have that ability; they can manipulate air. The mental abilities and strength came from the darkness."

"What about the darkness and the force that my mom can push out of her?" Eloi asked.

"Each possessed unique abilities, but the Aoibhan wanted more power. One of the Royals corrupted their magic, and the darkness has haunted their...your...bloodline ever since. That's where your strength and communication come from, though you could argue that communication is another way of manipulating air." She looked thoughtful. "Your bloodline has control over it, but when it is taught outside the bloodline, it will send the user mad. The Aoibhan are the ones who created the shifters."

"But all the royal bloodlines are shifters." Eloi frowned.

"Thanks to your ancestors, they made the first shifters. Before that, everyone was human, though I'll never understand why they chose wolves." Rosa shrugged.

Eloi sat down next to Rosa on the bench. "I'm confused."

"Well, I guess that the Aoibhan hid the history to stop it from happening again. The dark wolves, as you call them, were the original creation before shifters came into being. The changes divided the packs, especially the Aoibhan." She took a breath. "The half that denied the shifter gift became hunters."

Eloi felt Lachlan jerk next to her; Liam, who had wandered over at some point, gaped in astonishment.

"Shifters and hunters are the same? Just chose different paths?" Eloi looked into the distance and shook her head in amazement. "Are you sure?"

"Yes, dear, it's why I'm so excited the hybrids have come forward. They were in early prophecies which said they would appear at a time of the greatest need. Our future is on the precipice of something significant. You've felt the change. We will all come together to fight one common enemy. If that enemy isn't destroyed, then all shifters will suffer."

Eloi groaned. "How ominous." Daniel stood next to the bench and put a hand on her shoulder.

"It will all come down to one powerful shifter. She will have some relation to all the bloodlines. Only she can end this."

"Three guesses as to who that is!" Girvan guffawed behind Liam, who growled at his nephew.

"But if my mom is a descendant of all four bloodlines... then so am I." Everyone went silent. The tension in the air could have been cut by a blade as they all stared at her.

Rosa gaped. "I didn't even think about that."

"You're right." Lachlan put a hand on her shoulder and squeezed.

"Other clues are surrounding the prophecy as to the identity, not just the bloodlines."

"Do you know what these are?" Eloi pleaded.

Rosa scratched her chin. "I used to know them by heart,

but I have to admit I'm getting on a bit. I'll have to look through my research."

"Convenient," Eyolf mumbled, clearing his throat. "Aine can't be a descendant of all four bloodlines. I can trace Aoibhan and Tivaci in her ancestry, but not Xerxes or Torak."

Eloi sighed in relief and looked at Rosa. The older shifter moved on the bench and hugged her granddaughter to her again; the young girl had fallen asleep.

"I know that she will mate a hunter and bring together humans and shifters," Rosa spoke carefully.

"That's the prophecy I've heard in our teachings." Eloi gulped. "Mom has already started to do that with Lachlan's help. He is a hunter and her mate, so if what you say is true and she does have all the bloodlines, then at least it indicates we are heading in the right direction."

"Not necessarily; there are two interpretations. It could go either way, either harmony or the destruction of all shifters." Rosa paled.

Eyolf shook his head. "I can't believe that. What you're saying is we've only had part of the history all this time?"

"I guess so." Rosa glanced in Eyolf's direction and spoke loudly. "It seems some of your elders decided to hide some of *your* history."

"Dark magic has only emerged again in the last few years—" Eyolf started.

"You're wrong." Eloi looked at her mentor. "What about Solus? It looks like he's been involved a lot longer." Eyolf swallowed and fell quiet.

Eloi rose and took a few steps, turning to face the group. "If my bloodline caused this, then it is up to mom and me to make this right. First thing's first, we need to get her back."

Lachlan nodded, and she looked around the rest of the group.

“At least we’ve had a warmup.” Daniel’s eyes twinkled, and he gave her a lazy grin. Eloi didn’t return it. She walked away to see if there was something she could help with. Rosa had given her plenty to think over.

18

"Where is she?!"

Rolan was in his room, lying on his bed and staring at the ceiling. Sleep had evaded him, but he jerked as Solus's shout carried down the tunnel. It echoed around the walls, and Rolan heard others in the corridor scramble. He had been fantasizing about how Aine would suffer from bite's effects and eventually turn into one of the wolves in the cavern. He also thought about the hunter's offer. He tried to straighten his face and shrugged when Solus finally found him.

"I don't know. Did she escape?" Rolan kept his tone calm and clenched his fists behind his back. He lifted his lip into a half-smile and shrugged. "She can't have gone far. It's like a maze down here if you don't know your way around."

"She's not in her cell." Solus paced the room and growled in Rolan's face. "What did you do?"

Rolan smirked. "She's nothing; why do you even want her?"

"It's all for her; this is all for her. You don't know what she will become, she is the most powerful shifter ever born, and we need that power!" Solus grabbed Rolan by his shirt and lifted him off the ground.

Rolan felt each jagged rock dig into his back; the air in his lungs blew out in a long breath, and he squirmed as he was slammed against the wall. He braced himself, and when he caught his breath, he laughed at Solus.

"You're losing it, old man. Your power is weakening!" Rolan gripped Solus's wrists and pulled them off him. With a push, Solus staggered backward, and his face paled as Rolan glared at him. "I can feel it draining from you. Spending time with your daughter has bled your power from you, or is she getting to you? Fortunately for you, she won't be an issue anymore."

"What did you do?" Solus's voice shook, and he stood firm before Rolan.

"She won't be a problem; I took care of it." Rolan shrugged and walked out of his room. Solus caught up to him.

"Where is she?" he growled and lunged for Rolan again. He sidestepped.

"Check the tunnels; she might turn up eventually." He shrugged and walked away but could feel Solus vibrate with rage behind him. He wondered if Aine had turned yet.

A scuffle down the tunnel caught his attention, and a scout appeared; he pushed shifters out of the way as he made his way toward them. He looked past Rolan to Solus and hurried toward him; Rolan could feel the heat of Solus's body behind him. The scout skidded to a halt, and his chest heaved as he tried and failed to catch his breath.

"Sumter has attacked and taken back the Tivaci lands. They've rescued the prisoners, everyone is dead, and they destroyed the cuffs. There's nothing left!" the shifter panted.

"WHAT!?!" Rage burst from Solus in a wave, and Rolan

flinched at the concussion of air in the tight corridor. The scout cringed; he ran his hand through his greasy hair and cowered, eyes darting along the tunnel.

"The dark wolves were defeated, I-I barely escaped..." the scout stammered.

Solus stepped forward, and a crack echoed through the tunnel as he broke the scout's neck. He threw the body aside and turned to Rolan.

"Where is she? We need her now more than ever!" he demanded. "You take me to her, or you will pay Rolan."

"Let me show you." He let his glee bleed into his expression and didn't wait for Solus to follow. It wasn't far down the dark tunnel from their chambers, and Solus growled as they walked deeper into the cavern. Rolan froze when he saw the gate was open. When they reached the dark wolf cave, he frowned and continued down the sloped tunnel into the cavern.

There was no sign of Aine, just a pool of blood and the bloody mouth of the guilty one before them. Rolan turned back toward the tunnel. A trail of blood shone, reflecting the light from the entrance. He swore.

"Where is she, Rolan?" Solus gripped his arm and turned him around. Another wave of rage hit Rolan, and he cringed. "She can't be infected by them—they are of her family's power!"

"I'll find her." Rolan looked his mentor in the eye, more power present than he expected.

"You better, and she better be unharmed. She must be protected at all costs," Solus snarled and stormed from the cavern.

Rolan sneered at his back. He turned to the wolves and summoned the darkness within him. Tentatively, he reached out and touched the minds of the dark wolves, grinning wickedly; the hold Solus had on them had crumpled. They stood dormant and ready for him to control. He sent the command through them.

Attack Sumter, none left alive.

Rolan turned his back on the wolves and walked back to his room, triumph shining in his eyes. The noise of the wolves sprinting out of the cavern echoed behind him.

~

ELOI SAT with Daniel on the flat rock at her place; their arms touched, and her heart leaped. He sat close to her and leaned in. They had been sitting in silence awhile, and Eloi sighed. Daniel shifted even closer, and she studied him from the corner of her eye. His tan skin and dark hair were beautiful in the sunshine. She could stare at him all day.

"Why didn't you tell me about your pack?" Eloi quickly turned to face him and searched his eyes. "You could have trusted me."

"Not my secret to tell. The hybrids have been hidden for generations. I'm surprised Michael actually did it and came out of hiding. It took some persuading, Lachlan tried to talk him into it before I brought him here, but it was what you said about the Tivaci that tipped the scale." Daniel smiled at her.

He lifted his hand and pushed a curl of her hair behind her ear. She shivered and looked up into his gaze.

"I think Liam is feeling rather foolish. His family has basically been killing off their own kind for centuries. I wonder how it all got so mixed up." Eloi's breath hitched when he leaned in.

"I wonder if hunters and shifters ever got on before all

this when the shifters and hunters first split. Or if they ever will again," Daniel sighed.

"I think your pack and my parents are evidence of that they can, in the future at least." She bumped his shoulder.

"True, it just feels like wasted time." He shuffled closer to her and lifted his other hand to caress her face. Eloi leaned into the touch; his scent tickled her nose, and she sighed contentedly.

"Do we have to go back?" She nuzzled his hand, and he drew her face closer. "Can't we just stay here?"

"Yeah, Lachlan might come and find us if we are away too long. I don't want to be on his bad side; I've seen him wield that battle-ax." Daniel stood up; the quick movement made her jump. He reached a hand down and dragged her to her feet, and she reluctantly stood. He pulled her close and pressed his body into hers. She giggled, her body heating at his touch, his lips only an inch from hers. Their breath mingled, and she felt her cheeks blush; she pushed away, embarrassed.

"Let's go," Eloi said quickly and walked toward Sumter. Daniel laughed and followed her, and he threw an arm around her when he caught up, pulling her tight to his side. Eloi huffed and rolled her eyes at him. They took their time and strolled back without shifting. The walk still went too fast, and Eloi wasn't surprised to see Lachlan head in their direction when they walked back into Sumter.

She sighed. "Here we go, now look what you've done."

Lachlan stopped and leaned against a wall with his arms crossed as he waited for them to approach.

"Is it too late to turn around?" Daniel's lips tickled her ear as he spoke, and Eloi smiled.

"I think he's already seen us."

Lachlan's frown deepened with her words, and Eloi stifled her laugh with a cough.

"Hey!" She smiled and waved at Lachlan, and he scowled.

"Don't 'hey' me, young lady, no more going off on your own. You know it's not safe outside the settlement. Not until we've stopped the Faction, and I know you'll be safe. What if they had taken you too?" Lachlan matched their stride and accompanied them. He glowered at Daniel, who refused to move his arm from her shoulder.

"What? I can't help it." Daniel stared Lachlan down.

"You can't talk; this is a little payback for you constantly slobbering all over my mom all the time. I can't look at you both without you two making ga ga eyes at each other." Eloi smirked at him.

"I don't slobber or make 'ga ga' eyes," Lachlan grumbled.

"Pffft, please, yes, you do," Eloi chuckled.

Nyko crossed from the training area ahead and jogged over. He gave Eloi an incredulous look when he saw Daniel's arm around her, then looked over at Lachlan and grinned.

"Yes, you definitely do," Nyko laughed as Lachlan looked between the two of them grumpily.

"I can't wait for Aine to get back so you two can't gang up on me anymore. You're both getting too much for me alone." He scowled at them and crossed his arms.

Eloi laughed at his expression, but her face fell, and she froze. She had kept a mental touch with each pack member, especially those on the border. She pushed out more power with her mind; one of the mental connections to a shifter on the perimeter had just winked out. She searched for the others and felt their fear. It spread through her, and she inhaled sharply. She pulsed a warning through the pack and started to run. She felt Lachlan and Daniel follow her.

"What's wrong?" Daniel asked, barely winded.

"The perimeter shifters are under attack. Feels like dark wolves again, but a lot more than we've dealt with so far." Eloi aimed for the side of Sumter she'd felt the attack but skidded to a stop when she felt a shifter mind cut off behind her. "They're coming from two directions—make that three." She twirled and looked to Lachlan.

"At least the hunters and hybrids are still here," he shouted. "Take the shifters east; I'll take the hunters north. Daniel, head west with the hybrids."

"I don't like splitting up," Eloi grumbled. "We need to start training together; each group has an advantage—"

"I know, Eloi; no time for that now." Lachlan took off. Daniel brushed a quick kiss across her lips before he left and when Lachlan couldn't scold them. Eloi shifted, and Nyko joined her.

Nice boyfriend you got. Nyko nudged her as they sprinted.

Not the time, Nyko, she snarled at him.

They ran for the east side of the settlement, and Eloi called all able shifters to help. They formed a barrier to protect those that couldn't fight as they ran further into the village for cover. The group that burst through the trees was smaller than the one that attacked over two weeks ago.

Eloi grinned. They had divided their forces to attack Sumter, and it was a mistake. She charged in with a snarl, and the warriors followed her; they worked in pairs to disable and kill each wolf. The steady stream kept coming, but the shifters didn't tire. Eloi twisted and pinned a wolf to her left. Nyko went in for the killing blow. He immediately pinned the next, and Eloi took her turn. The dark wolves had no chance to defeat them, and it didn't take long for Eloi, Nyko, and the warriors to destroy the wolves on that side.

That was a bit anticlimactic, Nyko said moodily.

Be glad for that, everyone—to the hunters, they will need support if the dark wolves have got in close, she mentally instructed.

She could feel their elation as they raced with Eloi to the north in time to stop the hunters from being overwhelmed. Nyko leaped and caught a wolf around the neck that was about to strike Owen; it fell dead at his feet with a quick move. Elijah joined Ian, and the four of them formed a defensive guard near the front of the hunters. This allowed the marksmen at the back to concentrate on their weapons.

The main force of the enemy came from the north, and some had broken through. Eloi saw a group of dead hunters, their bodies broken and rifles cast aside. She cringed but didn't stop; they'd had casualties in Tivaci, but she hadn't seen them. Bile rose in her throat, and she had to force herself to focus.

She saw Cillian struggle with two wolves. He whirled and kept them at bay, so she charged to his side and tackled one of the wolves to the ground. Mildly dazed, she saw it gave Cillian the advantage with the other, and he turned to finish the one she'd knocked down.

"Thanks, little wolf."

She snorted and shook her head. They fell into a similar rhythm to the one she had with Lachlan, and Cillian grinned at her when they took out a wolf together. The hunters fought ferociously, the shifters amongst them covering any gaps in the defense. Eloi paused to watch the final pair finish one last wolf. The hunters looked about in wonder at the shifters beside them, and Eloi couldn't hide her shock when she saw the warriors shift back and shake hands with the hunters; some even embraced.

"I can't believe my own eyes." Liam came to stand next to her and stared out at the group.

"We can't change the past; best to draw a line and look to the future," Eloi said to him.

"Very wise, little wolf." He put a tentative arm around her shoulders and pulled her into his side.

"Aw, Gramps, I didn't know you cared," she smirked at him. He looked at the ground.

"I need a drink," he grumbled, then he turned and left. Eloi watched him go, Lachlan moving to her side.

"The hybrids took out of the others. I don't think they expected our numbers; otherwise, they wouldn't have split themselves." He pulled her into a hug. "Let's get ready to leave; it'll take them time to realize they've failed. Then, we can take them by surprise."

"Finally," Eloi grinned. She turned quickly and slammed into a hard chest. She stumbled, and Daniel's strong arms caught her.

"Careful! God, you're like a whirlwind."

"I was—are you okay?" She blushed.

"Peachy, it was easy. They weren't expecting the numbers." He looked into her eyes, and Lachlan cleared his throat.

"Seriously, you two, do I need a bucket of cold water or something?" He stormed off.

"He's just grumpy because my mom has been gone too long. Want to come and get her with us?" she asked with a smile.

"Wouldn't miss it." Daniel leaned in toward her, and she closed her eyes.

"Glad to see you two are okay and have your priorities right! Don't mind me," Vivienne chuckled.

"Mom!" Daniel groaned.

"You going to introduce me, you know, officially?" Viv made quotation marks in the air with her fingers.

"Mom, Eloi, Eloi, Mom." Daniel gestured between them.

"Yes, son, we've actually already met." Viv laughed and walked away.

"She's a menace." He glared after her, raising his voice. She waved a hand over her shoulder.

"That she is. Hello, I'm Michael." The large hybrid held out his hand and engulfed Eloi's as she shook it.

"Hello—I can't thank you enough for risking everything to support us. I hope that we can return the favor." She smiled.

"I hope you never have to." Michael looked around curiously. "I heard a lot about Sumter from Jason, but I have to say. It certainly is something."

"It has changed a lot in the last few years, thanks to my mom and Lachlan. You'll always be welcome. Thank you for saving Jason and Lachlan. I don't know what I'd do without either of them. How can I ever repay you?" she asked.

"No need, keep doing what you're doing, bringing hunters and shifters together." He raised an eyebrow.

"I can sure try," she laughed.

Daniel squeezed her hand. "I should go and help with preparations. Sounds like Lachlan is raring to leave."

"He misses Mom, and so do I." Eloi sighed and squashed the guilt she suddenly felt. "I better get things ready too."

"See you soon." Daniel grinned and left.

19

"Now strike again," Solus told Aine. She tried the move once more and felt the smoothness in the maneuver. She punched his flat palm, and it felt less awkward than previous attempts. Arwen clapped near their house as she watched her husband and daughter train.

"Well done, Aine." Arwen smiled at her, and Aine grinned back.

"Great, let's try this again," Solus said.

"I'll be the best fighter here, Father." Aine grinned.

"I know you will, baby, but you have to keep at it. Practice, practice, practice." He gestured in front of her, and she took up her stance again. She tried the strike again, and Solus adjusted her technique.

"Now remember—" He stiffened, and Aine frowned. He gaped at something over her shoulder, and she turned to see what had made him stop.

Grandfather Conrad strode toward them; Aine shrunk away at his gaze. He looked livid, scowling at Solus and his daughter.

"Arwen, Solus, we have something to discuss. Now!" He gestured toward their house.

"Come on, Aine, we will have to call it a day here." Solus held out his hand, and she took it.

Arwen crouched down in their home's entranceway and put her hand on Aine's shoulder. "Aine, go and play in your room." She gave her daughter a nudge, and the girl obeyed.

Aine watched her parents talk to her grandfather through a crack in the door. She was very small, so they wouldn't see her. They argued, but it was worse than usual.

"Did you really think you could keep this from me?" Conrad growled.

"We knew you'd be mad; we can't change the past," Arwen said calmly.

"Why didn't you tell me this sooner?" Conrad's face was contorted in anger.

"We didn't know; I don't really understand how this changes anything." Solus stood in front of Arwen protectively. "You can't undo a child, Solus."

"Do you realize what this means? It changes everything!"

"No, because you won't tell us." Arwen stepped around Solus. "Father, if you won't enlighten us, then how are we supposed to know what we've done wrong?"

"Your child should never have been allowed to be born. She's too dangerous; her existence could destroy us."

"How can you say that? She's just a child, Father!" Arwen screamed, and Aine cringed. A tear leaked down her face, and she held back a sniffle.

Her grandfather turned to face Solus. "How long have you known?"

"My grandmother died recently. I found our ancestry when I was going through her things." Solus crossed his arms. "How was I supposed to know we had Xerxes and Torak in our bloodline? I thought we were Aoibhan; I didn't even realize we hadn't come from this area. We joined the pack a few generations back, and I

didn't know that."

"Arwen and I have a Tivaci ancestor. That means she's born of the four bloodlines! There are prophecies that doom us if she is allowed to live."

"No! Father, you can't be serious. You are talking about killing your granddaughter!" Arwen stood firm, and a growl vibrated through her. She moved toward Aine's bedroom. "You will not harm my daughter."

Conrad's eyes flicked toward Aine's bedroom door; they narrowed when he saw the crack, and Aine jolted when her eyes met her grandfather's. He lurched toward her bedroom door, and Arwen was thrown to the ground.

"Father, no!" she shrieked. Solus helped her up and growled when Conrad dragged Aine out of her bedroom.

Aine cried and sobbed as Conrad roughly yanked her into the room. Her grandfather knelt before her, looking into her eyes, and tears streamed down her face.

"I'm sorry, Grandfather," she sniffled. Conrad sighed as her lip trembled, and she tried to stand straight before him.

"I won't kill her, but we must do something." Her grandfather stroked her hair, and Aine stopped trembling. "She must never have children. This will be the end of our line, Arwen, and she must never remember what she is."

His face hardened as he placed both hands on the side of Aine's head. She felt a cold touch in her mind and screamed. Arwen lunged toward her, but Solus held her back.

"This will wipe our conversation from her memory. I'm also going to block the powers for the other three packs. I hope it's enough," Conrad explained as Aine struggled in his hands. "I'm sorry, sweetheart, I know it hurts."

Aine screamed again as the cold became painful, and she fell to her knees. The pressure on her head eased, and she looked up at her grandfather with a frown.

"Sleep, child." Aine fell against him, and Conrad lifted her up. He handed her to Arwen, and Aine felt Arwen squeeze her tight against her body. Conrad left, and she felt herself being carried to her room. Darkness enveloped her, but she could still hear her mother's voice.

"We will need to help her when she's older." Her mother paused and sighed. "I'll have to teach you how to wield the darkness if anything happens to me. She will need protecting."

OLIVIA'S HAND felt cold on Aine's forehead. The penetration of her grandfather's power gave her a headache as she pulled herself from the dream. The memory twisted her insides as she realized what she had overheard; she needed to talk to Eyolf when she returned. There was no way she could be of the four bloodlines—the royal bloodlines had been forbidden to mate. The chance of her having two was rare enough, let alone four. She thought about the bite and how she had pulled the poison back. A vague memory of the different powers of the bloodlines made her pause, but the thought disappeared as she tried to sit up.

"How long was I out?" she asked Olivia.

"Just a few hours." She smiled weakly. "Apparently, Rolan is turning the tunnels upside down trying to find you."

Aine grimaced. "I better get back to my cell. If he discovers me here, he will kill you." She glanced up at Taylor. "Both of you."

Olivia paled but set her jaw. "We could help you escape, and he won't know it was us. There are tunnels in the main cavern that lead out of the caves."

"Olivia!" Taylor gasped.

"No." Aine put a hand up. "I need to stay. I'm not leaving the shifters here for Rolan to take his anger out on. Lachlan will come, then we can all escape in the confusion."

"How do you know he will come? He's a hunter; maybe he's the one that betrayed you."

It saddened Aine that Olivia felt the need to ask that question. "He will." She reached out a hand to touch Olivia's arm. "We won't leave anyone behind, and you will be safe with my pack."

"What about the hunters?"

"They won't hurt you; the ones with my pack work well with us," Aine pleaded with Olivia to believe her. Taylor grumbled near the door.

"What about you? Still think you're on the right side?"

"I'll follow her. Where she goes, I go." Olivia looked up at him, her face slack. Aine nudged her and smiled.

"We could try and start sneaking some out." Olivia stood, her head tilted and her gaze relaxed as she thought. "The tunnels through the cavern—let's start moving people through. At least then they will be away from any fighting."

"If you think you can do it safely, but leave me here. If anything, I can always distract my father and Rolan." Aine stood slowly. "It's the least I can do after you looked after me."

"No! What will they do when they find you?" Olivia asked.

"Well, they've kept me alive so far. Take the shifters to Sumter. I know you have reservations, but they will keep you safe." Aine watched Taylor. "Look after her."

"Rolan just tried to kill you. Look at your shoulder!" Olivia gestured to her, and Aine pulled back the shirt she had on. Olivia must have redressed her. The wound was gone, and Olivia gasped.

"See, I'll be fine." Aine held out her hand to take Olivia's and squeezed it gently. "Get as many out as you can. It'll take time, but hopefully, they will be distracted looking for me, and by the time anyone notices, my pack will be here to support you."

"I can take care of the guards. Most aren't happy, and it won't be hard to persuade them to help us." Taylor shrugged. "Take care, lady." He saluted her and left. Olivia gaped at his back.

"Well, he wasn't too hard to bring to our side." Aine nudged Olivia, who grinned at her.

"Take care; I'll do my best to get everyone out." Olivia squeezed Aine's hand back as she left.

Aine watched Olivia go and sent positive thoughts out to the group of shifters she would lead out. She hoped they wouldn't resist leaving. She tried to reach Lachlan, but a dull throb behind her eyes warned her against it. Her body still ached from the attack in the cavern. She slowly moved along the tunnel and used the wall to support herself, stumbling several times.

She wandered aimlessly through the tunnels, hoping to create a trail away from the other shifters. She came to a dead-end just as she heard heavy footsteps behind her. She sighed in exasperation and turned to see her father approach her, his hands held out in front of him. She relaxed slightly. Solus was a better option than Rolan.

"Are you okay?" His brow furrowed as he scanned her.

"Fine," she snapped.

Aine stepped to walk around him and froze as he took her arm.

"Let's get you back to my rooms; you're very pale." Solus gently pulled her down the tunnel. She tried to resist but gave in when the walls started to spin.

"What, you're not throwing me back in the jail cell? I mean, it was so comfortable," she muttered.

"Don't be smart with me, young lady," he snarled and dragged her further. He slowed when she fell and helped her up. "I'm sorry, it's my fault you're so weak. I didn't protect you very well."

He helped Aine the last few steps into his rooms and gently lowered her onto the couch. He took a step back and rubbed his arms. She'd never seen him look so uncertain.

Once she was laid on the couch, she sighed. "Where is Rolan? Terrorizing the other shifters by any chance?"

"On his way here, we have things to discuss." Solus's lips thinned, and he tilted his head. She flinched when he reached out to touch her shoulder; as he touched her skin, she felt energy pour into her. She gasped, feeling the darkness within him flow with it. She pushed some of her own power back in him and searched. She pulled the last dregs of the infection within him, and the last of the darkness drained away.

Solus gasped. "What just happened?" He shook his head, and when he opened his eyes, she stared into them. They looked clear, with no sign of the mania. She slumped back on the couch.

"I think your head finally cleared." She gave him a small smile.

He sat heavily on the other sofa and put his head in his hands. "It's like I was living in a fog." He shook his head and lifted a hand to stroke her hair. "I lost so much time." Silence fell between them.

"Why did you join the Faction?" Aine eventually spoke. She frowned at him as he continued to stroke her hair.

"I was trying to create an army for you. You will need protection," he answered.

"That doesn't really make sense. Why attack us if you were trying to protect me?" she grumbled.

"I needed to swell our numbers, and Rolan made it sound like a good idea to take shifters from your pack." Solus stopped and put his head in his hands. He heaved a heavy breath and didn't continue. Aine shifted into a sitting position and watched him.

"I got so lost." Solus shook his head and looked up at her hopelessly.

Aine sighed. "Maybe we can change that; you're here now."

Solus shook his head slightly and stared at her. "You're right, together we can forge a new pack. With us leading the Aoibhan and Rolan by your side, we will be unstoppable."

Aine's eyes widened. She shifted and opened her mouth to speak.

"How did you survive that bite?" Rolan marched into the room and froze when he saw Aine. She glared at him.

"I'm sorry, Father, but I can hardly work with someone who has tried to kill me more than once." She stared at Rolan.

"But you are married! Surely you can work this out together. Didn't you try to kill him too? You have a daughter together; don't you want her to be happy?" Solus glanced between them.

"I didn't try to kill him. He tried to kidnap Eloi, and Lachlan protected her." Aine crossed her arms and tried to sit up.

"I'd rather have no wife than have to bow to her. She isn't fit to lead. She's violated our shifter laws and tainted herself." Rolan looked disgusted.

"And you do not have the power to stop me." Aine stood

up, fists clenched, and Rolan took a step toward her. Solus stepped between them.

"Stop this nonsense. We will forge a new pack, one that will be stronger for the war to come."

"What war?" Aine threw her hands in the air. "There is no war, just the one you've created."

Rolan sneered. "She is not fit to lead. She won't fight the hunters, and she's got her human filth." His eyes hardened. "I just want Eloi back. She is my daughter, too, and I have the right to raise her. You've had her three years now—it's my turn."

Aine gritted her teeth. She felt her eyes change, and a growl escaped her. "If you go near her, I will rip your head off with my bare hands."

"Aine and Eloi are of the Royal bloodline, Rolan. You wouldn't be able to help her with her power the way Aine can. You need to remember your place; I'm your master here." Solus spoke firmly and turned to face Aine.

Rolan bristled and glared at Solus's back. "You are past your usefulness, old man."

Solus turned to face Rolan, and his eyes widened when Rolan took a step forward. Aine heard a sickening squelch, and her hand flew to her mouth. She didn't have much time to react as Rolan spun toward her, but she managed to dodge the slice from the dagger in his hand. From the corner of her eye, she saw Solus slump to the ground, a hand held to his chest and blood gushing through his fingers.

She threw all her strength into her power and thrust her hands toward Rolan; he was flung across the room. With a glare, he scrambled to his feet, fists clenched at his sides and growling. Aine stared back but didn't move toward him.

Rolan's eyes flickered to the ground behind her, and he smirked before turning his back and fleeing.

Aine threw herself at her father's prone figure and held a hand against the wound on his chest.

"You'll be okay; it's going to be fine." Aine pressed harder, but the blood pumped through her fingers faster.

"The dagger..." Solus coughed, and blood spattered along his chin. "It drains power; he pulled my power into it. It's his now, just like when your mother died, except then, she pushed the power into me... He has her power now, Aine."

"Don't speak, I'll get help and—"

"It's too late." He lifted a hand to touch her face. "You are a marvel; Rolan will never beat you." His hand dropped back to the ground, and she watched the life drain from his eyes.

"Father." A sob escaped her, and a tear leaked from her eye. She looked up at his face, his eyes glazed and lifeless.

"Father," she whispered and dropped her head. Her soul ached at the idea that he could have been saved.

~

IT HAD TAKEN time for the pack to prepare to leave after the attack on Sumter. Lachlan counted nearly a hundred dark wolves. He didn't want to risk another attack, though he doubted the Faction had any attackers left. Nyko and Jason would stay with Tania and half the warriors to clear up the damage and the bodies. Jason tried to insist they needed him, but even he had to admit he was still weak. Lachlan wondered who they had been before they were brainwashed.

The Aoibhan, hunters, and hybrids trekked to the caves

where they thought the Faction resided. Eloi came to stand next to Lachlan and watched the entrance.

"It seems so quiet." She closed her eyes and her brow puckered. "I don't sense many shifters." She opened her eyes and looked to her left.

"What is it?" Lachlan followed her gaze.

"I'm not sure. Elijah and Ian, come with me." She hesitated. "Eric, do you know the area or the rough layout of the caves?"

Eric shook his head. "I never left them without the bag over my head, but I have an idea of what is where in the cave system." He stepped forward, eager to help.

Eloi put her hand on Lachlan's shoulder. "I need to check something out; keep an eye on the entrance." He nodded and looked pointedly at his father. Liam came to join him.

"Eloi needs to check something out." Lachlan shook his head at Liam's quizzical look. "Can you see any other entrances? You've had experience with caves and shifters."

Liam rubbed his jaw and looked out over the cave system. "There's usually the main entrance, easy to defend and obvious. But we used to stake out a system like this for months and find where the hidden entrances were. We don't have time for that."

"So full frontal assault, all guns blazing?" Lachlan sighed and turned to look at their allies. "We don't have the numbers for that."

"Let's watch for now. It might be better to wait until dark and sneak in through the main entrance under the cover of night."

"I hate waiting." Girvan shifted behind Liam and groaned. Cillian bumped his shoulder with his, and Girvan scowled at him.

"Let's see what Eloi comes back with and keep an eye out for now." Lachlan settled in for a long wait, and Girvan groaned again.

20

Eloi crept through the trees, impressed by Ian's stealth as he carefully picked a path through the uneven ground behind her. Eric didn't have the same skill, and she flinched at every sound he made.

She loved the stealth training as she grew up; banned from using her mental abilities, it was a great challenge to hide from the warriors. She reached out before her to feel the small group of shifters. There weren't many, but they appeared to have settled outside the cave system. A large shifter stiffened at her mental touch, and she pulled back. She signed to Ian to flank around to the side and tilted her head to Elijah.

Let's approach with caution. They won't trust a hunter, but maybe two shifters... She let the thought trail off, and Elijah nodded; Eric followed them.

Eloi approached the group with caution and held her hands out in what she hoped was a non-threatening way. The large shifter turned to face her and took a defensive stance; he pushed a petite woman behind his back.

"Eric?"

"Olivia?" The large shifter frowned at Eric as he took a step forward, and Eric stopped. He looked at the woman Eloi presumed was Olivia. "What's going on?"

"We've had to leave. Rolan is insane, and the dark wolves...." Olivia hiccupped a sob. "We were so wrong."

The large shifter pulled her to his side and tried to soothe her. He looked up at Eric.

"Why are you here?" the muscular man growled, his arm tightening around Olivia.

"The Aoibhan have come for their Pack Leader." He gestured at Eloi, who stepped forward.

"I am Eloi. The prisoner taken is my mother."

Olivia gasped. "Aine told me about you."

"Is she safe?"

Olivia shook her head. "She was bitten. I tried to help her heal, but she was very sick. She told me to start getting the shifters out. Taylor here and some of the other guards helped, but there's still some inside. We couldn't find everyone."

"We can help. How did you get out?"

"A small tunnel that leads to the main cavern."

Eloi nodded and looked at Elijah. "Tell Lachlan and take Ian with you." The group of shifters before her huddled and exclaimed in fear when Ian stepped from the trees. There were murmurs of "hunter" among them.

"Ian, accompany Elijah back. We will follow shortly." Eloi spoke firmly and slightly louder than necessary. Ian and Elijah nodded before they quickly left.

"Did you see that?"

"She was commanding a hunter!"

"What's happening?"

The whispers of the group came to her, and she ignored them. To Taylor, she said, "What do you need? We have a mixture of hunters, shifters, and hybrids all here to help."

"Hybrids?" Taylor frowned at her, Olivia still clutched to his side.

"It's a long story." Eloi looked at the group of shifters; there were about fifteen of them. "Are any of you injured?" There was no reply, so she looked to Olivia.

"We are all fine, just confused and fed up, I think." Eloi nodded at her and looked back in the direction she had sent Ian and Elijah. "Hopefully, we can get you out of here and settled somewhere safe soon," she promised. Olivia peeled herself away from Taylor and approached Eloi.

"Are the hunters really safe?"

"The ones with us have been working with us a while. We've recently discovered a good history between hunters and shifters." Eloi sighed. "Another long story, I'm afraid."

Olivia nodded, distracted. "Do you think you can defeat Solus and Rolan?"

"It depends on how many dark wolves they have left. The recent attack on Sumter, we killed over a hundred." Olivia stared at her, pale and wide-eyed.

"That's all I saw in the cavern we found. Aine tried to tell me, and I wouldn't listen. Then she was bitten. I felt so helpless, and she made me leave her." Olivia burst into tears, and Eloi shifted. Taylor was at Olivia's side in an instant, but Eloi moved away toward Eric.

"What has been going on here?" She looked at him, and he shrugged.

"Everyone seemed happy when I left—sounds like your mom has done some stirring up. She doesn't wait around, does she?"

Eloi smiled. "No, she doesn't. How is she?"

"She's weak. She refused to eat in case they poisoned

her." Olivia glanced at Eric, who looked guilty. "And then Rolan used one of the dark wolves to attack her. I think he thought she'd turn, but she healed. I've never seen anything like it."

Eloi fidgeted. "It's not the first time Rolan has tried to kill her. Let's hope she can last a little longer." She looked back over her shoulder impatiently and sighed with relief when she saw Lachlan approach with Ian.

"You said there's a small tunnel?" Lachlan spoke to Eloi, but his eyes darted over the group. They shriveled back from his gaze.

Eloi nodded to Olivia and nudged her gently. The petite woman stared up at Lachlan, and the blood drained from her face. "I…" She looked to Taylor.

"I can show you; there are still some inside we need to find. How many will you take with you?"

"As many as we can sneak in." He turned back to Ian. "Tell Michael and Liam—five each, that should be enough, and the rest can approach via the main entrance. Hopefully, that will be enough of a distraction." He turned to Eloi, and she nodded.

"I select the five shifters." Eloi closed her eyes and summoned Elijah and four others. She wished Nyko was there.

The group gathered, and the shifter refugees watched them curiously. Lachlan had given instructions on how to reach Sumter, and Eloi had warned Nyko they were coming. She watched them retreat then stepped toward the hidden tunnel. She exhaled a deep breath and rolled her neck.

Water dripped from the tunnel and trickled down the walls; the sound grated on Eloi's nerves as she listened ahead. Daniel stalked beside her, and they edged forward slowly. Once inside, they split into pairs and searched for

Aine, with Daniel firmly partnered with her. When the tunnel widened into the cavern, Eloi looked around at the deserted area. She scanned each space and saw that they were set up for different skills. There were no shifters here, and the quiet put her on edge. She turned to nod at Lachlan and picked a tunnel, Daniel shadowing her.

Daniel insisted on being the first to enter each cave, and they explored what appeared to be living quarters for the refugees. Olivia had left Aine here, and they eventually found the cave with Aine's scent.

"She was here." Eloi brushed her fingertips over the cave entrance and followed the scent further down the tunnel.

"This place is like a maze. Do you think we will be able to find a way out?" Daniel stayed close behind her and kept his voice quiet.

Aine's scent stopped at a dead end, and Eloi frowned. "There's another scent here, male, powerful. They must have backtracked." She turned to look at the direction they'd come from.

"Think we missed a turn-off?" Daniel followed her gaze.

"We must have." Eloi slowly trailed back and looked each way. Aine's scent had led them to a widened area, and the first turn had led to the dead-end. She searched the others and found one with both the male scent and her mom's. "This way."

Eloi reached back and touched Daniel's hand; her face heated when he took hold of it and wouldn't let her go. They walked on, the eerie silence doing little to mask their presence.

"Something doesn't feel right." Eloi squeezed Daniel's hand, and they continued down the tunnel. It looped back around to the main cavern. None of their teams were in sight. Eloi looked around and tried to track her mom's scent, but there were too many in this area to pick out a single smell. Eloi looked around and threw up her free hand.

"Aargh, now what?"

"Now what, indeed." Rolan stepped from the shadows not far from the tunnel they'd entered through. Eloi's heart leaped to her mouth, and she froze; Daniel winced when she gripped his hand harder. "I thought that I would have to come and steal you away, but here you are. You came to me, my daughter."

"You are not my father! You gave up that right when you tried to kill my mother!" Eloi spat at him.

"She hid you from me, Eloi. Believe me, if I'd known your potential, you could have become so much more by now." Rolan grinned at her, causing Eloi to grimace.

"Now, who is this you're with?" Rolan sniffed the air and glared at Daniel. The boy stood up straight and held Rolan's eyes. "He looks like a hunter but smells like a shifter. Interesting."

Daniel growled and shifted. His posture remained upright, but he became more muscular, and his head became a full wolf. The whole effect should have been disturbing, but Eloi stared at him with wide eyes. She tried to shift herself but cried out in dismay when a metal cuff clinked around her wrist. She struck out at the shifter who had snuck up behind her and snarled when Rolan smirked at her. Daniel released a deep growl, almost a roar. Rolan shifted his hands and grinned at him.

"Careful! He—" Eloi yelled as Daniel charged at Rolan. On impact, dark smoke billowed from them, and Eloi lost sight of them. She spun at a heavy footstep behind her. A group of shifters approached from the corridor behind her, and she turned to face them. Even without the ability to shift, she had trained extensively with Lachlan and smiled at the challenge before her.

The leader of the group charged, and she spun, blocking his strike. A swift kick pushed him into a wall, his head snapping back and a loud crack echoing in the tunnel. The three remaining guards held back, shifting uneasily. Eloi stared at them and dared them to move. A thud behind her caused her to spin; she sensed movement from the guards and shifted her center of gravity. Gracefully, she turned and disabled the first guard, directing his body toward the other unconscious shifter.

The last two guards charged at her. She pivoted and caught one by the arm. She used her weight to slingshot him into the other guard. They fell in a tangle of limbs and struggled to get to their feet; one took a last look at her and fled. The other quickly followed. Eloi swiftly turned to where she'd last seen Daniel and Rolan. A crash further into the cavern caught her attention, and she ran forward. She gripped the cuff on her hand and yanked as she ran, but it wouldn't budge.

"Daniel!" she shrieked and squinted into the darkness before her. She reached out and tried to touch it, but pain shot through her as she reached for her power. The cuff felt like a hot iron, and she blanched as her skin felt like it blistered under it. She slowly walked toward the sound of the fight. Snarls and howls pierced the air. Daniel fell at her feet, and his chest heaved as he struggled to catch his breath.

"What the hell is he?" Daniel leaned on her, and Eloi staggered under his weight.

"We need to get out of here!" Eloi tried to pull him toward the tunnel they had used to enter. She turned to make sure he followed and cried out. Rolan leaped forward with a knife in his hand. Daniel grabbed her, his arms wrapped around her body, and he pushed her against the wall. She grunted as the wall hit her back, and he trembled against her.

"Daniel," she whispered. "Daniel!"

His eyes glossed over, and he slumped to the floor before her. Rolan's knife protruded from his back.

"Daniel!" Her voice was thick. She sighed when she saw his shoulders move with each breath. She crouched beside him and examined the knife; from the position, it didn't look like it had hit anything vital. She looked him over and found another knife strapped to his thigh.

"Come, Eloi, we have places to be." Rolan held his hand out toward her.

Eloi slowly reached for the knife at Daniel's thigh.

"Eloi!" Rolan barked impatiently.

She screamed in rage when she touched the knife and yanked it free. Then, she lunged at Rolan and sliced at his outstretched hand. He flinched back, batting away her second attack.

"Don't be stupid; I'm your father! It's my right to raise you!" Rolan dodged again.

She ignored him and focused on his moves, each twitch or step he took, and how he maneuvered. A quick pivot, and she was past his guard; she elbowed him, and he staggered back, winded. He then baited her, and, in her anger, she didn't notice her mistake. She raised the knife to plunge it into his chest, and with a quick sidestep, he was behind her. A cold hand gripped the back of her neck, and the feel of ice crept through her whole body. Every muscle and joint locked up, and she couldn't move. The knife clattered to the floor; she willed every part of herself, but the feel of ice slithered through her inch by inch.

"That's better. Now you'll come along with me. We have

a lot to catch up on."

Eloi couldn't stop herself as her body rose of its own accord and followed Rolan. A tear silently fell as she fought internally. His hand never left the back of her neck, and she couldn't even turn to look back at Daniel. Pain lanced through her when she tried to reach out mentally to her pack members. Rolan led her into a dark tunnel, and she couldn't see ahead of her.

~

AINE SAT beside her father's body. She was shocked no guards had come to discover him yet. She mentally prepared herself to get to her feet and traipse through the tunnels, hoping enough time had passed for the others to escape. Her heart ached with the need to get to Lachlan; his absence left a hole within her. She groaned as she stood and held her hand to her shoulder, the bite still aching. Her feet dragged along the floor and scraped the rock as she started toward the tunnel.

Her body felt like a dead weight, and it was an effort to take each step. A noise ahead in the tunnel made her stomach lurch, but heat infused her body pleasantly. A small smile appeared on her face, and she eagerly leaned forward to get to the tunnel faster.

"Lachlan!" She laughed as his face appeared around a bend ahead of her. He charged toward her and lifted her into his arms. His smell filled her nose, and she breathed out a sigh. As they touched, their minds connected, and energy poured into her. She put a hand to his chest, over the rifle shot, and held back a sob. "It is so good to see you."

"And you! Is Rolan here?"

"No, he left after—" Aine hesitated. "My father is dead. I

don't know how, but I managed to clear some of the madness from him. It took time, then Rolan killed him."

"Is that why you wanted more time here? To try and cure him?" Lachlan asked, incredulous.

Aine nodded and leaned into him. "Did the others make it out? Olivia?"

"Yes, Eloi found them, and we've sent them to Sumter. They will be safe there, though they're a little skittish."

"They did believe we were the bad guys, so it's hard to blame them." Aine looked behind Lachlan, and her eyes met Liam's. She frowned.

"Your incredible daughter has managed to do in a week, what we couldn't do in years," he whispered in her ear. "Let's get out of here. Eloi and the others will meet us in the cavern."

"What about Rolan?" Aine looked up at him.

"Knowing him, he ran off—it's what he does best." Lachlan slid an arm around her waist and helped her down the tunnel. It took time to return to the large cavern, and sweat dripped down Aine's back by the time they made it there. She stopped short at the smell of blood. Her head swept back and forth at the broken equipment and chairs before her. Rolan's dagger, the one she had seen him use to remove the power from Solus, lay near a tunnel entrance, and a trail of blood led further down.

Lachlan frowned, handing Aine over to Liam. "Stay here."

Aine lurched after him. "Eloi was supposed to be here! I'm coming." She walked toward the blood, a bit steadier on her feet, and looked down. She sniffed. "It's male." She let out a relieved breath and picked up the dagger, feeling it pull on the dark magic within her. She would need to keep it safe and show it to Eyolf.

Lachlan continued down the tunnel, and she watched him approach a still form; her eyes fell on a male she didn't recognize. Blood slowly seeped out of the wound at his back, though it looked to have healed some.

"Daniel!" Lachlan exclaimed and lunged toward him. Aine watched him as he shook the figure, but he didn't stir.

Aine looked around the area. "Where are the others? Was Eloi with him?" She gestured to the unconscious man Lachlan shook.

"I believe they were paired up," Liam spoke behind her; Aine turned to face him and looked down the corridor as it disappeared into pitch black.

"Daniel?" Michael's voice boomed in the tunnel as he arrived, and he looked down on his pack member. He crouched and put a hand over his back; the blood slowed, then stopped, and the skin knitted together, the wound completely healed. Michael sighed and shook him. "Wake up, buddy," he said shakily, his voice tinged with worry.

Daniel looked up groggily. "What happened?"

"We need you to tell us that," Michael said gently.

"Where's Eloi? She was with you?" Aine helped him up frantically. Daniel rubbed the back of his head, and his eyes flashed.

"I'm sorry, I tried...I...." He looked at the ground, and his shoulders shook.

"Daniel, please," Aine begged him.

"Rolan took her. She couldn't shift. He put a cuff on her."

Blinding pain flashed through Aine, and she felt her blood heat. Her whole body shook and pressure built within her.

"No." The word slipped past her lips.

"Aine, we will get her back." Lachlan put both hands on her shoulders, and she shrugged him off.

"Don't touch me!" Aine shrieked. She stumbled back into the cavern and looked around wildly. The pressure built inside her, pain shredding her heart, and her blood felt like it boiled. Her anger raged through her like a storm; her hands shook, and her vision darkened. She fell to her knees and held her hands to her head.

"Aine—" Lachlan's voice sounded far away.

"NOOOOOOOO...." The word transformed into a scream, and the pressure exploded out around her. The cavern walls shook and the air concussed. The shifters around her cried out, and she felt her power surge once more inside her. A sudden calm took over her, and her vision darkened.

"Her eyes are completely black!" someone in front of her whispered.

"What was that?" A hunter pushed himself up off the ground. Lachlan came into view, and she stared at him blankly.

"Aine, I promise you, with everything that I am and everything we have. I will do everything in my power to find her." His voice cracked. "Come back to me."

Aine continued to stare blankly in front of her. She looked through him and felt the power pulse with her heart.

"Aine, come back." Lachlan shook her slightly, but she didn't respond. He slowly bent and touched his lips to hers. The heat in her surged through that point of contact, slowly at first and then with a rush. She kissed him back and felt a balance form between them. His hands felt hot on her shoulders, and she looked him in the eyes. His blue gaze pierced her.

"She is strong. We will get her back." He swallowed, his voice thick. She nodded and walked toward the exit of the cavern silently.

21

A search of the area brought no hope; there was no trace of how Rolan had left the caves. His trail led to a dead-end. A pile of rubble blocked the tunnel, and no one could find a way through. The shifters searched the surrounding area with no luck. As the sky darkened, Lachlan looked at his exhausted pack, the weary hunters, and Daniel's broken silhouette. Aine hadn't said a word since they'd exited the caves.

"We need to head back." Lachlan tried to catch Aine's eye. "We are losing the light, and we need to rest. We can come back with more teams tomorrow and search the surrounding areas. Then, we can all take a different direction." Aine didn't reply.

"We might lose the trail." Liam gripped his son's shoulder.

"We can't risk trampling something in the dark." Lachlan gestured to the ground.

Liam nodded. "I'll take Cillian and Girvan; we will each pick a direction and pray for a bit of luck. We are used to tracking twenty-four seven; it's what we've trained for."

"Thank you." Lachlan gripped his father's arm. "I appreciate it."

"You would do the same for me, and I need to hear that little wolf call me 'Gramps' again." Liam nodded.

Lachlan smiled weakly. "Stay safe and keep in touch. Don't approach. If Rolan can take down a hybrid...." He trailed off.

Liam smirked. "He was only a baby hybrid."

"Don't let Daniel hear you say that." Lachlan pulled his father in for a hug.

"Stay safe," Liam said. "Join us when you can."

Lachlan approached Aine; she stared into the caves and didn't move. "We need to return to the pack. You're drained and...."

"I know, I heard." She stood slowly and headed over to the shifters that prepared to leave. Lachlan followed her and scanned the area. Everyone was ready to go.

"Let's move. I bet we will all appreciate being home," he called to them. The atmosphere was tense; it should have been a triumph, but Eloi's disappearance had affected everyone. Lachlan followed the shifters with Aine and glanced at her to see how she was doing.

"Stop gawking at me, Lachlan," she said impatiently.

"I haven't seen you for days, Aine. Can you blame me? You're beautiful." He smiled sadly. "I'm sorry I didn't protect Eloi. I will look for her. I don't expect you to forgive me—"

"There's nothing to forgive." She put her arm through his.

"It's just been a long...however long I was there." She sighed. "I want to be home with my baby, but she's gone."

They fell silent as they walked. The journey dragged out and the group was subdued on the way back. It was fully dark by the time they entered Sumter. Eyolf and Nyko were there to meet them, each frowning as they took in Aine's condition; slumped against Lachlan, barely awake.

"Take her to Tania." Lachlan gave her a gentle push and ran his hands through his hair as Nyko supported her. He caught up to them in the medical building once he'd made sure the refugees were settled and the shifters were sent home. Most of the hybrids left for their own settlement, though Daniel and a few others refused to leave. Daniel followed Lachlan until they met up with Eyolf.

"Lachlan, I'm so—" Daniel started.

Lachlan put up his hand. "Don't say 'sorry,' you did your best to protect her. I know how you feel about her, and I don't believe you would have just let Rolan take her without a fight." Daniel followed him through the door of the medical building.

"Is it true? Rolan took Eloi?" The old shifter's eyes begged Lachlan to deny it.

"I'm sorry, Eyolf. I should have been with her." Echoes of old guilt pulsed through Lachlan, and he collapsed into a chair as he watched Tania fuss over Aine.

"Tania gave her a sedative; she will be out until the morning. Probably for the best." Eyolf shook his head, and his shoulders slumped. "I tried to tell Aine about what we've discovered about the four bloodlines, but she's...not herself." Eyolf looked unsure, and Lachlan nodded. Daniel crept to the edge of the room and sat on a chair by himself.

"Daniel?" Lachlan asked gently. "We need to know exactly what happened."

Daniel nodded and told them about the fight with Rolan. "I tried to protect her, but Rolan looked half-mad when he charged us." He wiped his eyes and sniffed. "I'm so sorry."

"It can't be changed now. I've trained Eloi for years. She's not helpless."

"The cuff, it was the same as the ones we destroyed in the Tivaci settlement." Daniel shook his head. "She couldn't shift—he took it away from her. Can he control her if she's still wearing it?"

Lachlan swallowed. "I don't know. You did your best; Aine knows that. But it'll take time. Hopefully, my family can find a trail, and we will have her back soon. It isn't hopeless." Daniel nodded meekly but didn't reply.

"Lachlan, I need to talk to you," Tania softly spoke. Lachlan stood and walked over to stand beside Aine's bed. "I think you should stay with her; proximity to you will help her heal physically. It's like when she tried to heal Gary. She's completely drained."

"Thank you, I'll stay with her." Lachlan settled beside her bed. Eyolf dragged his chair over, but Daniel remained where he was with his head in his hands. Nyko came to stand next to Tania, and he led her away.

"You need to rest, too." He took her hand, and Lachlan heard her mumble something about test results as she left the building. When he was left alone with Eyolf, he cleared his throat.

"Something weird happened in the cave when she realized Eloi had been taken. Aine released a massive amount of power, more than I've ever felt from her before. Then, her eyes went completely black."

"Black?"

"I couldn't bring her back. It's like she wasn't there. I saw a stranger stare back at me."

Eyolf rubbed his chin. "I've heard of such a thing. A way for her to expel her grief." His eyes flashed up to Lachlan's. "Did you promise her anything?"

"Yes, that we would find Eloi." Lachlan frowned. "She came back after that."

"And you were touching her at the time?"

"Yes." Lachlan elongated the word and scowled at Eyolf.

"She transferred power into you and then returned to normal?" Eyolf nodded thoughtfully when Lachlan nodded. "I see."

"Don't give me that, old man." Lachlan gritted his teeth. "What does that mean?"

"Time will tell." Eyolf shrugged, but Lachlan noticed the glimmer in his eye. He looked back at his mate and let it drop. Eyolf rose as if he sensed his melancholy; he left without a word, and Lachlan lowered his head to the bed.

"I've spent too much time by your bedside recently, Aine," he grumbled and sighed. "I promise we will find her."

He woke when the light shone through the window onto his face, the delicious heat a contrast to his dark mood. It was quiet in the room. Tania hadn't returned yet, and Daniel had disappeared. Lachlan shifted to find Aine's eyes; she watched him carefully and lifted a hand to brush his hair.

"You need a haircut; you're starting to look wild."

"Like a fierce beast." His laugh was halfhearted. Aine let out a deep breath and shuddered.

"We will find her," Lachlan said roughly. He cleared his throat.

"We have to." Aine was quiet. She stared at the ceiling, and Lachlan took her hand. She squeezed it, and Lachlan blew out a breath. He jumped when the building door opened, and Tania approached them.

"Oh good, you're awake. How do you feel?"

"Pretty lousy."

Tania's eyes shone sympathetically. "Well, I need to give

you some medication. Vitamins and such." She shifted uncomfortably.

"Okaaaay." Aine drew out the word.

"Erm, well..." Tania hesitated.

"What's wrong?" Aine asked sharply.

"Nothing is wrong as such, just I have to tell you...well, you're pregnant."

"What?" Aine jerked, and Lachlan fell off his chair.

"You have been avoiding me." Eyolf caught up to Aine, and she huffed at him.

"Yes."

"Powers still haven't returned?"

"Not one bit." Aine turned from him to head home; she didn't want to talk to him about this.

"It's been a month, and I've been doing some research. I think it's the pregnancy, a way to protect your unborn child."

"Honestly, with what this baby had been through, I'm surprised it survived." Aine's hand unconsciously touched her stomach. She was three months along now, and she smiled weakly at the bittersweet news. With the attacks and being taken by her father, she hadn't exactly kept track of her cycle. She closed her eyes and thought of Eloi, trying in vain to reach her again. She hadn't been able to connect with anyone; it reminded her of when she met Lachlan. The trick of the mind when she'd forgotten something important but couldn't remember what.

"It'll come back, Aine, with time. Power like that doesn't just vanish." He reached out to touch her, and she stepped back.

"To be honest, it might be for the best it stays gone after what we discovered."

"You mean the four bloodlines, but we still don't know what that means. We need to find the other royal packs—"

"Yes, you keep saying." Aine focused on her door and cringed at the empty room she would return to. She put a hand to her chest, a hollowness causing it to ache. "I need to go home before the meeting. Have you just been researching my power, or did you look at the dagger I brought you? The one Rolan used to take the dark power."

"I have done some research," he grumbled, "but I've had other priorities."

Aine sighed. "Please look into it; it might be the only way to remove the power from Rolan. He's got my mother's power and his own; he might be too strong even for me now. I'll see you in the meeting."

Aine entered her house, her tread soft as she pushed Eloi's door open. She tried to be strong when she was with her pack, but it was exhausting. She curled up on Eloi's bed and pulled the pillow close; she hugged it to her chest and lay still until Lachlan shook her awake.

"They're here."

She nodded. "Good, I'll be there in five." She quickly went to that bathroom and splashed water on her face. The meeting room crowded when she got there; it immediately fell silent as she entered. She tried to soften her voice. "Report."

Cillian stepped forward. "We traced them north from the caves. Liam got lucky and kept on their tail but lost them a few days ago. They checked into a motel and then disappeared in the night. He nearly had them."

Aine nodded slowly, her fist shaking behind her back. She looked at Michael.

"Daniel thinks he's got a bead on the Xerxes on the east coast—he's using buses to get there. He will keep us updated. No news on the location of any of the Torak."

Aine nodded, looking at Elijah. "Training?"

"Shifters and hunters are working well together. The natural synchronicity seems to work with everyone but some pairs bond better than others. Almost like a mating of skills. It's been interesting to investigate."

"Good. I don't know what Rolan is planning, but he's always been good at charming the desperate into following him." She looked across at Olivia, who quickly glanced down.

"Tania?"

"The medical information we've got from the Tivaci has been invaluable. We don't have their innate skill, but we've improved our knowledge by an incredible amount in a short time."

"Have they reconsidered the offer to join us? As natural fighters, we can protect them."

"Rosa is reluctant; she thinks it's disastrous to mix bloodlines...." She trailed off and looked at Aine apologetically. "She's not been any more forthcoming about the prophecy."

"Probably means she's told us all she knows."

They continued to discuss various topics, but even Aine started to get bored as some arguments circled around several times. Lachlan eventually called an end to the meeting and put his arm around her. He kissed the side of her head and leaned down to whisper in her ear.

"Eyolf keeps grilling me about powers he thinks I might have after what you did in the cave."

She frowned. "And?"

"Nothing to report." Lachlan laughed when Shauna shoved into him.

"How's it going?" She put her hand on Aine's stomach, and Aine growled. "Okay, okay, jeez."

"Don't touch. Why did you tell everyone, Lachlan? I hate the attention."

"Couldn't keep his excitement contained!" Shauna said. "I never thought you'd be a dad."

Lachlan couldn't stop his grin, and he pinned Aine to his side tighter; she let herself smile back at him. But her face relaxed, and when she closed her eyes, her thoughts were with Eloi.

"Aine, Lachlan," Eyolf shouted behind them.

"Quick." Aine picked up speed. "Maybe we can pretend we didn't hear him."

"Even without your powers, you still have shifter hearing, Aine. He's never going to believe that."

They made it home as Eyolf caught up to them. "May I?" He gestured toward their front door.

Aine sighed. "Of course."

Eyolf sat at the table in the kitchen and waved his hands at the chairs, Aine rolling her eyes before sitting down. Lachlan joined her, and they waited for Eyolf to speak. The old shifter looked between them, practically bouncing in his chair.

"I figured it out."

"Figured what out?" Aine huffed.

"You transferred your power to Lachlan or at least some of it. It's instinctual during a time of grief. It enables Lachlan to keep the promise he's made you."

Lachlan shifted uncomfortably under Eyolf's gaze. "What are you talking about?"

"Well, let me see if I'm right. Give me your hand."

Lachlan reached forward and put his hand in Eyolf's. He noticed the old shifter wore gloves.

"Wait!" Aine's warning came too late. Eyolf placed the medallion in Lachlan's hand, and it felt like the metal was on fire. Lachlan flinched back, but Eyolf held him firm; the sensation wasn't painful and happened quickly. A delicious heat coursed through him, and he closed his eyes. His body felt warm, and when he opened them, Eyolf grinned at him.

"As I thought."

"What just happened?"

"I used the medallion to activate the power Aine gave you."

"How come he's not unconscious? I was out for two days." Aine crossed her arms. "That's not fair."

"He's not a full shifter." He paused. "Now, you'll have to teach him how to control it so that he can use it."

"Did you really just give me powers without my consent?" Lachlan gritted his teeth. Eyolf wouldn't meet his eye.

"I did it for the good of the pack. You will need every advantage if we are to get Eloi back and keep everyone safe." He put the medallion in his pocket. "I'm uneasy about the prophecy. Both of you have the four bloodlines, and further research suggests that the prophecy has an outcome where we live in harmony or shifters are destroyed entirely."

"You still could have asked." Lachlan stood so quickly his chair fell over, and he walked out of the room. Aine heard the front door slam and winced.

"He's right," she said. "You should have asked."

~

WHEN AINE FOUND LACHLAN, he was sitting on a flat rock next to a pool with a small waterfall trickling down the rocks to feed it. It had taken her some time to figure out he'd left the village.

"I see why she always comes here. It's beautiful." She sat down next to him.

"It's where she met Daniel."

"Why didn't you tell me about Daniel?"

"Eloi said she would tell you, but you were taken. I assumed she had." He blew out a long breath. "I'll need to go and start searching for her, but I can't leave you while you're pregnant."

"You can't leave now. I need to teach you how to use your powers."

"My powers!" Lachlan laughed. "Manipulative old shifter. Why couldn't he leave it alone?"

Aine sighed. "I'm not saying what he did was right, but we do need every advantage we can get."

"If I can't leave, then we will have to carry on using everyone else to search, especially for the other packs. I don't think I'll just be able to sit back and do nothing."

"It won't be nothing. We will have to train. How about we see what you've got?"

Lachlan grumbled but nodded. Aine directed him to close his eyes and look at the power within. Their mental connection wasn't as strong as it had been. She searched and felt his mental caress accompany her as she looked at his center, the way she used to look at her own.

"Can you feel that power?"

"Yes." Lachlan swallowed.

Aine withdrew. "Can you find it yourself?" She watched him, his face relaxed at first, but after a few minutes, he frowned. Eventually, he growled and quickly stood. He paced the area and threw his arms up.

"What are we doing?" he growled. "I'm sitting here with my eyes closed when we need to be out there."

"I know you're frustrated; I want to be out there too. I miss her." Aine's eyes stung, and she looked out into the woods. She raised her voice. "I want to hold my baby girl. I want to run right out of here and search every inch of the world until she's back in my arms."

Lachlan stopped and was at her side instantly. He pulled her into a hug, and she buried her face against his chest. She heaved a sob. "What if we never find her?"

"We will—she will be trying to get back to us just as hard as we are trying to find her." He rubbed her back gently. "I'll try again. I'm sorry I got so frustrated."

"I'm frustrated too. I want to leave, but I can't leave the pack, and if I lost the baby, I would never forgive myself."

"You still don't believe, do you? That they will be okay?"

"You know the history. What if Eyolf is wrong?"

"He's rarely wrong, today being a prime example. I felt the power release, he's right about it being there, and we need to work on it. Come on." He held her at arm's length. "Teach me, oh wise master."

Aine hiccupped a laugh. "Some student you are. Couldn't even sit still," she teased.

Lachlan sat with her, and they tried again. This time Lachlan managed to feel the power, and she smiled.

"You won't be as powerful as me, but it'll definitely give you an edge."

"What will I be able to do?"

"I don't know; we will have to see." She leaned in and gave him a kiss, soft and sweet. He smiled at her, put his hand around her shoulder, and they both looked out into the woods.

22

They moved again. Rolan had lost track of the number of places they'd stayed over the last month. This room was larger than any so far, with a desk near the window and two single beds. A TV sat on a dresser on the opposite side of the room to the beds, and the décor was far too floral for Rolan's taste, but it was free. He had followed Finn's instructions when he left the caves; it hadn't taken him long to find the motel and get the information he needed. The clerk looked curious as he handed over the package, but Rolan had growled at him.

At each motel, he had picked up a new set of instructions. The rooms were already paid for when he got there. Rolan was grateful, as he'd never used money before or been out in the human world.

Eloi lay on one of the single beds. With the power he had gained, she was easy to control. He could still feel her fight him, but each time he entered her mind, she weakened. She had been in a trance since he took her, and he spent most of each night in her mind searching her memories. He learned a lot of the Aoibhan secrets. He raised one side of his mouth in a smirk as he watched her sleep, the cuff still on her wrist. That would have to remain in place if he wanted to keep her under his control.

"I will mold you into the greatest shifter of this age, and we will rule the world." Rolan approached her and placed his hands on either side of her head. He continued to search her memories and rewrite each one.

Aine would become the parent that betrayed her and let her down. Aine tried to kill her loving father and kept the medallion that would cure her father of the madness that gripped him from her. Her father only took on the power to stop Aine's tyranny despite the risks to himself, and he needed Eloi's help to cure himself. Aine had killed Solus and taken over the Faction to infiltrate the other packs. She had cuffed Eloi so she wouldn't threaten her power, using the excuse that it was for Eloi's own good.

Since he'd killed Solus, the power came to him quickly and in greater amounts; he hadn't been able to overpower Eloi all those years ago, but now it felt like child's play. The cuff she wore diminished her strength, and it would take time, but as he changed her memories, she would believe her mother was the enemy and trust only her father.

Rolan grinned as he removed his hands but tensed when a shadow crossed the motel window. The power came to him now and swirled around the doorway as the lock clicked. Finn entered, his broad frame large filling the entrance. The glint of menace in his blue eyes made Rolan wince. He wrapped his control around the power and swirled it around the stranger.

"That's no way to treat someone who has helped you get this far." The man raised his eyebrow and smirked at Rolan.

"I thought we were to meet tomorrow." Rolan frowned and didn't relax.

"I changed the plan. I like to do that; it helps keep us hidden for longer." Finn shrugged and entered the room. He approached Eloi, and Rolan growled.

"Don't go near her!" He lashed out with the power, and Finn dodged.

"Now, now. Don't attack your ally," he teased.

"You don't have a knife to my throat, and I'm a lot more powerful than I was last time we met," Rolan snarled. Heat surged through him as Finn held up a hand.

"True, but you need me," Finn grinned. "I figured you must have had a way to take more power, biding your time under the old wolf's thumb until you were ready to strike."

Rolan ignored the gleam in Finn's eyes. "Why should I trust you?" he spat, sweat forming on his brow as he kept hold of the power around them.

"Because I've led the hunters in circles and kept them away from you. They've lost the trail now, but it took some effort. I've also paid for each room you've stayed in. Be grateful," Finn said smoothly. "Now, it appears we have a common enemy. I want Lachlan destroyed."

Rolan dropped the power causing a growl to escape him. "That simple? You want him gone, that I can understand. For what he's done to me, he must pay," he agreed.

"Good. I don't particularly care for shifters, but the enemy of my enemy—you know." He waved a hand through the air. "I've been siphoning funds from my father for years, but we can't stay in motels forever. Leave that to me. What I need from you is information. What have you discovered about the prophecy?" Finn took a seat at the desk near the window.

"That one of the Aoibhan line will be born of the four

bloodlines; she will mate with a hunter and bring shifters and humans together," Rolan stated.

"Very vague and the same as what I've discovered." Finn looked at Eloi thoughtfully. "Bring shifters and hunters together how? In harmony or one side the superior?" he asked quietly; Rolan didn't think he expected an answer. "Or...bring them to destruction, together in death. That's kind of poetic."

Rolan didn't interrupt as Finn pondered the words. He wished he'd paid more attention to Solus. "Solus often said that Aine needed protecting." He shrugged.

"Ah, but it could mean either the mother or the daughter," Finn continued as if Rolan hadn't spoken. "Both are of the same bloodline, Lachlan controls one, and we control the other." He tapped his chin and stared at the wall over Rolan's shoulder.

"I think I can help. I haven't looked yet, but Eloi has some knowledge on the prophecy." Rolan approached his daughter and kept one eye on Finn. "Do not come near us while I do this, or I will kill you."

Finn laughed. "Sure." He took out his knife and started to pick at his nails.

Rolan put his hands on either side of Eloi's head and searched. Finally, he found the conversations with Rosa and Eyolf. They didn't know for sure if Aine had all four bloodlines, but it must be true from all of Solus's ramblings. He pulled himself back and glanced at Finn, who looked bored.

"Well?" Finn stared at him. He told him what Eloi knew, and Finn laughed. "Of course, there are conditions that must be met. Well, if one of them is that the woman must mate with a hunter..." He grinned, and Rolan cringed.

Rolan shifted his position and watched the hunter approach Eloi again. Finn kept an eye on Rolan and moved closer when he didn't react. He reached out and brushed some hair off her face. His mouth twitched into a half-smirk, and he seemed lost in thought.

Finn eventually came out of his reverie. "Now, I don't particularly care who wins, as long as Lachlan is destroyed. I like to cause pain, so that doesn't mean he has to die." He smiled maliciously. "I have a proposition. We could work together here. I think there are two sides to this prophecy, one of harmony and one for destruction."

Rolan frowned. "How can we work together? You've been killing shifters your whole life. You hate my kind, why the change of heart?"

"I don't care what I kill, as long as I can keep doing it. My beef was never with the shifters." Finn barked a laugh, and Rolan grinned. "I was a weapon my father could use. When he didn't want to kill shifters anymore, it made me obsolete. Now, what I suggest is that we create our own candidate for this prophecy, throw doubt into the mix as to whether Aine is worthy of fulfilling it." Finn looked at Eloi, his smile saccharin. "I will mate with your daughter. She has, after all, the four bloodlines and now a hunter to mate."

Rolan looked at the man, his eyes hard. "No."

Finn's face dropped. "No? Why not?"

"Why do you want to mate my daughter, and why would I let you?" Rolan growled.

"I like her; she's got spirit. I've had my eye on her for a while. Let's just say I took a liking to her when she visited my father in Burntwood Falls and because we want the same thing. I don't care for power; I just want to have the freedom to indulge in my...hobbies."

"She is not a hobby, and I will never let you harm her," Rolan declared.

"I won't hurt her, I want her for my own. I'll treat her better than family." Finn bowed mockingly.

"I've seen how you treat your family." He glared at the hunter.

"Well, if she's willing, there won't be a problem. I already know you've been rewriting her history." He paused. "No, don't deny it; I've been watching you."

"It's not that simple." Rolan crossed his arms.

"Yes, it is; just make her believe she's my mate, and we are meant to be together. She won't be able to resist me. Don't you want her with a strong man that will protect her?" Finn raised an eyebrow.

Rolan's stomach turned at the thought of her with a human; he scratched the back of his head. "I need to think about it."

"Don't think too long." Finn swept up dramatically from the chair and opened the door. He didn't look back when he left, and Rolan slumped on the bed.

He looked at his daughter. "Don't worry, Eloi, you will never mate with him. I just need him to believe that for now while he's useful. When he's no longer needed, I will let you deal with him as you see fit."

If she could harness the power of the four bloodlines, and he controlled her, then he would rise to where he deserved to be. She could still mate him and dispose of him after. The condition of the prophecy would be met, and Finn would be gone.

Rolan thought of the hybrid he'd fought at the cavern, a different type of shifter. The boy had been young but powerful. Rolan shuddered. If the boy had been older and more experienced, then that fight might have ended differently. Rolan thought of the pack he could build if he had hybrids on his side. Maybe the hunter would be helpful—but could he defile his daughter like that? He would sleep on it and decide in the morning.

Finn hadn't left details on how to contact him, but Rolan expected he would have another message from the motel in the morning. Instead, Rolan opened the door to find Finn standing there. He lurched back in surprise, barely stopping himself from tripping over the bed.

"Have you decided?"

"Maybe." Rolan looked at Eloi. "You won't hurt her? If you do, then I will hunt you down, and your methods of torture will be nothing to what I will do to you."

Finn stormed into the room. "What do you care? You're using her."

"Yes, but I still love her. She's my daughter. The corruption from her mother will never change that." Rolan narrowed his eyes.

"Every relationship hurts, you know that, Rolan. But I'll take care of her." Finn crossed his heart with his finger, a wicked grin on his face. Rolan paused.

"Fine, but I'm the leader," he declared.

"Fine, but you don't get to tell me what to do." Finn nodded. "Come on. There's an SUV outside. That'll take us to our next destination, where we can start putting together your new pack."

Rolan gently lifted Eloi into a sitting position and put his hand on the back of her neck. She came awake, but not enough to fight him.

"That is a useful trick. Any chance you could teach me?" Finn cocked his head.

"No." Rolan would not give this kind of power to the man, even if he could. He directed her outside, and once she was seated, he let her drift entirely under again. He opened the passenger door and sat next to Finn, his stomach twisted.

"Where to, oh mighty hunter?" Rolan put his seat belt on.

Finn grinned at him. "Mouthy today, I see, I like it. You're no fun when you're all meek and pathetic. Let's start by finding a base, then we are going after one of the other Royal packs. See what they are made of."

Rolan nodded, watching the road as they ate up the miles. Finn stuck some rock radio station on and proceeded to sing loudly to each song. Rolan tried to tune him out as he thought about their next move. He mulled over the four bloodlines and Eloi's link to each one. They could easily capture members of the Tivaci and force them to train her in healing. Finn could return to the pack and be allowed to roam the area if the hunters weren't too suspicious of him. The other two were a mystery.

"What do you know of the bloodlines?" he asked Finn.

"Well, when I left, I may have planted a bug or two in my father's house and the historian's house. Everything seems to happen there." He looked pleased with himself.

"And?" Rolan said shortly.

"Weeeelll." Finn sucked his teeth. "It turns out that the Xerxes control the weather. So I figured if we track obscure weather patterns, then we will find them. The Torak like fire, so I figured we should find an active volcano or something."

"Don't humans have a fire protection branch or something?" Rolan stared out of the window.

"Firefighters, huh?" Finn tapped a finger. "That's a great idea; we could look into units that have no losses or miraculous saves. Good one, Rolan! See, I knew you weren't entirely useless." He punched Rolan's arm, and the shifter flinched.

Finn eventually turned off onto more secluded roads. They headed deeper into the country, and Rolan felt queasy.

"Where are we going?" Rolan searched the trees and saw no sign of life.

"You'll see, it's perfect," Finn smiled maniacally at him.

Rolan watched the trees get thicker and thicker, and the SUV bumped about as Finn sped down a single-track lane.

"I'll have to have this resurfaced. Can't be doing this all the time." He glanced at Rolan. "Aw, come on, lighten up."

The road carried on until the trees opened into a clearing, and a dilapidated mansion was before them. Rolan looked around at the surrounding forest and realized Finn was right. For a shifter, this would be perfect.

"How did you find this?" Rolan stared in awe.

"The human way. I found someone to buy it for me. It's definitely a fixer-upper, but it'll do." Finn pulled the car up, and Rolan got out. "It won't trace back to me, but I had to *borrow* more funds than usual from my father's account. He might notice, though I haven't returned since I left them with the Tivaci, so they might not immediately think of me."

It was a mansion, and Rolan was more than happy to take advantage of Finn's family money. "Is it livable?"

"I've already had someone working on it. We can stay here, but if we want an army, then it will need more work. I can sort that; you concentrate on my future wife." Finn winked at him. Rolan resisted the urge to punch him.

~

ELOI WOKE. She scrambled up in her bed as she looked around an unfamiliar room. She fought the urge to scream and felt the cuff on her arm; she scratched and pulled at it, but it wouldn't come off. The door opened, and light streamed in. She blinked at it and held a hand up. A dark figure in the door approached.

"It's just a bad dream; everything is okay." Rolan pulled her in for a hug; she stiffened but relaxed as he held her.

"Father, where are we?" She clung to him and heaved a sob.

"I've found us somewhere safe. Do you remember what happened?" He stroked her hair.

"I... Mom... I don't know." Eloi pushed her father back and looked at his face. "How did we get here?"

He brushed the hair from her face. "Aine really did a number on you this time. But, it doesn't matter, for now; what matters is that we are safe, and we are together." He smiled at her, and she hugged him again.

"That's right, we are together," Eloi said automatically. She rubbed her eyes and brushed the tears away.

"Now, you've been through a lot. You must sleep. Can you do that for me?" His face softened.

"Of course, but...will you stay with me?" Eloi shrank back and fiddled with her sheet.

"I'll stay until you're asleep." He picked up a chair from against one wall and pulled it to the side of the bed. "Do you want me to help?" He reached for her with his hand.

She nodded weakly. "Yes, please." She lay back on the bed and closed her eyes. His cool hand touched her forehead, and she sighed as his power pushed into her.

"That's right, Eloi. Sleep, it will all be better next time you wake up." Her father's voice caressed her mind.

Eloi lashed out with her mind in every direction. She replayed the scene in her head and cringed at her meekness. Her father would pay for what he had done. His presence pressed in on her, and she turned to face him. His mental projection in her head made him look younger than he was, and she snarled at his image.

"You won't get away with this!" She tried to run at him, but an invisible force held her back. Even in her mind, the cuff pulled her power away. She rubbed her wrist and scowled at Rolan.

"You're wrong, my dear. You never remember these conversations when you're awake. It's only been a month, but you won't last long trapped in here as I replace your memories." Rolan reached toward her, and Eloi resisted the urge to snap at his hand. She had tried that once, and he had punished her for it. She raised the cuffed hand.

"This won't stay on forever, and when I take it off, you won't be able to hold me here!" She looked around; there was nothing here, just herself and Rolan. She had no way out and wandered aimlessly, a prisoner in her own mind.

"I'll just tell you the cuff is the only thing keeping you alive after what your mother did to you." Rolan's grin was wicked. "Your will to survive will stop you ever wanting it off."

Eloi looked at him with disgust. "I'll find a way."

"How? Over time you will weaken and no longer exist. My daughter will be powerful and strong. You will be what I make you."

Eloi screamed and lashed out at him. Rolan didn't flinch as the power washed over him.

"When will you learn that I am the one in control? Stop fighting, and it will be less painful for you." He rubbed his chin. "I don't want you to suffer like this. It'll be so much easier for you if you give in."

"I will never give in to you!" Eloi tried to reach her mother's mind; Rolan must have found a way to sever her from the pack. Her chest ached at the emptiness she felt, but she kept her face blank. "It's only a matter of time," she growled at him.

"Yes, it is." His image disappeared, and she watched her memories play out before her, powerless to stop the changes he made. She shut out the vision and concentrated on her mind. She needed to stay strong and find a way to break through his control.

One step at a time.

23

Six months later.

Eloi looked down the corridor. The mansion was far too big as far as she was concerned, but her father liked to have the space. She could appreciate the comfort, but it felt empty sometimes. They'd lived here about six months, and as far as she could remember, it was the only place that had ever felt like home to her. It had taken a lot of work; Finn had directed most of it, but it was now livable.

Rolan had told her they'd been forced to move a lot to avoid detection by the pack in Sumter, but they finally had the confidence that if they were found, he could defend this place. Not that it could easily be found.

"Stupid mansion in the middle of nowhere," she muttered.

She entered the large office at the end and found her father at his desk. The room was full of shelves; she felt sadness as she looked at their barren expanse with no books on them. Her father sat at a mahogany desk, which looked like it was from the early twentieth century. She loved the look of that desk; it was stunning. She waited patiently for him to finish reading what he was working on, and he didn't acknowledge her presence. Eventually, he signed the paper at the bottom and set it to one side.

"Thank you for coming. I wanted to let you know that I've been impressed with your dedication recently." He smiled at her and touched his fingertips together in front of him. "You've done a great job with the shifters we've managed to bring in. Do you think you're ready for more responsibility?"

"Yes, sir, I am confident I am able to do more if you'll allow it." She didn't let herself smile; her father liked discipline.

"It's your eighteenth birthday soon." Rolan watched her. She couldn't help the grimace on her face. "Not happy to be mated so soon?" He cocked his eyebrow at her.

"I just feel that it's too young. I have much more to offer before you mate me off to our ally." She resisted the shrug, but her hand twitched. His eyes glanced down, and he sighed. She held her breath.

"You can't put it off forever, but if you do well in this task, I'll delay until you're nineteen. I agree; you are too young," he whispered conspiratorially.

Eloi allowed herself to breathe. "I'm sure that is more than acceptable. What is it you'd like me to do?"

"I'm going to have you work one on one with some...." Rolan paused. "Tutors. They will be able to work with your abilities and help you control your powers."

He held up a hand as she opened her mouth to speak, then continued. "I know you think you've got a handle on them, but I'd like you to try to reach your full potential. You've worked with communication all your life, but not the air side of your power. I blame your mother; she wasn't prepared to train you properly."

Eloi sneered. "You're right. I'm sorry to doubt you, Father."

Rolan smiled. "Finn thinks he's found someone who can teach you water; we will then need earth and fire. Have you been trying to access air?"

Eloi shook her head. "I don't really understand what I'm doing. The telepathy has always seemed so natural."

Rolan blew out a breath. "Well, maybe mastering one of the others will help you with the foundation, and you can figure it out. Once mastered, I then have a special task for you."

Eloi looked at him hopefully. "Am I going back to Sumter?"

Rolan's eyes flashed for a second, which gave her pause. "I didn't realize you were so eager."

"It's about time they paid for what they did to you. Is it true they've completely integrated with the hunters?" She grimaced. "It's disgusting."

"I agree. Yes, I'm sending you to Sumter." He paused. "Are you sure you're up for this?"

"Absolutely. You want me to find the medallion? We need it to help you, Father. You have lived with what Aine did to you for too long. If the medallion can cure you, then I can get it," she said eagerly.

"Yes, my dear, you will need to retrieve the medallion—my only hope for a cure." He coughed. "And then I need you to do something which you may find difficult. I need you to assassinate Aine and her lover. Do you think you'll be up to the task?"

"Yes, sir, you know I have no reservations," she said with a firm nod.

"Good." He smiled at her and stood. When he walked over to her, he pulled her into a hug, and she frowned but hugged him back. "I'm extremely proud of what you have become, my dear."

"I would be nothing without you, Father."

"That's very true." He spoke so quietly, she wasn't sure he meant for her to hear. "Now, back to your duties. Finn is bringing some shifters here who want to join the cause." He dismissed her. She gave him a quick nod, then left.

As she walked down the corridor, Finn approached with a group of shifters that looked familiar.

"Catori?" Her old teacher approached her. This was the third family she'd seen arrive from Sumter.

"Oh, Eloi, it's so good to see you. I know you support your mother, but we couldn't carry on living in there with all those hunters. Rolan always took care of us, even when your mother wasn't there, so I hope you understand us coming here." Catori held Eloi's hands and gave them a gentle squeeze.

Eloi frowned. "Of course, why wouldn't I understand? I hope you settle in well." She smiled at the group behind her, including two younglings. She guessed it must have appeared she supported her mother to the other pack members. What choice did she have back then?

"It's good to see you here. We left after the attack on the Faction. I didn't know you hadn't returned with them. Is that cute hybrid here with you?" Catori looked expectant.

Eloi frowned and spoke carefully. "I left with my father; he needed me. What hybrid are you talking about?"

"Oh, dear, the one you were close to. I guess I made a mistake." Catori looked lost.

"I'm sorry, Catori, I have somewhere to be, but I'll catch

up with you once you're settled here." She nodded to her old teacher and carried on down the corridor.

What hybrid? Lost in thought, she didn't see the hand shoot out until it gripped her arm to stop her. Finn stepped so close she could feel the heat from his body invade her space.

"Hello, Eloi, lovely to see you."

Eloi tried not to cringe at his words; she kept her face blank. "Hello, Finn." She waited, but he didn't continue; he glanced up toward her father's office and pulled her against a door. His body pushed against hers, and she drew in a breath. His smile indicated he mistook her reaction, and he lifted his hand to cup her face.

"Not long now." He grinned at her, his eyes shining.

Eloi suppressed a shudder. "It will depend on the work I'm doing for my father. Now excuse me. I have somewhere to be." She tried to push past him, and his grip tightened.

"There's no rush." He leaned in.

"Exactly, there's no rush. I have work to do for my father, and it may take me away for longer than my eighteenth birthday. So it will delay our nuptials." She tried to keep her voice flat.

"Pity, no big deal. It's only a matter of time, my dear." He stepped back and released her, then blew her a kiss; she waited for him to turn his back before she shuddered. The man was more than twice her age. What was her father thinking? He looked after himself and had aged well, but she couldn't understand the match chosen for her.

She thought about the medallion her father needed and vaguely remembered that Eyolf had hidden it. She would have to find a way to get him to let her know where it was. Each time she tried to make the memory clearer of conversations they'd had, her mind felt like a fog. Eyolf will have probably moved it by now anyway.

She would have to watch them, learn their routines, infiltrate the pack, then make her move once she knew all the specifics. She smiled at finally being able to bring her father the cure he needed and the peace from knowing that he no longer had to worry about Aine.

She walked out of the house and took a deep breath; when Finn was near, she felt suffocated. She preferred it when he was on one of his hunting missions. Her father had sent him to find tutors for her. At least when he went to look, he was away from here.

~

AINE GROANED as she tried to get up from her kitchen chair. She struggled without her morning coffee and was looking forward to finally returning to her morning ritual. It wasn't long until her due date.

"Woah, Woah. Let me help you." Lachlan rushed into the room to give her a hand. "Why are you getting up? I can get you anything you need."

"Stop fussing, you big lout. The chair is not comfy. I need to walk around."

"But Tania said to stay off your feet." He rubbed her belly. "You're too big to—"

"Do not finish that sentence, Lachlan O'Reilly; otherwise, you'll be sorry." She raised a finger to point at him, and he caught her hand and kissed it. Aine slowly moved toward the door.

"Fine, but I'm coming with you. You should have called for me." Lachlan fussed, and Aine groaned at him. She huffed and continued toward their front door.

"I wouldn't be surprised if Tania doesn't move me to the infirmary soon. Twins will make things harder," she groaned. That had been an enormous surprise; she had never heard of twins being born to a shifter.

Fortunately, she was strong and hadn't struggled with the pregnancy as much as Caroline, a human from Burntwood Falls she'd met when she lost her memory, thought she would. She missed shifting, though, and looked forward to being able to run through the woods.

Her ability to shift had disappeared with her power. She vaguely remembered her power disappearance from when she was pregnant with Eloi, but she hadn't been as powerful then or used it as much.

"Eyolf says my control is coming along well." Lachlan smiled at her. She helped him finally release it and Lachlan's power had manifested differently from hers. There was no smoke or darkness; it was more like blasts of air. Purer than her innate abilities.

Phil appeared and grinned at them both. Aine waved as he approached, then turned back to Lachlan.

"I spoke to Rosa again when she visited. She thinks that the darkness and smoke come from the corruption my ancestors introduced when they created shifters. That's why your power is different."

"So, the Aoibhan originally controlled air, like I do?" Lachlan scratched his chin, his other arm through Aine's to support her. As Phil met them, he reached for Aine's belly; she slapped his hand away.

"No touching," she growled, and Phil laughed.

"Fine, fine. How are you both? Not long to go!" He fell in step with them, and Lachlan smiled at his friend.

"Not long. Still doesn't seem real that we are having

more children." Lachlan shoulder bumped his friend. "Ever thought of settling down and doing this yourself?"

"Nah, ya got to be joking right. I'm a free spirit," Phil chuckled. "How's the training going? Spoke to Cillian and he said you didn't have much free time. So figured I'd better come here to make you take a break."

"We were just talking about that. It's going well, but it's really different from Aine's power." Lachlan shrugged.

"I never realized we had more than the mental communication and influence." Aine closed her eyes and paused in their walk.

"I don't have that, though," Lachlan continued, "so I wonder if that came from the corruption too. Part of the dark magic."

They wandered further into Sumter, Phil looking thoughtful as they continued. Aine greeted a few of the shifters as she passed and had to slap a couple of hands away. Phil grinned at her when she scowled at his laughter.

"Don't you start." She pointed a finger at him, and he put his hands up.

"Can't blame them, really, can ya?" he chuckled again. Aine scowled at him, her face softening when he pulled her into a hug. "Ya should be resting."

"I need to keep up with the pack and keep an eye on their moods." She felt a pang of sadness at the families that had left. The hunters had fully integrated into Sumter; some remained in town but often visited like Phil did. Aine was wary of Liam, but Lachlan was more relaxed around him, which she took as a good sign. She could understand some shifters not being comfortable with them being here but didn't see any other way if they were going to integrate and learn to work together.

A twinge in her side caused her to pause, and she rubbed at it with her free hand.

"Pain?" Lachlan's eyes widened, but she shook her head.

"A rather hard kick to my bladder." She tilted her head to the medical building but then hunched over as pain shot through her. "Okay, maybe not."

Lachlan's eyes widened, and Phil looked around frantically.

"What do ya need? How can I help?" Phil shifted from foot to foot, and Aine would have laughed if the pain hadn't intensified. Instead, she leaned heavily on Lachlan's arm as he helped her toward the medical building; Phil barged through the door and shouted for help.

Aine rolled her eyes as she followed him through. Tania approached as she gently lowered herself down into the nearest bed, still leaning heavily on Lachlan. When she looked up into her mate's eyes, she was touched to see the glisten of a tear. He grinned at her, and she couldn't help but smile back as the pain eased.

"This is it," she said.

~

LACHLAN HELD one of his twin boys, and Aine the other; his heart swelled more than he ever could have imagined. Aine had returned to their home and rested in bed after a long labor. She managed to deliver both their sons naturally, and Lachlan couldn't have been prouder of his mate.

"It's like the amount of love I have has tripled." Lachlan stared at the small boy in his arms with wonder.

Aine smiled at him. "I know what you mean." She swayed the baby in her arms. Both were quiet, and he wasn't sure how long that would last, but this moment was almost complete bliss. A tear fell from Aine's eye silently down her cheek, and she shuddered slightly.

"I just wish Eloi was here to meet her brothers. I dreamt of her when I was in labor. It might have been the pain, and I was being delusional, but I felt her with me."

Lachlan's face dropped, and he sat down on the bed next to her. "Don't give up hope. Girvan and Liam are chasing another lead."

"It's been months, Lachlan. Where could she be? Rolan could be hurting her." Aine's pain lanced Lachlan and his heart ached.

"I know, love, but she is strong. She will fight him as long as she can, we will just have to be there for her when she comes back and support her as much as she needs." He shifted the baby to free an arm and wiped her tears with his thumb, his hand cupping her face.

"I love you, I will do everything I can to find her," he went on. "I have more control over my power now. If you promise to stay and protect our sons, then I will go and search for our daughter." Lachlan lifted his mouth into a smile. "She's just like you. Trust that she will be fine."

Aine lifted her chin, her lip wobbling slightly, but she nodded. "I wish I could come with you."

"Stay with the pack; they need you just as much. They will help you with the boys. It'll break my heart to leave them, but I know how important this is. Eloi needs to be back with her family. I'll..." He paused. "I'll have to leave in the morning."

Aine stared at him. "I don't know what I did to deserve you."

Lachlan laughed. "Me too. We've had enough trials over the last four years."

"Knock, knock." Eyolf knocked on the door and entered as he spoke. Lachlan cocked an eyebrow at him.

"You should really wait for a reply to the knock." Lachlan couldn't help the huge grin on his face.

Eyolf shrugged. "I'll remember next time. How are you all doing? Two will be hard work, though I'm sure you'll have plenty of help around Sumter."

"You know what they say about it taking a village to raise a child...maybe we should find another village for the second boy."

"Have you decided on names yet?" Eyolf sat in the chair in the corner. Two bassinettes were on the floor next to it, but Lachlan hadn't been able to put the baby down yet. He held the boy close to him and nodded.

"Aine wanted to go traditional and use names from pack history. I'd like to use more modern names so that they can fit in better with humans. Maybe integrate into society. If we can ever end the differences between shifters and hunters, then maybe they can have normal lives."

"They will never be normal, Lachlan. They are born from two powerful families."

"What are the options?"

"Izen, the oldest, and Arlen." Aine nodded toward the baby in Lachlan's arms and then the one in her own.

"Okay, fine, they aren't too bad," Lachlan smirked.

"Those are fine names." Eyolf nodded. "Izen, a fighter of justice. Arlen, oath, or pledge. Your boys will pledge to fight for justice."

"Alright, they do sound pretty perfect," Lachlan conceded.

"It's official, then." Aine's face shone with joy, and Lachlan couldn't help but smile. The baby in his arms started to stir. He walked around and swayed to settle him.

"Do you have any news?" Lachlan asked as he passed Eyolf.

"Liam has a suspicion that Rolan has help—he's had some funds go missing."

"He thinks a hunter is helping Rolan? That doesn't make any sense." Lachlan turned quickly at Aine's exclamation. The baby in her arms cried in protest, and she shushed it. Arlen quickly settled again, and she sighed. "What's wrong?"

"Finn." Aine sagged.

"No, Finn wouldn't leave my father, and he's always liked to torture shifters. Rolan wouldn't put up with that."

"But you said he disappeared after you freed the Tivaci and argued with your father. He would have access to your father's accounts. Plus, Rolan would torture shifters, you know what he's capable of." Aine's voice sounded desperate.

"I don't believe that he would betray our father."

"He didn't take Liam's declaration for succession well. Both of you have said that."

"I'll pass your suspicions on." Eyolf rose. "I hope you're wrong, but it makes sense."

"I can't believe it," Lachlan said. A heaviness settled in his chest and he blew out a breath.

"You have to admit there's a good chance...." Aine had paled.

"If it is Finn, then I need to leave and join the search for Eloi. I need to find her." Lachlan handed the baby to Eyolf and looked at his family wistfully. His heart broke as he left the room to prepare for his journey.

EPILOGUE

Daniel had traveled alone for months. At first, he had journeyed with the hunters and followed Eloi's trail. Since it had gone cold, he had used the research Michael had done on the other packs and tried to track down the Xerxes and the Torak.

He had heard rumors of the Xerxes on the east coast and tracked freak weather occurrences that didn't seem naturally possible. This was why he now sat in a diner near the coast of Florida. It looked like it had been decorated in the fifties and was far too pink for his taste. His cell rang, and he considered ignoring it, then sighed and pulled out the burner. He let it ring once more.

"Hello, Mom." He grimaced.

"Daniel, it has been over a week since I heard from you."

He held the phone away from his ear. "I'm sorry, I didn't realize. How're things in Sumter?" He stirred his coffee idly.

"Good. Aine had twin boys. You should have been here; they are Eloi's brothers." He heard his mom close a door.

Daniel swallowed a pang at Eloi's name. "I know, but I'm

more useful here. I need to do this, if I can't search for her... then I need to be useful."

"I understand," she sighed.

A chime sounded as someone entered the diner, and Daniel ignored it. He stared deep into his coffee. "I can't—" He stopped.

"I know how you feel. Now, don't be mad, but I sent you some help." He could feel her grin and scowled.

"Hey, little bro, want some company?" Shauna sat opposite him in the booth.

He rolled his eyes. "Mom, you set Shauna on me? That's not fair."

"Oh good, she's there. Say hi for me!"

Daniel passed the phone to Shauna.

"Hi, mom," Shauna said. "Yes, he looks grumpy. I'm good; it didn't take as long as I thought. Sure." She held out the phone for him, and he shook his head. "He says bye. Love you." She hung up.

"I know you don't want me here, but we all know you will wallow by yourself. This way, you have my pretty face to cheer you up." She beamed at him.

"Okay, number one, eeew. And number two, I don't need anyone. I'm fine, plus I reckon I know where to start looking." He crossed his arms.

"Well, we can go together." Shauna pulled the coffee toward her and sipped it. "Urgh, where's the sugar?" She proceeded to add four sugars to the drink.

"So, what do we have?" She looked at him expectantly.

He huffed. "A hurricane was supposed to sweep into Florida but swerved in the final hour. It missed the coast and stopped about fifty miles out. It then turned around and went back the way it had come from; the weather channels are going nuts."

"Subtle, okay. So where do we start?" She leaned on the table.

"There's a bar on the coast; apparently, a weird group were stuck to the news and then disappeared the day the hurricane turned tail. So I figured that would be a good place to start." Daniel shredded a napkin in his hands.

"Excellent. When are you heading there?" She raised her hand to the waitress, who picked up her pad and came over.

"After breakfast." He sighed when she ordered a huge meal.

"You're going to have to help me; coffee for breakfast does not a meal make," she said brightly.

"Try telling Aine that," he grumbled.

"Ha, good one. I bet she loved that first cup after the twins were born." Shauna's smile was forced.

"Stop being so chirpy; it's annoying." He got up from the table and went to the restroom, splashing water on his face and scowling at his reflection. He looked too thin in the face, and his hair had got too long. Finally, he sighed and returned to the table, where Shauna had started to devour the most enormous breakfast he had ever seen.

She pushed a plate toward him. "Here." She heaped bacon, eggs, and mushrooms onto it. "Your favorite," she spoke with a full mouth.

After finishing the food, they left a generous tip, and he led Shauna out of the diner. "The bar isn't far from here," Daniel said. "Let's go."

She constantly commented on her surroundings and Daniel tried to ignore her; once he spotted the bar, he quickened his pace.

"Oh, look, can we get cocktails later. Those look fun!" Shauna pointed at the sign outside the bar, and Daniel glared at her.

"What is with you? It's like you're on drugs." He pointed at her face.

"Just bored, no fun when you don't reply." She shrugged.

Daniel rolled his eyes and pushed open the door into the establishment. He spotted the barman and took a seat at the bar.

"What can I get you?" He came to stand in front of Daniel.

"Just a soda and some information, please." He pushed a one-hundred-dollar bill toward the man; he eyed it.

"What kind of information?" he asked slowly.

"About the group in here that you thought were weird." Shauna fluttered her eyelashes at him, and he relaxed.

"Yeah, sure, they were an odd crew. We had the hurricane on the TV back there." The man behind the bar gestured to the television behind him. "Came in every day and requested the weather channel. We were just considering evacuation when they packed up their boat and set out toward the hurricane. Didn't think we would see them again; it should have been suicide."

"Boat," Daniel groaned. No wonder they were so hard to track down.

"Sorry?" the man asked.

"Nothing, did you see them again?" Shauna nudged him.

"Yeah, the day after the hurricane headed back out to sea. They came back for a night and then left."

"Any idea where they were heading?" Daniel held his breath.

"Just north; why do you want to know?" He eyed them both suspiciously.

"I think we have relatives among them." Daniel gestured to himself and Shauna.

The man's smile turned to a scowl. "You a traveler like them?"

Daniel's brow furrowed. "Traveler?"

"Don't settle anywhere, live on the sea, and move around," the barman said.

"No, not like that. I'd just like to track them down and meet my long-lost relatives." Daniel shrugged, and the man relaxed.

Shauna leaned on the bar. "They didn't leave anything behind or a way to contact them by any chance?"

"No, paid in cash and left after that one day. Not seen them since."

"Damn." She winked at him. "Oh, well, let's go."

"I thought you wanted to stay for cocktails," Daniel called after her.

"Nope got something better to do!" She grinned at him. "Let's go hunting, little brother."

AUTHOR NOTES

Hello again! I'm so glad you've stuck with us on this journey into The Royal Pack Trilogy. I really hope you're still enjoying this series and are looking forward to the final installment. I have loved how the characters have led us on a wonderful journey, new ones joining them and where we have been led. We try to plan our stories but sometimes the characters do not behave how we want.

I completely fell in love with Daniel and I hope you do too as you get to know him even more in book 3. If you'd like to see more of him, we have a bonus story available if you join our Clan Whelan Publishing - Reader Community on Facebook.

Anne and I love writing stories and we believe that every story deserves to be shared. Because of this belief we have started a small publishing company designed to help less known PNR authors take that first step into publishing.

We have some incredible authors releasing in the future and what and experience it has been working with them. We can't wait to bring you more in the PNR genre and hope you stick around to see where we go.

As for us, we are working on a few more series that we can't wait to share with you. But first, Prophecy will be out soon to end this wonderful trilogy. Our head are spinning with ways we can expand this universe, as neither of us are quite ready to leave it. Especially after writing the bonus novella for Daniel.

Stay tuned to see what happens next and thanks for being here,

Liz

REVIEW AND READ MORE

Review

Thank you for reading the book. We hope you enjoyed it 🩶.

If you liked the book and want to share the love, we'd be thrilled if you could leave a review on Amazon and recommend it to your friends and family. As you probably know, reviews and word-of-mouth recommendations can make a huge difference for authors and readers alike.

Read More

Explore more books from this series here.

CWP NEWSLETTER AND PARTNERS

Our Newsletter

At CWP, our mission is to help readers like yourself to discover new fantasy romance and paranormal romance, including paranormal women's fiction, authors and books.

Join CWP newsletter. You'll be the first to know about our new authors, releases, and receive exclusive invites and special offers.

Our Partners

For Readers
Book Dragon - an app for discovering new books and keeping on top of your reads. Easily explore what books your friends and family loved. Save time, and track all the books and authors you love in one place. Pick and choose which books you want to recommend for others to read. Have fun along the way by earning Dragon Coins. If you

wish, with a click of a button, disable the social features of the app - you are in control.

For Authors

Kuprik - a one-stop shop for indie authors to find verified service providers. If you are searching for affordable and reliable people to work with, look no further.

CWP AUTHORS AND BOOKS

We have more thrilling stories you can choose from and that are coming your way. Check out our authors and books 🩶.

With love,
Anne & Liz

CWP Authors: https://clanwhelanpublishing.com/authors/

CWP Books: https://clanwhelanpublishing.com/cwp-books/

Printed in Great Britain
by Amazon

40457487R00175